# HOUSE IN THE WOODS

# HOUSE IN THE WOODS

### JESSICA AIKEN-HALL

**MOONLIT MADNESS**
**PRESS**

ISBN-13: (paper) 978-1-955071-01-7

Library of Congress Control Number: 2021910804


Moonlit Madness Press

Cover Design © Shower of Schmidt Designs

Editor: Silla Webb


jessicaaikenhall.com

*For Michele, thank you for your support and love.*

# CHAPTER ONE

"Mom's missing." The silence on the other end of the line made me question my decision to get my older brother involved. "It's fine, don't worry…"

"What do you mean she's missing?" Marc yawned with the last word.

"It's nothing, really. Don't worry about it. I know you're busy." I closed my eyes to hold back the tears.

"Molly, knock it off. You can't call me in the middle of the night and say shit like that and then say not to worry. I'm twelve hours away."

"It's morning, Marc. We're in the same time zone. Forget about it."

"Sorry, guess it was a long night. I'll be there as soon as I can."

"Wait, she's probably fine. She's done this before."

"What do you mean? This is the first I've heard of it. What's going on up there?"

"She's sick."

"Sick? Like with the flu?"

"No, like with dementia. It's not a big deal. She always comes back. I'm sorry I bothered you."

"Molly, I'm on my way. Call my cell if anything happens."

My body shook with emotion. It's been years since I've seen Marc, since any of us have. Dad told me not to call, but I don't think I could live with myself if we'd lost her, and he didn't get a chance to say goodbye. She was his mother too.

I wiped my eyes dry with the sleeve of my favorite sweatshirt. I'd waited my entire life to be able to wear a university logo and have it mean something. In just a couple more years I'd be able to say I did it when I walk across the stage and receive my diploma. Then maybe Dad will be proud of me.

I shook my hands at my sides and took a look in the mirror hanging in the entryway. My emerald green eyes stared back at me. *"Who are you?"* The feeling of not belonging was never too far away. This wasn't the time for self-pity, not when Mom needed me. I grabbed my keys and got into my silver Ford Focus to start the search. I loathed this car, but my parents were still making payments on it; my high school graduation present. At least it started today.

Dad never wanted to get the police involved. He said they'd have to put her in a home if they knew she wasn't safe. I couldn't imagine her being a prisoner in one of those places, but this time was different. She'd been gone almost two days. The last few times she'd return within a few hours.

As I drove through the quiet streets of our neighborhood, I was grateful summer was on the way. There was no way she would be able to survive out here this long in the bitterness of Vermont winters. The smell of lilacs reached my nose as I peered out the window. The beautiful purple blossoms always brought hope with them, a signal of summer vacation and longer nights. Two of my favorite things.

Two hours of driving around in circles was all I could take before I needed to get out of my car and stretch. The sinking feeling of what was to come was all I could focus on. I wasn't ready to lose Mom; not yet, and not this way. I turned my car into the high school parking lot and reminisced about the days not too far behind me. The funny thing was when I was a student here, I couldn't wait to leave, but now I missed how simple life used to be.

The heavy car door fell shut after I got out and pushed my arms above my head. Looking around, I noticed the big white tents in the football field. Graduation was only a few days away. I took a few steps toward the building and noticed a piece of paper with its edges folding over in the wind. I smoothed it out to get a better look. *Help us find our friend. Class of 1999 search party for Lucy Minor* was written in bold lettering, a picture of a girl with jet black shoulder-length hair and emerald green eyes stared back at me. Goose bumps swallowed my body whole. I looked around before I tore the flyer off the bulletin board and folded it up.

With every step around campus, I was greeted with the same green eyes. Who was Lucy? And why did she look like me? Marc graduated with the class of 1999. He never mentioned a missing girl, but that wasn't surprising since he didn't really talk to me about anything. He moved to Virginia before I was born, and he barely looked back. He was more of a stranger than a brother.

I found my way to the bleachers on the field and opened up the folded piece of paper that had fingernail marks imbedded in it. I looked at the face looking back at me, and a jolt of electricity shot through me. How was it possible that I grew up in this town and never once heard about Lucy Minor? I did the math; it was twenty years ago. She had been missing for two decades, and people were still looking for her? That seemed like a waste of time. I mean, who really thought she was still alive after all that time?

The vibrating of my phone in my back pocket pulled me out of my head. When I pulled it out, I saw Dad's name light up my screen. "If it were still 1999, I might be able to hide from him." I clicked on his name. "Hello."

"Molly, where are you?" The agitation in his voice made me regret answering it.

"I'm looking for Mom; where else would I be?"

"Well, you can stop. She's home now."

"She's back? You found her? Is she okay?"

"I'm not going to play twenty questions with you. Just get your ass home and see for yourself."

I wasn't sure what I ever did to make my father hate me, but after all these years I expected his harsh words, almost craved them. I stood and looked around one last time before getting my ass home as Dad so eloquently demanded. I missed this place, when life was simpler and all I had to do was go to class and do my homework. Now I had to do all that and take care of Mom. I missed how it used to be.

# CHAPTER TWO

"I was so worried about you." I rushed over to my mom and wrapped my arms around her.

She took a step back. "I'm not a child."

"I know, but I didn't know where you were. I missed you." I kissed her cheek. "Where did you go?"

"It's none of your damn business." Dad's harsh tone boasted through the kitchen.

Without acknowledging him, I took Mom's hand and took her outside. "Come with me. I want to show you something."

Mom's feet slid on the linoleum as she followed me. "I'm tired."

"I know, but it won't take long." I pulled her through the sliding glass door and into the back yard. "Look, Mom." I leaned into the lilac bush and inhaled the sweet fragrance. "It's our favorite." I plucked a branch off and handed it to her.

"Oh, I love these." She closed her eyes as she put the blossoms to her nose.

"How about we get some tea and sit out here to enjoy them? They never last long enough."

Mom nodded as a smile spread across her face. "I'd like that." She followed me back to the kitchen and placed the lilac sprig into a glass of water while I made our tea. I handed her a cup, and we headed back outside where we sat at the picnic table.

"I'm glad you're back." I took a sip of tea. "I was really worried about you."

"I know." She dropped her head. "I got kind of lost."

"Where were you going?"

"I'm not supposed to say." Her eyes wandered back to the lilacs. "But it's beautiful there."

"I'd love to go with you next time." I scooted closer to her on the bench and rested my head on her shoulder. "I miss the time we used to spend together."

She picked up my hair and let it fall through her fingers. "So silky." Her gaze was off in the distance.

"You used to say that when I was little. Remember?" The word I knew I shouldn't have used. "I mean..."

"Hush, Molly. Let's just enjoy our time together." Mom put her arm around my waist. "I can remember. I hate how everyone says that I can't. I'm not some old lady."

"I know, Mom. It's just that I worry about you. We all forget sometimes."

"Yes, but not everyone gets lost." She dropped her head on my shoulder. "I wasn't lost, though. I knew right where I was going."

"Where?"

She lifted her head, and her eyes darted around the yard. "I'm not supposed to say." Her voice was barely above a whisper.

"It's okay; you can tell me." I matched her volume.

"The house in the woods." Mom put her finger to her lips as she looked behind me.

"Is that where you stayed? In the house?"

"Nope. I can't tell you. He'll be mad." She put the cup to her lips.

"I won't tell. I promise."

"What the hell are you two doing out here?" Dad's arrogant voice made me about fall off the bench.

"We're enjoying the sunshine." Mom gave me a squeeze. "The lilacs are out."

"Well, someone needs to start making some food. I'm starving." The door slammed closed.

"He's a good man. He just gets angry. That's all." Mom tried to fix the situation like she always did.

"Yeah, he's a peach." I got off the bench and took my mug. "Come on. We should go make the king his lunch."

"Molly, you know he's a good man. I know you know it."

"I know." Except I didn't. I didn't have one memory of him being a good man. He was always at work or the bar. What kind of father and husband did that? Not a good one, that was for sure. "Come on, Mom. Let's go make some of your famous grilled cheese sandwiches."

"Oh, that sounds like a good idea. Now I'm even hungry." She laughed as the door closed behind her. The kitchen was the only place Mom still seemed like Mom. She hadn't forgotten many of her recipes, and being productive seemed to give her a purpose. She always loved cooking. Most of my memories growing up took place in this kitchen.

I grabbed the bread, butter, and cheese out of the refrigerator and put them on the counter in front of her. "Let me get the pan." I turned around to see it already on the stove. "You beat me to it."

"Guess I'm good for something." Mom wiped her hands on her jeans.

"That's not true, Mom. You're good at everything." I put my hand on the middle of her back. She let it rest there for a few seconds before she pushed it off.

"Molly, I'm not stupid. I know I'm not the same." Moments of clarity came less and less these days. It was heartbreaking to watch the mom I knew slip away.

"You're right— you're not stupid; you're sick. It's not your fault." I opened the bag of bread to try to avoid the conversation we'd been having the last few months.

"I know. I hate it." Mom took the slices of bread from me and started to butter them. "I wish there was some way to make it stop. I wish I didn't have to forget all of the important stuff."

"Isn't there a pill or something you can take to help slow things down?" I knew the answer, but I hoped she'd agree to take it if it seemed like a new idea.

"Molly, I said I'm not stupid. I know what you're doing."

"Then why don't you take it? If it could help?"

"Because you and I both know the pharmaceutical companies are only after our money. They don't care if they help me or not. I don't want to put poison into my body, not when there's no evidence it will work." The bread sizzled as it hit the hot pan.

"But, Mom, what do you have to lose? You'd want your patients to take it if it helped them."

"I don't have patients." She layered the cheese onto the bread. "Not anymore."

"But when you did, you would have wanted them to take something that would have helped them. I heard you were one of the best nurses on the unit."

"Molly, it's not going to happen. You and I both know there's no use."

"Okay, Mom. I'll drop it." I took plates out of the cabinet and opened a bag of barbeque chips, Dad's favorite, in hopes he might calm down enough to be civilized.

Smoke filled the kitchen. Mom stood over the sandwiches as she stared off into the distance, oblivious to the fact that she was still making lunch. I turned off the burner and took the pan off the hot surface to stop the smoke from spreading. I didn't say anything. What was the point? It would just upset her.

"Jesus Christ, Catherine, what the hell are you doing?" Dad stood in the doorway and waved the smoke away from his face. "Why can't you just pay attention?"

Dad's remark pulled Mom back to us. "Oh, I'm sorry. I was just..."

"Yeah, you're always just something. Maybe you should stay away from the stove? Huh? How about that?" He plopped himself down at the table and dumped some chips onto his plate. "I just don't want you to burn the damn house down."

Mom rushed past me. "Why don't you just shoot me?"

"Way to go, Dad." I followed after Mom to try to calm her down. She never used to be this emotional; it was like she was a totally different person. The doctor warned us this could happen. Her bedroom door was locked. "Mom, can I come in?" With my head against the door, I listened. I could hear her crying and imagined her in a heap on the bed. "Mom." I placed my hand on the wood that separated us. "I just want to see you. I promise I won't say anything."

The floor creaked before the doorknob turned. "Come on." She scanned the hallway behind me and pulled me in before she closed the door and locked it.

"Are you okay?" I stopped myself from asking everything I wanted to know when I remembered my promise. I sat on the bed and looked around the room. Clothing was tossed all over the place. I'd never seen their room in this state before.

"I've got to get out of here," Mom whispered as she stuffed clothing into a suitcase.

"Mom, you just got back. Where are you going?"

She paused and looked at me. "I can't tell you. He'll find me."

"Who will?" I got off the bed and put my hand on her back. "Mom, you're safe here. You don't have to go anywhere."

She pushed my hand off of her and dropped her belongings. "You're right." She pushed the bag off the bed and sat down. "I don't know what I was thinking." She put her face in her hands.

"Dad can be kind of a jerk sometimes, but he doesn't hurt you, does he?"

"No, of course not. Your father's a good man." She got off the bed and clapped her hands. "Let's go eat."

"Wait... Mom, are you sure you're okay? You were pretty upset. You don't have to just drop it."

"No, I'm fine. Don't you worry about me." I wasn't able to tell if there was any truth behind her smile. I didn't know her anymore.

"You're not going to leave again, though, are you? I was really scared."

"I'm sorry. I was just looking for something, and I must have got lost. I won't do it again." She took my hand between hers. "I love you, but you don't have to worry about me."

"What were you looking for? Maybe I could help you find it. I can go with you the next time you want to get out of here."

"Okay, honey." The smile was still plastered on her face as she opened the door. She placed her finger to her lips and winked at me.

I took that as my sign to be quiet. Don't let Dad know. That was always the way. Even when I was little.

CHAPTER THREE

In my bed I couldn't help but think about how upset Mom had been earlier. She seemed scared, but of what? Mom and Dad always fought, but she had never acted like she was afraid of him. What was she running from? And where was she going? The questions were endless, and there was no one to ask. Mom was easily agitated now, and Dad always had been. I closed my eyes to try to get some sleep.

Through my bedroom window I heard the crunch of gravel. My heart shot up into my throat. *Shit.* I forgot to call Marc. I threw the covers off and peeked out the window. Marc reached his arms over his head as he looked around the yard before he reached for something in the backseat. I slipped on my sweatshirt and hurried to greet him. I unlocked the front door and closed my eyes as I shut it. "Hey, Marc. I'm so sorry I forgot to call you." I stuffed my hands into my sweatshirt pocket.

"Is everything okay? Is Mom..." His grip tightened on the strap of his duffle bag.

"Yeah, yeah, she's fine. She came home on her own. I just got so caught up with everything that I totally forgot to let you know."

Marc looked up at the sky. The crescent moon poked out behind the clouds, and the stars sprinkled throughout the darkness. He rubbed his face with his hand. "It's fine. I'm due for a visit anyway."

"So you're going to stay?" The giddiness of having my big brother home made me feel like a little kid at Christmas.

"I might as well. I'm exhausted. Think I can come in?" Marc took a step closer to me.

A squeal of excitement filled the night's air as I jumped up and down. "I'm so glad you're here." I threw my arms around him and squeezed.

"Are you alright?" Marc brushed my arms off him.

"I'm fine. Really. I just missed you."

"I missed you too, Molly."

"You did?" I felt my hands settle onto my hips and dropped them to my side.

"Yeah. Now move it." Marc swatted me as he walked by.

I blocked the door with my body. "Wait. I didn't tell anyone you were coming, and Dad will kill me if he knows I told you anything."

"Relax. You think I don't remember how Dad is?" Marc shook his head. "I won't let them know you called."

"Then what are you going to say?"

"I don't know. That I missed my family." He took a step closer to me.

"No, that won't work. He'll never believe you."

"Come on, Molly, it's not that big of a deal."

"Oh, I know. It's your twentieth high school reunion. Tell them that."

Marc tilted his head. "It is? How do you know that? You weren't even alive when I graduated."

"I'm not stupid, I pay attention. I know things." My hands gravitated back to my hips.

"Fine, I'm here for my reunion. Now move. I'm too tired to play games."

I opened the door and let him enter before I followed behind him. I held my finger to my lips. "Don't you dare wake them up yet. Dad's a bear when he doesn't get a full twelve hours of sleep," I whispered.

"Some things never change, huh?" Marc shook his head. "Good night, Molly."

"Good night." I mouthed the words as he walked away. With Marc home,

everything felt okay. It wasn't like he was going to be able to fix Mom or make Dad stop being a jerk. But having him here helped ease my nerves.

On my way back to bed, I stood by Mom's room and pressed my head to the door. I used to do this after arguments to make sure she was still breathing. I guess I watched too many *Dateline* episodes, but something always had me on guard. An uneasy feeling hung in the air like the smell bacon leaves behind.

* * *

The slamming of cupboards pulled me out of my slumber. "Where the hell is it?" The sound of Mom's frantic voice brought tears to my eyes. I already knew today wasn't going to be a good day for her. The good days seemed to be few and far between lately. I dried my eyes and found Mom in the kitchen. Her nightgown hung on a woman I barely recognized.

"Mom?" She didn't turn to look at me. "What are you looking for?" I stood behind her and placed my hand on her back.

When she turned around, there was a wild look in her eyes. "I need to find it before I can get out of here. We have to go."

"Mom, you're home. You don't have to leave. It's safe here."

"You don't know what you're talking about." Her scowl grew. "We have to get out of here."

"Mom?" Marc appeared around the corner.

Mom jumped back at the sight of him. "Who are you?"

"Mom, it's me, Marc." The look in his eyes pierced my heart.

"She knows that. It's just early, and she wasn't expecting to see you. Isn't that right, Mom? You know who Marc is." I said the words I needed to believe.

"Marc?" The question seemed to bring calm with it. She took a step closer to him, and he did the same. Her hand went to his face. "It's so good to see you, honey."

"Are you okay, Mom?" His voice broke as he looked over at me.

"Of course, I am. How about some breakfast?" A smile pushed up her cheeks. "I can make you some pancakes."

"No, it's okay. I'm not hungry." Marc blinked his eyes to fight off the emotion bubbling inside.

"It's no trouble. I remember how much you love to eat."

She shuffled her feet to the counter where she stood and stared ahead. "Pancakes it is." She opened the cabinet and rummaged through the contents before she pulled a box of mix out.

"Mom loves to cook. Isn't that right?" I joined her at the counter and took out the mixing bowl.

"I'm not a child. I can do this. Go sit down." She pushed me away. I hovered to make sure she had the right burner on and that the correct ingredients made it into the batch.

Marc sat at the table as he waited for breakfast. He didn't say a word and didn't even make eye contact with me again until Mom brought him a plate. "Here you go, honey." She ran her hand through his messy brown hair. "Looks like someone needs a haircut."

"Thanks, Mom. These look delicious. I forgot how much I miss being home." His eyes glistened in the sunlight.

Mom returned with a fork and a napkin. She sat next to Marc and smiled. I turned the burner off and joined them. "Isn't this a nice surprise? It's been ages since we've all been together."

"It's the best surprise." The smile looked like it was painted on her face.

"I'm glad I decided to come for a visit. It's been too long." With all eyes on him, Marc took a small bite of his breakfast. "Mmm, these are just how I remember them."

Mom's head dropped and was followed with a sigh. "Has Molly told you?"

"Told me what?" Marc set his fork down and wiped his mouth.

"That I ... can't remember."

"No, she didn't tell me anything. I'm sure you're fine. Lots of people can't remember. It's normal." He reached his hand out for her to take. "Hell, I can't remember shit these days."

"I think it's more than that. But I'm trying to get better. If I just take it one day at a time, I might get better. That's what the doctor said." She was lying or was telling him what she wished to be true. She wasn't going to get better.

"That's great, Mom. I know you will." Marc resumed eating.

"What in the hell is going on out here?" Dad joined us at the table; his threadbare boxers and stained t-shirt completed his ensemble. "Marc? Why the hell are you here?" He shot me the look I was expecting. The one that said he'd be talking to me later.

"What? A guy can't come home for a visit?" Marc shrugged his shoulders. "It's my high school reunion. I figured I should go."

"You never go to those things." Dad stood behind a chair, which helped hide the parts of him I didn't want to see.

"Yeah, well, this one seems special. Twenty years. I'm not getting any younger."

"Where's Stephanie?" Dad looked around the room.

Marc cleared his throat. "She's not here. We broke up."

"Figures. I knew you wouldn't be able to keep that one." Dad smirked as he shook his head.

"What does that mean?" Marc squinted his eyes.

"Nothing. I just knew you'd blow it. Jesus, you're almost forty, and you've never been married. People are going to start talking." Dad scratched his butt cheek.

"Are you serious? Is that all you're worried about? What

people will say? You know what? I don't give a damn what people think. Maybe you should give that a try." The tone of Marc's voice brought me back to the last time he had visited, and I remembered why it had been so long since I'd seen him.

"Oh, don't get your panties in a bunch. You've always been so sensitive." Dad shook his head. "If I didn't know any better, I'd think you were my daughter. I think Molly's more of a man than you are."

"Dad." I took a deep breath to try to elevate the tension building inside my stomach.

"Molly, it's okay. You don't have to get involved. I should have remembered why I never come home. Some things will never change." Marc got up and pushed his chair in. "I'm just going to get my shit and get out of here. It's clear that I'm not wanted here."

"Marc, please don't go." Mom stood up to go after him.

"Let him go." Dad went to Marc's plate and picked at his food. "Must be nice to get a hot breakfast."

"Why do you have to be so awful?" I regretted asking the question as soon as it left my mouth, but I couldn't keep it in any longer. "Marc drove all day and night to get here, and you have to treat him like that. Why can't you just leave people alone?" I followed after Marc and found him stuffing his clothes back in his bag.

"I'm sorry, Molly, but I can't stay here. I'll get a room at the Shady Lane for a few days, but there's no way I can stay here with him."

"Marc, you don't want to stay there; that place is so gross. Don't you remember? The bedbug incident?" I shook the memory out of my mind.

"I don't see any other option." He turned the light switch off as he walked past me. "Do you want to come with me? So we can talk?"

"Yeah, sure. Let me get dressed, and I'll meet you there."

CHAPTER FOUR

When I arrived at Shady Lane, I found Marc's car parked in front of room four. The lot was empty, so I pulled in next to him. The chances of me being in someone's way were slim. It was amazing this place was even still open. The door in front of me opened, and Marc emerged talking on his phone. I gave him a quick wave, not sure if I should give him space or get out and join him.

The awkwardness kept me in my car. He looked upset. I tried to read his lips to figure out who he was talking to, but no luck. He waved me over to join him. "What was that about?" I asked as he slipped his phone in his back pocket.

"Oh, just one of my old friends, Chris. I wanted to see if he was going to the reunion." Marc kicked at the welcome mat in front of his room. "Want to come in?"

"I don't know if it's worth the risk." I laughed as I took in the filth around us. "I guess it might smell better inside."

"It doesn't." Marc hung his head. "Why does Dad have to be such a dick? God, you'd think after twenty years he'd get sick of it."

"Was he always like that?" I dusted off the chair before I sat on the edge.

"What, a dick? Yeah, well actually, no. When I was younger, there were moments of normalcy. You know, where he was fun and stuff."

"No, I don't know. I've never met that Dad." I scanned the room and felt my nose turn up as I noticed the dirt around the room. "Marc, have you had your tetanus shot? This place is absolutely disgusting."

"Molly, knock it off. Don't gross me out." He tossed a pillow at me.

"Eww, I'm going to have to shower again. Get that thing off of me." I threw it back onto his bed. "So, is Chris going?"

"Going?" Marc raised his brow. "Oh, to the reunion. Yeah, he is. I'm going to meet up with him later. He said a bunch of our old gang is getting together before."

"Must be for Lucy."

Marc whipped his head around to look at me. "What did you just say?"

"Lucy. I think that's her name. I saw the flyers up at the high school."

"Flyers? For what?"

"For a search party. Did you know her?"

He nodded as he looked through me. "It was a small class. I knew everybody."

"I know that. But did you know her? Like, were you friends?"

"Yeah." His gaze went to the ceiling. "I loved her." A tear rolled down his cheek.

"Really? How come I've never heard you talk about her?" I perched on the edge of my seat as I awaited his response.

"I don't. She's the reason I moved away. I couldn't stand the thought of not knowing what had happened to her."

"What do you think happened to her?"

"I don't know. I always hoped she'd come back. I figured she just took off and she'd come back one day, and we could talk about where she went and what she did." He dropped his eyes to avoid my stare. "I guess she's probably dead."

"I'm sorry, Marc. I didn't mean to bring it up."

"It's okay. I've never stopped thinking about her. I guess that's why my relationships never last." He picked at the side of his thumb. "It was my fault."

"Don't say that. It was not. You were just a kid when she went missing. How could it be your fault?" I rocked in my seat, not knowing what I should do next. I wanted to hug him, but our relationship wasn't like that. We were more like strangers.

"No, it was. I should have never left her at that party. If I had stayed with her, she would have made it home. I would have made sure of it." Marc cracked his knuckles. "If I could do that night over, I would have made her come with me. I would have found someone else to bring Rick home."

"Marc, you can't change it now. It wasn't your fault."

"It was. You weren't there. You don't know."

"Tell me about it. What happened?"

"It was the night of our graduation; a bunch of us went out to the quarry for a party. We were all drinking and being stupid. Rick drank too much or smoked something he shouldn't have, and he started getting sick. I brought him home, and when I got back to the party, Lucy was gone. I asked around to try to find her, but no one knew anything. I didn't even have time to tell her goodbye or see ya later. I was just in a hurry to get Rick home, and I didn't take time to find her before I left. I was coming right back."

"Marc, that doesn't sound like it was your fault. There were other people there; it's not all on you."

"But Lucy went with me. It was my job to make sure she got home safe." Marc squeezed his eyes closed. "I should have never left her there."

"But you didn't; you went back for her. Maybe she left before you did."

"Hmm. Maybe she did. But it still doesn't change that I left her. I should have made sure. There's nothing I can do to change how much I fucked up."

"It was twenty years ago."

"Exactly. Twenty years of not knowing where she is, or if she's okay. Twenty years of hating myself."

"I'm sorry." I dropped my head as I tried to imagine how much pain he had been drowning in. "I had no idea you were hurting so much. You know you can always talk to me."

"Thanks, Molly. I don't talk to anyone about it. Lucy is always on my mind, but I never talk about her. I guess the guilt is too much. And I loved her so much."

"Are you going to help with the search party?"

"I guess. I don't really have a choice. It'd look pretty weird if I didn't."

"Can I come with you?" I asked as I twisted the back on my earring.

"Sure. I guess the more the merrier." Marc stood and stretched his arms over his head. "Do you want to go for a ride? I haven't been through town in ages."

"Yeah, anything to get out of here. I think I'm starting to smell like this place."

Marc pulled his shirt up to his nose and sniffed. "Aw man, I think you're right."

"See, I told you. Don't you think dealing with Dad would be better than this place?"

"Maybe, but I already paid for two nights." Marc grabbed his keys, and I followed him out the door.

"Where are we going?" I asked as I waited for my door to unlock.

"I don't know; wherever the car takes us."

"Alright, that sounds fun." I buckled my seat belt and checked my phone. Mom hadn't tried to call. I guessed I should have expected that; she never called me anymore. "Hey, does Mom call you?"

"No, not really. I guess I haven't talked to her in a while. I lost track of time and didn't really notice, not until you told me she's been sick."

"Didn't she used to call you all the time?" I rolled down the window to let the smell of fresh cut grass fill the car.

"Yeah, I guess so. I really should have come back sooner. It must be hell for you."

"It's okay. I'm used to it."

"What do you mean? How long has she been sick?" Marc took his eyes off the road long enough to look at me.

"It's probably been a couple of years." I focused my attention to the passing trees as I remembered the first time Mom went missing. "The first time happened the day I'd graduated high school."

"Shit, Molly. You should have called. I could have come home and helped you."

"You have a life in Virginia. I didn't want to bother you with the drama of Pine Grove."

"But you should be able to count on me. I'm your big brother."

"I know. I know you would have come if I'd called, but I didn't really know how bad it was, or that I should even be worried. It all happened so fast. Sort of. Time just stands still sometimes."

"That's for sure." Marc hit a button on the radio. "How about some music?"

"What is this." I raised my eyebrow. "You call this music?"

"Get out of my car right now."

"What?"

"If you can't appreciate music from the God of Rock and Roll, we can't be related."

"The God of Rock and Roll?" I laughed before I noticed he was serious. "Oh." I settled back into my seat.

"Tom Petty has gotten me through some pretty shitty times. I just crank it up and let him take me away." Marc's head moved with the music.

"Okay, well, it's growing on me."

"Kids today have no clue what real music is." Marc shook his head and turned up the volume. "Here's one of my favorites, *Mary Jane's Last Dance.*"

"I've heard this before. I love this song."

A smile spread across Marc's face. "You can stay."

We circled the neighborhood as the music played. I was grateful the words replaced the ones I couldn't find. How could I have not known how much pain my own brother was in? He was even more of a stranger than I ever knew.

CHAPTER FIVE

"Dad, did you work on that missing person's case in town?" I sat on the couch as I waited for him to put the newspaper down.

"What missing person's case?" he asked as he turned the page.

"You know, the girl from Marc's class. Lucy."

"Why in the hell are you digging up the past?" The newspaper crinkled as he lowered it.

"It's not really the past if she's still missing. Right? Shouldn't the department still be looking for her?" My throat closed as I waited for his response. I knew better than to poke the bear.

"The case was closed years ago. No one is looking for her. You should do yourself a favor and mind your damn business."

"Her friends are looking for her." I twisted my ruby ring, focusing my attention on the sparkly red stone.

"How in the hell do you know that?"

"There's flyers up all over town. It's been twenty years."

"Huh." Dad picked up the paper and returned to reading. "Not like they're going to find anything. Just a waste of damn time."

"You're probably right." I left him to his reading and went to get ready. I had to meet Marc in an hour to help with the search. I should have known it would have been a waste of time to ask Dad anything.

With forty-five minutes to wait, I took out my iPad and entered Lucy's name into the search bar and waited for the results to populate. The underwhelm of results sent a shock wave of disappointment through my body. How can no one be missing her? I guessed the internet wasn't a thing back then. I scrolled through the page and saw an article in the newspaper from ten years ago. The same flyer I saw at the high school appeared on the screen. I enlarged the photo to get a better look. It was hauntingly eerie how much she had looked like me. How come no one had ever mentioned it? Marc and I had some of the same teachers at Pine Grove High School. Someone must have noticed. Unless I was hallucinating or something.

I took my iPad and stood in front of my mirror, holding Lucy's picture by my face. *We could be twins.* How am I the only one who notices this? All these years living in this town, and no one speaks about her? Something just doesn't add up.

I couldn't bear the thought of waiting another minute. With plenty of time to spare, I grabbed my keys and drove to Shady Lane. Marc would understand more than anyone why I couldn't last at the house. Between the stress of Mom deteriorating and just Dad's overall presence, it was no wonder I hadn't moved across the country too. Nope, I had to be the responsible one. There was something keeping me here, if I wanted to be or not. I envied Marc's ability to just throw us away, but now I understood why. All those years of resentment I held just make me feel guilty now. I couldn't imagine living with the guilt he had.

Marc was in his car when I arrived at the hotel. Just in time. I grabbed my purse and joined him in his front seat. "Hey."

"Jesus, Molly, you scared the shit out of me."

"Sorry I'm early; I just couldn't last another minute at home." I looked over and saw the moisture in his eyes. "Are you alright?"

He rubbed his eyes dry with his hands. "I'm good."

"Marc, you can talk to me. I…"

"I'm fine. It's fine."

"Come on; just talk to me. You must be hurting. Let me help you."

"Molly, I'm fine. I'm just tired, that's all."

"It looks more than tired. You were crying. Just let me help. I want to hear about Lucy."

"Jesus, Molly, you're just like Mom." Marc laughed as he looked at his eyes in the rearview mirror. "I just miss her, that's all. Being back here is hard. The demons I've been running from have caught up to me. It just sucks."

"I'm sorry. I can't imagine what you're going through, but maybe this is what you need. Facing it head-on might bring you some peace. And you'll be with your friends; that will be nice, right?"

"When did you get so grown up?" Marc looked over at me, and his tears returned. "Jesus, I must be tired." He blinked his eyes.

"You see it too?"

"See what?"

"I look like her, don't I?"

"Yeah, you do. It's crazy. I've never noticed before."

"It was like staring in the mirror when I saw her picture on the posters. I don't understand how it's possible."

"I don't get it either." Marc took his attention off me and started the car. "Let's get going. Maybe there will be others just as eager to get this over with."

"You're not looking forward to seeing your friends?"

"Not really. I haven't kept in touch with anyone. This is going to be super awkward. But it's for Lucy, so why the hell not." He looked over his shoulder as he backed out of the parking space.

"Do you have any pictures of her?" I watched his face harden as he stared straight ahead.

"No." His knuckles turned white as his grip tightened on the steering wheel. "I lost a box of my stuff before I moved. When I started unpacking, I noticed it was missing. I called Mom and asked her to look for it, but she said it wasn't there."

"What was in it?"

"When Lucy went missing, I packed up all of our pictures and the notes she wrote to me. I guess I felt too guilty to have it around. I didn't want to get rid of it; I just didn't want it in my face, you know?"

"I'm sorry, Marc."

"Yeah, so I don't have anything from our time together. It was like we never happened."

"Maybe some of your friends have pictures or something."

"It doesn't really matter anyway. It's been so long. I should just get over it anyway."

"That's crazy! This isn't something you get over. You don't even know what happened to her."

"It's pretty obvious, though, isn't it?" Marc turned to look at me as his car came to a stop at the only traffic light in town.

"I mean, no one knows for sure. She could still be alive."

"That would make me feel even worse. She hated me that much that she would fake her own death to get away from me."

"She didn't really fake it. Maybe she was abducted or something. I've watched enough true crime stuff to know anything is possible."

"I don't know, Luc... I mean, Molly." Marc pulled his car into the high school parking lot. "Looks like we're not the only ones with nothing else to do on a Saturday."

"Do you recognize anyone?" I unbuckled my seat belt, trying to ignore the name slip.

"Unfortunately." Marc ran his hand through his hair. "Come on, let's go."

I followed Marc to the crowd of people standing by the bleachers. "Well, if it isn't 'ol Marc Jackson." A short, round man had his hands on his hips as Marc joined them.

"Still a pain in the ass, I see." Marc put his hands into his pockets.

"Yeah, some things will never change." A pretty blonde woman appeared behind the loud man. "Don't mind James; he doesn't get out much."

"Hey, Beth, it's nice to see you." Marc rocked on his heels.

"Keep your dirty paws off her." James grabbed Beth around the waist.

"Oh, wow, you guys are still together, huh?" Marc pushed up a smile.

"Yup, at least until something better comes along." James shrugged his shoulders.

"You're such an ass." Beth slapped him before peeling his hands off of her. "Looks like I'm up for grabs if you know of any decent men. Preferably ones who finished growing."

"Feisty as ever. I like that in a woman." Marc laughed as he waited for a reaction from the short man.

Beth made her way over to Marc and wrapped her arms around him. "It's so nice to see you. I've missed you." She kissed his cheek before pulling away. "Who's this?" She squinted her eyes at me.

"This is Molly, my kid sister."

"Hi." I looked at the ground, hoping no one else noticed the resemblance.

"Hi, Molly. I didn't know you had a sister, Marc." Beth reached her hand out. "I hope your big brother didn't tell you any of our secrets." She winked at Marc.

"What secrets are you talking about?" James joined the conversation.

"Oh, don't you worry about it. Just a little history between friends."

"Beth? What the hell are you talking about?" James crossed his arms.

"Calm down; she's messing with you." Marc put his hand on James' shoulder.

"I just mean all the trouble we all got into as kids. That's all. Don't get your panties in a bunch, honey." Beth kissed her husband's cheek.

"Seems your secrets are safe with Marc. I didn't even know about any of you."

"I don't really talk to anyone. Just keep myself busy with

work. Besides, Molly doesn't want to hear about all that stuff." Marc pulled me close to him. "Big brothers have to lead by example."

"Do you live here, Molly?" Beth asked.

"Yeah, I still live at home. I'm in college, so I can't afford my own place yet."

"That's cool. We still live here too. I'm surprised I've never seen you around." I felt Beth look me up and down. "You must have gone to school here too."

"Yeah, class of 2017."

"You're just a baby." Beth smiled. "It's nice to meet you. I'm glad you came to help with the search."

"Yeah, I saw the posters around. It must be hard not knowing after all these years." I kicked at the gravel.

"It really is. Lucy's sister, Angie, has never gotten over it."

"I don't blame her. It'd be all I could think about if Marc was missing. I mean, he practically is, but at least I know he's safe." I bit the inside of my cheek to try to distract myself from how stupid I must have sounded.

"Is Angie here?" Marc looked around the crowd.

"Not yet, but I expect she will be. She's the one who organized this, just like ten years ago."

"I haven't talked to her since everything happened." Marc hung his head. "I really fucked things up."

"Marc, knock it off. None of this is your fault. Everyone knew ... knows how much you love Lucy." Beth put her arm around Marc.

"Yeah, but I never should have left her there. I should have made sure she knew I would be right back. I..."

"No, Marc, you can't go there. You can't change what happened. You were just a kid. We all were." Beth closed her eyes and paused. "It was my fault. I'm the one who brought the peppermint schnapps. I'm the reason Lucy was drunk."

"What are you talking about? Lucy wasn't drinking." Marc raised his head to look at Beth.

"She was." Beth pushed a tear off her cheek. "I've never told anyone that before. I didn't want anyone to think whatever happened to Lucy was her fault. I figured if the cops knew, they'd stop looking."

"Yeah, well, they didn't really seem to care, even back then. That's why I just had to get out of here. I felt so helpless. There was nothing I could do." The color drained from Marc's face as he looked behind me.

I took a step closer to him before I turned around. A woman in a denim jacket with shoulder-length blonde hair approached us. She had a large blue tote bag tossed over her arm that looked heavier than she was. "Who is that?" My thought formed into words. I put my hand over my mouth as I realized who it was.

"Long time no see." The woman dropped the bag on the ground in front of Marc's feet.

"Angie, hi. How are you?" Marc stuffed his hands into his pockets.

"Really? That's all you have to say after twenty years?" Angie looked at her wrist before she scanned the football field. "Where is everyone?"

"Oh, you know, it's a nice day. They probably just want to spend it at the lake or something." Beth's smile didn't ease the tension.

"Must be nice to be able to not give a shit. Some people never change." Angie knelt by the tote bag and pulled out a stack of paper. "Here." She handed a pile to Beth and Marc. "Put these up while you're out looking today."

A tear rolled down Marc's cheek as she stared into Lucy's green eyes. "I can't believe it's been twenty years."

James took the fliers out of his wife's hand. "Jesus, Angie, don't you think you should give it a rest? I mean, it's been twenty years. There's no way we're ever going to find her, and if we do, she sure as hell isn't going to look like this."

"What the hell is wrong with you?" Beth kicked her husband in the shin. "Don't mind him; he's still the same asshole from high school."

"You can all think I'm crazy, but there's no way I'll ever be able to rest until we find her. She deserves a proper burial if nothing else." Angie's gaze met mine. "Who are you?"

"Hi, I'm sorry about your sister." I pulled my eyes away from her and tried to make myself invisible.

"Who are you?" I felt Angie's piercing stare.

"This is my little sister, Molly. She wanted to help with the search." Marc pulled me close to him.

"I didn't know you had a sister." Angie squinted her eyes, still not taking them off of me.

"Yup, guess I'm full of surprises." Marc squeezed my shoulder. "So what do you have planned for today? Where are we going?"

"Well, I was thinking we should start at the quarry." Angie picked up her tote bag and put it over her arm.

"The quarry?" Marc covered his mouth to catch his cough. "I don't know."

"What? It's where Lucy was last seen. Why wouldn't we start there?" Angie's grip tightened on her bag. "If you don't want to help, you don't have to."

"No, no, I want to help. It's just that I haven't been back there since…"

"Since Lucy went missing?" Angie pulled out more flyers before she left to gather up the others.

"Wow. She still hates you." James hit Marc in the chest.

"You really are an ass." Beth gave James a push. "Angie's always been intense. You know that. Don't let her get to you."

"She's right, though. I shouldn't have left. I should have stuck around and helped look for Lucy." Marc looked down at the photo in his hand. "I can't believe it's been twenty years."

"You keep saying that. It's like you're trying to say we're old." James laughed. "Don't be so hard on yourself. It was hard on all of us."

"He's right, for once. We were kids. Nothing like that had ever happened before. None of us knew what to do. We all know you loved her, and none of us blamed you for leaving town." Beth put her hand on Marc's back. "We don't have to go to the quarry; we can just hang these things up. Angie will never know. She'll be too busy to notice who's there and who's not."

"No, I want to go. I need to go." Marc looked over at me. "Have you ever been to the quarry?"

"Me? No, that's not a thing for kids my age. We have the internet. We don't need to party outside."

"Really? You have no idea what you're missing." James looked over at his wife as he awaited the smack that was coming. "What? We used to have a lot of fun there." He winked at Beth.

"We did, didn't we?" Beth smiled as the memories flooded

her. "I'm so glad we grew up without all this damn technology. It's so hard to keep up with."

"I don't know. I can't imagine living without it." I pulled my phone out of my pocket. "But I guess it would be nice to go somewhere without people always being able to reach you." I looked down at the screen. "Mom called."

"Should you call her back? Do you think she's okay? Should we go home?" Marc's questions added an extra layer of panic I wasn't ready for.

"I don't know. She doesn't call anymore. I guess I should check to make sure she's okay." I dialed the number and waited. "I got the answering machine." I tried to push all of the what-ifs out of my head. "Mom, it's Molly. I'm with Marc; I'll be home later. Are you..."?

"Molly? Is that you?" Mom's voice trembled, and I couldn't tell if she was scared or just confused.

"Yeah, Mom. I saw that you called. Are you alright? Do you need me to come home?"

"I don't remember calling you. I'm fine. Don't you worry about me. Just have fun with your brother."

"Are you sure? I can come home."

"Don't be silly. I'm fine. I love you, Molly."

"I love you too, Mom." I turned my phone off before I put it back in my pocket. "She's fine, I guess. It's just weird; she doesn't usually call."

"It's cool if you want to go home." Marc pulled out his phone. "No calls here. Guess you're still her favorite."

"Don't be a bonehead. I want to come with you guys. I want to see what this quarry is all about. See what I've been missing."

"I like her." Beth laughed. "I didn't think anyone else knew what a bonehead you were."

"Come on, guys; let's go. I want to get there before everyone else shows up." Marc took his keys out and dangled them in front of me. "Let us show you what you Gen Z's have been deprived of."

I followed Marc to his car and waited until the doors were closed before I let out the breath I was holding. "Are you okay?"

"Yeah, I'm fine. Why?" Marc's grip tightened around the steering wheel.

"Oh, I don't know. You just had a bunch of crap thrown at you. It's alright if you're not okay."

"It's just a lot. I came home because I was worried about Mom, and now I'm going back to the one place I vowed to never go again. Everything I've been running from is now right in front of me." Marc rested his head on the back of his seat.

"We don't have to go. Want to ditch them and go get pizza?"

"Nice try." Marc laughed. "You saw Angie; she'd hunt me down and kick my ass. She already hates me."

"I don't think she hates you. She just misses her sister."

"I know. I was just a real pussy. I should have stayed here."

"Stop that. You were a kid. You were taking care of yourself. I can't imagine losing the person I love like that."

"Wait, hold up. You have someone you love?" Marc scrunched his nose up. "Do I need to kick someone's ass?"

"No, that was a hypothetical someone." I hit his arm. "Come on, let's go."

"Uh huh. I believe you."

"You know Dad won't allow me to date."

"Molly, you're an adult. You don't have to listen to him anymore."

"Yeah, I do. I still live in his house. Trust me, I hear about it all the time."

"I don't know how you do it."

"I have no choice. Mom needs me." I looked out the window to try to push back the emotion building behind my eyes.

"See, I am an ass. I left you here too. I just took off and left everyone I loved the most behind to fend for themselves."

"To be fair, I wasn't even born when you left."

"I'm still a lousy big brother. I know how Dad was. I should have come back home after Mom told me about you."

"Told you about me? What do you mean?"

"You were a surprise. They weren't trying. I didn't know she was pregnant until you were almost born."

"You didn't know about me?" I turned to look at my brother's face. He really was just a stranger.

"I knew about you. I guess I just didn't talk to Mom about her sex life."

"Gross. Don't talk about it like that."

"Well, would you want to know about that stuff? If you were away at college, would you want the details?"

"Yeah, I'd want to know. Not the details, but I'd want to know how she was doing and help her get stuff ready for a baby. I think it'd be fun."

"Well, you're a girl. That's normal. But I didn't want to help her shop for baby clothes or decorate the nursery."

"When did you meet me? Did you come home after I was born?"

"I don't know, Molly."

"You didn't want me, did you?"

"It's not like that. I was an only child for almost twenty years. I figured Mom didn't need me anymore. She had you."

"For real, Marc? Am I the reason you stayed away? You didn't want to be around me?"

"No, it's not like that. Everything was just so screwed up. I was the one who was supposed to be starting a family, not my parents. It was like they were laughing in my face. I left, and they replaced me."

"That explains a lot." I squeezed my eyes closed. I couldn't look at him.

"Molly, it's not what you think. I was still so upset about Lucy. I couldn't let myself get close to anyone again. It hurt too bad. I love you, Molly. I'm glad you're my baby sister."

"You don't even know me."

"I know. I hate that. Why don't you come back to Virginia with me? There are some great schools down there."

"I can't leave Mom here. Some of us give a shit about other people."

"Ouch." Silence swarmed around us for the rest of the drive. I never knew I was the reason he'd stayed away. I was a mistake. That was all I'd ever be.

# CHAPTER SIX

"Looks like this is still the party spot. Do you have something you're not telling me, Molly?" Marc's attempt to break the silence only added to the tension.

"I'm not the one keeping things from people. Seems like you have enough secrets for both of us." I unhooked my seat belt and opened my door.

"Molly, I don't want you to be mad at me. You're not the reason I stayed away. I just couldn't stick around this town without Lucy. Something in me thought maybe she'd come back if I stayed away."

"How does that make sense? Why would she come back if you weren't around?"

Marc let out a heavy sigh. "Close the door." He rubbed his face. "Truth is the reason I left Lucy at the party that night was because we were fighting."

I turned to look at my brother's face, still unable to feel sorry for him.

"I've never told anyone that before." Marc avoided eye

contact as he continued. "It was our first real fight. We'd always been so good together."

"What happened?"

"She wanted to talk about something, but I didn't. I just wanted to have fun, and she got mad at me. She told me she never wanted to see me again, so I left."

"So you didn't take your friend home like you told me before?"

"I did. That was the first excuse to get out of there, and after I had some time to think, I was ready to hear what Lucy wanted to tell me. But she was gone."

"Did you hit her?" I wished the words didn't leave my thoughts.

"No, of course not. I loved her. I never would have hurt her. But I did. I was such an asshole."

"What did she want to talk to you about?"

"I don't know. I shut her down before she could get started. I told her it wasn't the time for it. We were supposed to be celebrating. I've always wondered what she wanted to tell me." Marc closed his eyes.

"You don't have any idea at all? You never tried to guess?"

"I've been trying to guess for the last twenty years, but I have no idea. Everything was so good between us. She was who I wanted to spend the rest of my life with. I'd do anything to go back and let her talk."

"This may sound stupid, but have you ever thought about seeing a medium?" I raised my eyebrow as I tried to read his face.

"It's crossed my mind, but then I'd have to admit she was gone. I'm not ready to go there."

"Not necessarily. I've watched some of those shows, and

I'm pretty sure the medium would be able to tell you if she was still alive or not. And if she's not, maybe she could tell you what she wanted to all those years ago."

"I guess the truth is I don't really want to know. The chase is always better than the catch." Marc blew the air out of his lungs.

"Don't you think you've been running long enough?" I put my hand on my brother's shoulder.

"When did you get so grownup?" Marc studied my face. "I just can't get over how much you look like Lucy. It's like I've been transported back in time."

"It's eerie. I wonder who else notices."

"Probably no one. It's probably just something I put in your head. All this talk about her, and it's bound to get weird."

"Seriously, Marc, look at me." I pulled down the visor and opened the mirror. "I don't look like anyone else. Just Lucy. And I didn't even know about her until a few days ago."

"It is a little strange. I mean, what are the chances you look like her? There are so many other people you could look like. Mom for one."

"I never noticed how different I look from Mom before. I don't think anyone else in the family has black hair."

"Or those eyes. I have lame blue ones."

"Your eyes aren't lame. They're the color of the sky, just like Dad's. It's the only part of him that makes him approachable." I laughed as the image of my father being friendly filled my head.

"What's so funny?" Marc raised his brow.

"I was just imagining Dad being nice." I spit out more laughter.

"That's definitely something to laugh about."

"I wonder why he's such an asshole." I blew the last of the image out with my breath.

"Probably something to do with being a sheriff all those years. I guess he had to be an asshole in that job."

"I guess, but do you think they're all assholes?"

"All the ones I've met." Marc shrugged. "Come on; let's go look around. I have no idea what they expect us to find twenty years later, but why the hell not."

"You never know. I've watched lots of *Dateline* shows where evidence is still hanging on after all these years."

"Damn, Molly, you need a life. All you do is watch TV?"

"What else is there to do in this town." The crunch of sticks under my feet made the kids in the quarry look up. "Shit, I know those guys." I pushed up a fake smile. "Can we please get out of here?" I whispered as I tugged on Marc's shirt.

"Why don't you go say hi?" Marc gave me a little push.

"No way. I'm not here for them. They're just a bunch of morons anyway."

"Oh, sounds like someone has a crush."

"You're impossible. There's a reason I'm single. I'm waiting for the right guy at the right time."

"There's no such thing as either. You just have to live a little." Marc shoved his hands into his pockets.

"Good advice. Maybe you should give it a try."

"Touché." Marc surveyed the area. "Over there." He nodded in the direction of the trees. "That's where Lucy and I made it official."

"Official? Like where you asked her to be your girlfriend?"

Marc's face grew red. "Not exactly. Forget I said anything."

"Eww. Gross. You guys did it?"

"Yeah, that's what you do when you're in love."

"But outside? And here?" I stuck my tongue out.

"What, it's what kids of the 90s did. We were bored. What can I say?"

"Let's go over there and see if we can find anything."

"What? Used condoms?" Marc laughed. "TMI?"

"A little. You're sick. Come on; let's at least take a look around."

Beth and James came up behind us. "Find anything?" James gave Marc a little push.

"Nope. You?" Marc turned to face James.

"Yeah, your sorry ass." James pulled an amber bottle out of his sweatshirt pocket. "Want one?"

"Jesus, it's not even noon." Marc pushed the beer out of his face.

"Come on, man, like old times." James twisted the cap off and held it up in one last attempt.

"No. I don't want this to be like old times. Let's just do what we came here for, and get out of here."

"What are we here for?" James took a sip. "You really don't know what you're missing."

"What? Piss warm beer? I'm good." Marc took my hand and dragged me away. "We're going to look in the woods."

"You're such a buzzkill." James tilted his head back and finished the beer with one long chug.

I heard Beth slap her husband as we ventured away from them. "Yikes. Old people are lame."

"Hey, I take offense to that." Marc dropped my hand and stood still before we reached the line of trees. "I don't know if I can go in there."

"You don't have to. I'll go and look around, then we can leave." I started for the wall of pine trees and felt Marc tug at my shirt.

"No, don't go in there. What if you don't come out? I'd never be able to forgive myself."

"Marc, it's fine. Nothing is going to happen to me. It's daytime, and there's a bunch of people here. Just relax."

"I can't. I'm coming with you." Marc followed behind me. "You know I love you, right?"

"I know." I let the lie hang in the air as the branches scratched my face.

"I hate how fast life gets away from you. One day I'm a teenager, and the next day I'm a lame old guy."

"I didn't mean you. I was talking about him." I turned around and saw Marc pressing his hand into the trunk of a tree.

"Lucy and I carved our initials into one of these trees. I was going to marry that girl."

"Did she know that was your plan?"

"No, I never got the chance to ask her. I was going to do it at the end of summer, after I saved enough money to buy her a ring. Instead, I used that money to get the hell out of here."

"I'm sorry life went to shit for you. You know it's okay to move on and be happy. You don't have to punish yourself anymore." I put my hand on his back and felt his body tremble.

"But I do. I'll never be able to move on without knowing what happened to her."

"Come on; let's get out of here." His sadness radiated through me. I knew what I needed to do. Find Lucy.

# CHAPTER SEVEN

Before we reached Marc's car, my cell phone vibrated in my pocket. My heart fell to the pit of my stomach when I saw the number. "It's Dad. I have to answer it."

"No, you don't. Let it go to voicemail."

"I can't." I exhaled the emotions I had been harboring before I accepted the call. "Hey, Dad, is everything alright?"

"What do you think?"

"I don't know. That's why I'm asking. Is Mom okay?"

"No, she's gone again. She must have left when I dozed off. She took her purse but left her cell phone."

"Do you know how long she's been gone?"

"No, I just told you I didn't see her leave."

"Okay, I'll start the search." I rubbed the bridge of my nose. "Mom's gone. She left her phone this time."

"Why do you all freak out when she leaves the house? Doesn't she ever get groceries or anything?"

"Not alone, not since Dad retired. If he doesn't go with her, I do. She gets lost."

"Does she? Or is she just sick of being a prisoner? She was smart enough to leave her phone behind; that was planned."

"Or she could have just forgot it. Come on; I have to get back to my car." I pulled on the door handle.

"No, I want to help." The lock shut up with a click. "Get in, and tell me where to go."

"The thing is I don't know where she goes. I've never found her. Dad always does."

"Isn't that weird? How come he always finds her? He probably has a GPS tracker on her or something."

"I don't think so, or she wouldn't be missing. We'd know where she was."

"Where does Dad say he finds her?" Marc peered into his rearview mirror as he backed out of the row of cars.

"He doesn't. It's always a big secret."

"Have you ever asked Mom where she goes?"

"I always ask her."

"And?"

"And she never really says anything."

"Nothing?"

I thought back to our last conversation just a couple days ago. "Actually the last time she was gone she said something about the house in the woods, but then Dad came in, and she wouldn't say anything more."

"The house in the woods? That sounds like a song." Marc tapped his steering wheel to the imaginary beat playing in his mind.

"I have no idea what she was talking about, and I didn't dare ask Dad."

"Good call. She probably doesn't want him to know." Marc turned on the radio and hit a few buttons until something other than static came on. "Do you think Mom's scared of Dad?"

"I never would have thought so before, but the last couple of years she does seem afraid. I don't know if it's because she doesn't remember him or because he just gets meaner with age."

"He does seem to be a new level of asshole these days."

"And you haven't seen anything yet." I kept my eyes on the road as I searched for Mom's car.

"Where should we start?"

"I have no idea. Why don't you just continue driving and see where the road takes us."

"You think that's helpful? Should we call the cops? Do they know Mom gets lost?"

"No, Dad won't let me call the police. He gets a whole new level of asshole if I even mention it."

"Why? That doesn't make sense. He was a cop; he should know they just want to help."

"I think he's embarrassed. She's not the perfect wife he painted her to be."

"I guess, but wouldn't you think he'd want their help?"

"Right, but don't even think about it. He'd have your ass. And, I think he can take you."

"You're just full of compliments today. Lame and weak. I think I need a nap."

"I'm sorry. You don't have to help. You have so much stuff on your mind; you don't need to be worried by this right now."

"Molly, she's my mom too. I want to help. It's the least I can do." Marc circled Main Street and slowed down when he hit a line of cars. "I'm gone for twenty years and Pine Grove gets traffic?"

"Don't get too excited. This only happens on Alumni weekend. Typically, there is no action on these streets. Unless someone's cows get loose, or a herd of turtles cross the road."

"I kind of miss this."

"What, the turtles or the cows?"

"The quietness. Even with the traffic, it's still way calmer than Virginia. It takes forever to get anywhere."

"If you miss it so much, why don't you move back here?"

"I was thinking the same thing. Maybe you can help me find an apartment. There's no way I'd be able to move back home, and I don't know if I'll be able to make it both nights at Shady Lane. I know how it got its name now."

"Really? You want to move home?"

"Not home, but back here. You could move in with me."

"Oh my god, that's so exciting. But what about your place down there? Your job? Your stuff?"

"One thing at a time, grasshopper. Let's find Mom so I can tell her the news."

"She'll be so happy." My cheeks lifted into a smile too big to hide as I continued my lookout. "I can't wait to get to know you."

"You know me."

"Not really. I don't really know anything about you. I didn't know about Lucy."

"I'm sorry. I promise to be there for you from now on." Marc slowed the car down. "Is that Mom?"

"Where?" I squinted my eyes as I looked in the direction he was pointing.

"Over there, by the telephone pole."

"It is. Holy crap, you're magic. I've never been able to find her before. See, we do need you."

Marc pulled his car onto the side of the road behind Mom's car. "What is she looking at?"

"I don't know." I pressed my face against the window to try to get a better look. "It looks like one of those flyers that Angie had. What the heck is she doing with it?"

"It looks like she is tearing them down. Look at her hand, she has a stack of them." Marc looked over at me.

"Why would she be doing that?" I opened my door.

Marc held my arm. "Wait, let's see what she's doing."

I closed the door and watched as my mom looked at the paper she had taken off the pole. She walked back to her car and looked around before she got into her car. "Come on; we have to go before she leaves."

"No, let's follow her and see where she's going." Marc pulled out behind Mom as she headed south.

"What if she notices we're following her?"

"Then she notices. Don't you want to know where she goes when she takes off?"

"Yeah, but what if she gets mad?" The heat from the sun made my brow start to sweat.

"Then she gets mad. We're not doing anything wrong. She's our mom; it's not like we're just stalking random old ladies."

"Okay, but I'm throwing you under the bus if she gets pissed off."

"Fair enough." Marc slowed down to let Mom get further ahead of us. "Where do you think she's going?"

"I have no idea, but she's headed out of town. Don't you think we should try to get her to pull over? What if we lose track of her?" I fidgeted on the seat as I thought about Dad finding out we'd lost her, again.

"I'm not going to lose her. I can see her. Let's just see where she's going." Marc increased his speed to ease some of my worry.

"I don't like being sneaky. I want Mom to trust me."

"Molly, we're not following her to be sneaky. We just want to make sure she's okay. Don't worry; everything is going to work out."

Mom turned onto a dirt road, making Marc come to a stop. "What are you doing?"

"There's no way she won't notice if I follow her down there."

"So now what?" The anger started to fester. "You should have let me talk to her back there. At least it would have looked normal, like we were driving through town, but no. Why doesn't anyone ever listen to me?"

"You're right." Marc turned onto the road behind Mom. "She's just going to have to get pissed off. I'll take the blame."

"What the hell is out here? Why would she travel this road? It goes nowhere. Look, it's dead-end."

"I don't know. I guess we're going to find out." Marc slowed his speed until we could only see the tail end of Mom's car. "Look, she's stopping."

"Yeah, probably because there's nowhere else to go."

"Calm down." Marc sat on the edge of his seat, his head as close to the windshield as he could get it. He pulled in next to her. "Wait here." He got out and walked over to Mom's window and gave a wave.

I leaned over as close to Marc's window as I could to try to hear what they were saying. Mom rolled down her window and said something I couldn't make out.

"Hey, Mom, is everything okay?"

"What are you doing here?" Mom's voice was louder with each word. I couldn't tell if she was angry or afraid.

"We just saw you in town and wanted to see where you were going." Marc ran his hand through his hair. "I just wanted to see if you needed help with anything."

Mom stuck her head out the window. "Who's with you? Is that Molly?"

"Yeah, she was with me. But this was all my idea; she didn't want to follow you. She told me to leave you alone."

Mom smiled and waved at me. "I'm fine. I was just going for a drive."

"What are you doing here?" Marc leaned down to look into her car.

"It's a nice day. I was going for a walk."

"Here?" Marc stood back up and looked around. "Why would you come all the way out here?"

"Oh, never mind. Why don't we get back home?"

"Are you sure? Why don't we just walk with you? This looks like a nice spot."

I couldn't hear what Mom said, but her car started. Marc stepped back as Mom turned the car around in the clearing. Marc was left standing under the pine trees. "What did she say when you told her you wanted to walk with her?"

"Don't be silly. And then she told me to get home for lunch." Marc lifted his shoulders before he followed Mom's lead.

"That's it? She wasn't mad?"

"I don't think so. She didn't seem confused either. It seemed like she came here on purpose."

"Why would you say that? Why would she come here?"

"I don't know, but she seemed to know what she was doing." Marc rolled up his window. "Do you think she was going to meet someone?"

"Meet someone? What do you mean? We were the only ones there."

"I don't know. Do you think Mom could be having an affair? You said her and Dad haven't been getting along lately. Maybe there's someone else."

"Are you trying to say she doesn't have dementia? This is all a show because she's dating someone else?"

"No, I don't know what I'm trying to say. Obviously if the doctor thinks she's sick, then she's sick. I just think there may be more to the story than we all know. There always is." Marc turned the radio up to drowned out any chance of a conversation. Could he be right? Was Mom running away to be with someone else and pretending to be sick? Making me feel guilty so I didn't leave home?

# CHAPTER EIGHT

Marc asked me to be his date to attend his reunion. I jumped at the chance. I wanted to talk to Angie at the search, but we'd left before I had the opportunity. I grabbed my sweater before I rushed out the door. Marc specifically asked me to meet him by the road, so he didn't have to talk to Dad.

"Looking good, Marc. Are you planning on picking up a lady tonight?" I giggled as I got in the car.

"Oh god no. I just want to get through tonight. Thanks for coming with me."

"Anything to get out of the house." I pulled the seat belt out and buckled it. "You know you're going to have to talk to Dad eventually."

"I know. Tonight's just not the right time. I can only deal with one thing at a time, and I'm already about to hyper-ventilate."

"Relax. You know all these people."

"Exactly. I haven't seen these people in two decades. They're pretty much strangers."

"It won't be that bad. I think you'll be surprised at how much fun you're going to have."

"You do know we're going to hang out with a bunch of lame old people, right?" Marc's smile grew, accentuating his dimples.

"Old people? They're your age."

"Exactly."

"Oh, shut up. You're not old. Just try to have a good time tonight." I reached over and gave his knee a tap.

"What if they think I did it?" Marc's body stiffened as he stared straight ahead.

"Think you did what?"

"You know. Killed Lucy."

"Why would they think that? Everyone knew how much you loved her."

"Because I ran away. That's something a guilty person would do."

"Not necessarily. And you didn't just run away; you went to college. I'm sure you weren't the only person who left, at least for a while."

"Yeah, but their girlfriend isn't missing." Marc tapped his thumb on the steering wheel.

"I'm sure you're overthinking this. Don't worry. I'm sure you're the only one thinking anything like that."

"I don't know." Marc pulled into the back of the parking lot. "Just in case we need to make a getaway." Nervous laughter spilled out of him. "You ready?"

"The real question is, are you?" I'd never seen him this nervous before.

Marc got out of the car and stretched his arms over his

head before he shook his arms at his side. "Come on; let's get this over with."

I followed him onto the football field where tents were waiting for graduation tomorrow. "I never knew they let people drink here. I feel cheated."

"Cheated? You're not even twenty-one yet." Marc shot me a look of disapproval.

"Says the guy who drank at the quarry every weekend."

"Do as I say, not as I do."

"Always." I pulled my sweater on as we approached the crowd.

"Guess we're over there." Marc nodded toward the big 1999 sign in the back of the tent.

The tables were already filled with empty beer bottles and wine glasses. James and Beth waved for us to join them. "Marc, Marc's little sister, over here."

"Jesus." Marc mumbled before he smiled and waved at his friends.

I let him take the lead as I scanned the crowd. I didn't see Angie anywhere. A sinking feeling of disappointment settled in my stomach. She was my only hope of finding out what had happened to Lucy. I needed to figure it out now more than ever, before Marc let it destroy any more of his life.

"Hey, guys." Marc pulled out a folding chair and joined them.

"You're not going to get your sister a chair?" James jumped up to pull one out for me.

"What the hell; she's just a kid." Beth rolled her eyes. "No offense, Molly. It just seems James had one too many, and he needs to remember his wife is sitting right here."

I didn't remember Beth being so uptight the other day.

"It's okay." I took a chair closer to Marc as the dread my brother had been feeling was now circulating my body.

"Want a drink?" James pushed a beer over to me.

Marc took it. "Thanks."

Beth slapped her husband's hand. "Knock it off. She's probably not even old enough to drink."

I felt my throat tighten as I tried to drown out the tension. I pulled my sleeves over my hands and tucked them under my thighs.

"How old are you?" Beth's once friendly eyes turned cold as they pierced through me.

"Nineteen."

"See that. She's just a few years older than your daughter. Cut the shit, you fucking prick." Beth emptied her glass before she stormed away from the table.

"What was that about?" Marc rolled the bottle between his hands.

"Oh, she's just pissed." James took a swig of his beer. "She found out about my girlfriend."

"Girlfriend? I guess she deserves to be pissed."

"Oh, don't go all high and mighty on me. Everyone fucks around from time to time. It's what keeps things interesting."

"No, that's not how it works. Jesus, man."

"Don't tell me you've never fooled around."

"I haven't. Who is she? Someone Beth knows?"

James tossed his head back with laughter. "Yeah. It's our babysitter."

"Your babysitter? How old is she?" Marc scrunched up his nose.

"She's twenty-two now. I'm not a monster."

"How in the hell did you pull that off? A twenty-two-year-old?"

"What's that supposed to mean?" James tilted his head.

"You're a mess. How in the world did you talk her into it?"

I couldn't contain myself. "Maybe the beer." I slapped the table.

"Good one." Marc jabbed me with his elbow. "What's wrong with you, though? I mean, why would you do that to Beth? She's the mother of your kids."

"It just happened." James twisted the cap off another bottle. "Besides, it's over. Beth told me I had to break it off."

"And she's not going to leave you?"

"She said she needed time to think about it." James shrugged before he pressed the bottle to his lips.

"How'd she find out?" Marc asked.

"She found messages on my phone and then walked in on us."

"Walked in on you? Where were you?"

"At the Shady Lane."

Marc held his head in his hands. "Fuck, dude. I heard that. All of it. I had no idea it was you. Gross."

"See, I told you that place was nasty." My body shuddered as I tried to shake the image out of my head.

"It just gets old. I needed to spice it up. It wasn't a big deal. Well, not until Beth walked in."

"How the hell did she walk in? You didn't lock the door?" Marc finished off his beer.

"It was locked, but Beth's cousin, Frank owns the place." James leaned back in his chair. "When she saw my car parked out front, she demanded he give her a key, and then she let herself in. Thank god she doesn't know where any of my guns are."

"How the hell could you overlook that?" Marc shook his head.

"I don't know. I guess I wasn't thinking with the right head."

"Gross." I pushed myself away from the table. "I'm going to go the bathroom."

"Do you want me to go with you?" Marc stood to follow me.

"No, I'll be okay. I know my way around. Besides, it looks like you're sitting with the only predator here." I walked away before either one had a chance to respond. I left the tent and walked to the backside and found the porta-potties. Beth was talking to Angie. *Great.* The one person who hated me here was talking to the only person I needed to talk to.

I turned my back to them as I waited in line and thought about my options. It wasn't like I wanted her husband. He was vile. I didn't understand why she wanted him. As I inched closer to my turn, I felt a tap on my shoulder.

"Molly?"

I slowly turned my head and saw Angie standing next to me. I looked around to make sure Beth didn't follow her. The coast was clear. "Hi." My face flushed as all of the questions I wanted to ask her vanished.

"When you're done, do you have a few minutes so we could talk?" Angie's smile was welcoming, but it felt like there was more behind it.

"I don't know what Beth told you, but I don't want anything to do with James."

Angie laughed. "Who does? I never knew what she saw in him."

"Okay, I can wait." I stepped out of line. "I actually don't even have to go; I just wanted to get away from James. He's creepy."

"He really is." Angie folded her arms and started to walk away from the crowd. "So I just wanted to introduce myself and thank you for helping the other day."

"It's no problem. I wanted to help."

"It means a lot. The more people who help, the closer we are to finding answers."

"It sounds crazy, but I didn't even know about Lucy until the other day. I didn't know she was missing or that she and Marc dated."

"You didn't know? He never talked about her?" Angie turned up her nose.

"No. I went to school here too, and I'd never heard about her. Why wouldn't they mention her?"

"I don't know. Every chance I get to go inside, I cover the bulletin boards with the flyers. They must take them down as soon as I leave. I don't know why the whole thing has to be a secret. The more we talk about it, the more of a chance we have of finding her."

"Do you have any idea of what happened to her?" I crossed my arms to match Angie.

"No, there's never been any leads of any kind. She just vanished."

"I'm sorry. I can't imagine how hard that must be."

"Yeah, it's impossible to do anything else. I can't live my life until I know where she is. I'm pretty certain she's dead, but it'd still be nice to have her body so we could have a funeral, a place to visit her. Everything is just so…"

"Unsettled?"

"Yeah, how can I move on when I don't have any answers." Angie dropped her arms to her side. "I feel like I've wasted my life. Twenty years of just searching. I never got married or had kids. Time just slipped away from me."

"There's still time." I put my hand on her arm before pulling it away. "I'm sorry."

"No, it's okay." Angie smiled. "It's been so long since I've had a friend."

"Were you in the same class as Lucy and Marc?"

"Yeah. We were only eleven months apart. I think she hated having her kid sister in her class. Her friends were my friends. We didn't have anything of our own. We even shared our room."

"Were you at the party?"

"No, I was supposed to go, but my boyfriend and I wanted to be alone. His parents were out of town for the weekend, so we went to his house. I beat myself up over not going every single day. If I were there, I wonder if she'd still be here today."

"That's a lot to carry around. I'm sorry."

Angie brushed the tears off her cheeks. "It's okay. I should just get on with my life. But I can't."

"No, you shouldn't. You have every right to be sad. If I were you, I think I'd do the same thing. I don't know how I'd ever be able to stop looking." I took a step closer to her. "Can I give you a hug?"

"I'd like that." She opened her arms and welcomed my embrace. "Thank you, Molly."

"I really want to help you. I'll do anything you need." I tightened my arms around her before I stepped away. "I don't have any friends around here. It'd be nice to have someone to hang out with."

"Wow, Molly, that'd be great. Everyone wanted to help in the beginning, when Lucy first went missing, but as the years went on, they stopped coming."

"I'm glad you came and rescued me from my fake bathroom break." My heart sank when my phone vibrated in my back pocket. "I'm sorry; I have to check this." I pulled out my phone and saw an SOS text from Marc. "Oh, it's just Marc looking for me to rescue him from James."

Angie's eyes narrowed. "Is everything okay?"

I looked down at my phone and put it back in my pocket. "Yeah. It's just that my mom's sick, and I never know when my dad is going to need me to come home."

"Oh, I'm sorry. I didn't know about your mom."

"It's okay. I just hate to be rude and check my phone."

"It's not rude. I'd do the same thing if my parents needed me." Angie smiled. "Do you want to go rescue your brother?"

"I probably should. Do you want to join us?"

"No, I probably shouldn't." Angie pushed a strand of blonde hair behind her ear. "There's a few people I'm supposed to meet up with."

"Okay, well, it was really nice to talk with you."

"You too." She took her phone out of her purse. "Can I have your number?"

"Sure." She handed me the phone, and I entered a new contact before giving it back to her.

Angie sent a text. "Don't worry; it's just me." She winked before we went our separate ways.

I took my phone out and sent a smile face emoji back to Angie and a thumbs up to Marc. When I looked back at my phone, another message from Angie arrived. "Can we not let Marc know about this? Just not yet."

"OK." The only response I felt I could give. Why couldn't Marc know about it? If I wanted to help find Lucy, I knew I had to gain Angie's trust. Marc kept secrets from me, so what could it hurt?

"Where have you been?" Marc's eyes widened before he pushed up a smile.

"Sorry, there was a long line." I shrugged and took my seat next to him. Beth had returned, another empty wine glass in front of her.

"Hey there, Molly." She smiled, and this time it looked sincere.

"Hi." I gave her my biggest smile.

"I'm sorry if I scared you away. I was just in a bad mood. I'm not usually like that. I'm usually super nice. Isn't that right, Marc?" She leaned over the table and reached for his hand.

"Sure." Marc pulled his hand to his lap. "Molly, what time were you supposed to get home?"

I tilted my head to try to pick up the cues he was giving me. "Um, I don't know. Let me check." I turned my phone over and went into my messages to see one I had missed from Marc. "Oh no, looks like we're late. I have to get back home to babysit the neighbor's dog." I raised my eyebrow when I turned to look at my brother.

He stood and brushed off his jeans. "Aw, that sucks. Looks like we have to get out of here."

"Will you come back?" Beth batted her eyelashes at him.

"Maybe." Marc put his hand on my back and gave me a little push. "See you later."

When we were out of the tent, I turned to look at Marc. "What was that about?"

"I have no idea, but Beth was trying to get in my pants something fierce. I guess she's trying to get revenge on James, but he's too drunk to notice."

"Did you two ever, you know?" I wiggled my eyebrows.

"Beth?" Marc smiled. "Maybe."

"Hold on. You and Beth? Does James know?"

"No, and he never will, right?"

"Not like I'm going to tell him, but Beth might. She's pretty pissed off."

"She should be. What kind of creep does that?" Marc kicked at the grass.

"When did the two of you hook up?"

"It was before Lucy. It wasn't serious, but she was my first."

"That's pretty serious." I put my hands on my hips. "Do you still like her?"

"No. That ship has sailed, many moons ago. Besides, she's married."

"Apparently that doesn't matter. Just ask James." I waited by the car door for him to unlock it.

"No, I'm not a homewrecker." Marc got in, letting the door slam shut. "So are you going to tell me what you were really doing?"

"What do you mean? I was going to the bathroom."

"No, you weren't. I looked for you."

"I needed to get away from James. He was making me uncomfortable." I shifted in my seat as the lies poured out.

Although, they weren't really lies. He was making me uncomfortable.

"You and me both." Marc pulled out of the parking lot. "Thanks for coming with me tonight. I'm sorry James was such an ass."

"It's fine. Thank you for bringing me with you. It was nice to spend time with you." And it was. I liked being with Marc. Now if I could figure out a way to make my new friendship work without messing up the relationship I'd always wanted with my brother. Nothing was ever simple. That was life, I guessed.

# CHAPTER NINE

The sun cascaded over my body as I stretched my arms over my head. I tossed the covers off me and picked up my phone. It was too nice of a day to stay inside. Maybe I could convince Marc to go for a walk with me. A message from an unknown number pulled my attention away from my brother. "Hey, Molly. This is Angie. I was wondering if you wanted to go for a walk today."

"Hmm, is she a mind reader?" I reread the message until I knew what I needed to do. "I'd love to. Where do you want to meet?"

"Great! How about the park?" Her message appeared before I had a chance to set down my phone. Was she waiting for me to reply?

"I can be there in an hour." My heart raced as I waited for her answer.

"See you then."

I felt like I was James, and Angie was the other woman. Sneaking around didn't feel good. And why were we? I rushed around my room and pulled on my jeans and my favorite Green Day t-shirt before going to the bathroom to finish getting ready.

Mom was sitting at the kitchen table when I went in to find breakfast. "Where are you off to?"

I answered with my head in the fridge. "Just going for a walk."

"It's such a nice day. I'm glad." Her monotone voice made me take a second look.

"Mom? Are you okay?" I set the orange juice on the counter.

"Yes. I'm fine." Her gaze was fixed on the wall in front of her.

"Mom, what's the matter?"

"Nothing, dear."

On the counter next to the paper towels was a bottle of medication with the label torn off. "Mom, did you take these?" I brought the empty container to show her. I shook it in front of her face until I got her attention. "Did you take these?"

"No, why would I?" Mom's voice returned to normal. "Molly, I'm not a child. You don't need to treat me like one." She brushed my arm out of her face.

"I know; I'm sorry." I returned the bottle and poured my juice. "I just worry about you because I love you. I don't want anything to happen to you."

"You don't need to worry about me. I'm just fine." Mom's cheeks raised in an attempt to smile.

"Would you tell me if you needed help?" I sat in the chair closet to her.

"It's not your job to help me. I'm supposed to take care of you."

"You do, but why can't we take care of each other? That's what family does." I glanced over at the microwave clock and debated on canceling with Angie. I should take Mom for a walk. I should be taking care of my family. Then I remembered why I wanted to go with Angie; to help Marc.

"That's true. You're such a good girl." Mom put her hand on mine. "I love you, honey."

"I love you too, Mom." I let her hand linger on mine before I excused myself. I didn't want to keep Angie waiting.

Angie was already standing under the tall oak tree when I pulled in. "Hey, I'm sorry I'm late."

"You're not late. I just wanted to soak in all of the sun I could." Angie stretched her arm across her face. "I never remember to stretch."

"Yeah, me either. But I figure if we're just walking, what's the point."

"You're right." She tossed her hands up. "You ready?"

"Sure, where do you want to go?"

"Well, graduation is happening right about now, so maybe we can just walk around here? Nothing too strenuous."

"Sure, that's smart. I forgot about graduation. We should have a little while before the kids are out here causing mischief." I closed my eyes and dropped my head. "I'm sorry. I didn't mean to..."

"No, it's okay; don't worry. I know what you mean. Those kids can get pretty rowdy."

"Today must be hard for you, though." I fidgeted with my hair tie on my wrist.

"It used to be, but it gets a little easier every year. I try not to use up too much of my energy on the negative thinking."

"I'm sorry."

Angie put her hand on my arm. "Molly, it's fine. Let's soak up that sunshine."

"Alright." I followed her to the water fountain in the center of the park.

She reached into her pocket and took out some change. "Do you want to make a wish?" She handed me a shiny copper penny.

"Sure, why not." With the coin in my hand, I closed my eyes and made my wish. I looked over at Angie who was doing the same thing. We tossed our pennies in together. I knew in my heart we were wishing for the same thing. To find Lucy.

Angie sat on the edge of the fountain and focused her attention on the change in the bottom. "I think most of that's from me. I come here a lot and make the same wish. Well, different, but the same."

I joined her on the wet concreate. "I don't blame you. I believe in miracles."

"Well, that makes one of us."

"You have to keep your thoughts positive, which I know has to be next to impossible most days, but if you let that negativity creep in, you've already lost."

"Wow, those are wise words for such a young lady." Angie squinted her eyes to block the sun. "How old are you? I mean, if you don't mind me asking."

"I'm nineteen."

"You're just a baby." Angie smiled. "When's your birthday?"

"March seventeenth. My mom always told me I was lucky since I was born on St. Patrick's Day. She sometimes used to joke about finding me under a rainbow."

"That's cute." Angie's attention was pulled back to the water.

"When's your birthday?"

"August second, but I'm pretty close to twice your age."

"Age is just a number. What's that they say? You're only as old as you feel?"

"I hope not, because I'd be even older." Angie laughed. "This is nice. I love it here. I'm glad you could join me."

"I always walk alone. It's nice to have company."

"You should never walk alone, not in this town." Angie sighed. "Not while there is a killer or kidnapper roaming the streets."

"I honestly didn't know about that until last week. I guess I should be more careful, but this is Pine Grove; nothing happens here. At least, that's what I thought."

"I can't believe your parents never warned you. Your Dad was the sheriff." Angie shook her head.

"I usually just stay home, so maybe he didn't think I needed to know. Maybe he didn't want to scare me."

"Well, will you promise me that if you want to go for a walk, you give me a call? Or text; whatever it is you kids do these days."

"Text. I can't believe your generation actually had to have conversations on the phone."

"Yeah, and our phone was attached to the wall. There was zero privacy, unless you lucked out and got to be home alone." Angie smiled as she took in the memories. "But seriously, please don't go alone."

"Okay, I'll check with you."

"I just don't want anything to happen to you." Angie took my hand.

"Thank you. It's nice to be cared about."

"This is going to sound crazy, but…"

"I look like Lucy?" Chills traveled up my spine when I realized what I had said.

"Yeah. How did you know I was going to say that?"

"I saw the flyers you have up."

Angie smiled. "In a weird way it's like I have my sister back when I look at you."

I tried to smile, but my mouth wouldn't move.

"I'm sorry. I went too far." Angie covered her eyes.

"No, that's not it." I expelled the air trapped in my lungs. "It's just strange."

"Yeah, that it is." Angie stood up. "Hey, do you want to go back to my place? I can show you some of Lucy's pictures."

"Okay, sure. Where do you live?"

"On Lilac Avenue."

"That's by Shady Lane." I gave the elastic on my wrist a snap.

"Yeah, just past it."

"That's where Marc is." I took a step back.

"Do you want me to drive us there? I can bring you back to get your car later."

"Sure, that will work." I followed behind Angie. "How come you don't want Marc to know we're talking?"

"I just don't want to upset him. I know how broken up he is about the whole thing."

"Oh, okay, that makes sense."

"It's unlocked; you can get in." Angie opened the driver's door to her Volkswagen Jetta.

The bright red car was going to be hard to miss. I hoped Marc wasn't outside enjoying the sunshine when we'd drive by. I'm not sure how I could explain this to him now. Angie was right; it would be too hard for him to know, at least until we find Lucy.

# CHAPTER TEN

Angie handed me a stack of photo albums. "Here, start with the blue one; that's from when we were babies." She pointed to the book on top.

I flipped the cover open and saw baby pictures of Lucy. Some with her parents and some of her alone in different positions and outfits. "She was a cute baby." I smiled as I turned the page.

"She was. She was my parents' first child, so there are a ton more pictures of her than there are of me." Angie leaned closer to me to get a better look. "I think they felt guilty about that and put some of Lucy's baby pictures in my photo albums."

"Really? But you two look so different."

"We didn't as babies. Besides, all babies look alike. I didn't catch on until I saw the same pictures in here as I have in the albums my parents made for me."

"You said you're eleven months younger than her? They were probably exhausted taking care of both of you. Can you imagine? Two babies under one?" I ran my fingers over a photo of Lucy sitting up next to a tree. "She was adorable."

"You're probably right. I always just felt like she was their favorite." Angie took another book from the stack. "Here, look at this one."

I set the other album on the coffee table and opened the new album. "How old is she here?"

"She was six. It was our first day of school."

"Where are you?"

"In my own album. My mom separated our pictures into these books for our graduation gift. I'm not sure where the pictures of the two of us together ended up. Mom probably kept those."

"That's a sweet gift." I turned the page. "Oh, here you are."

"I guess I haven't looked at these in a while. I forgot what was in there." Angie pointed at her five-year-old self. "I can't believe my mother let me leave the house looking like that." She shook her head and laughed. "I bet you had way cooler clothes."

"I doubt it. I think parents have fun making us look ridiculous."

"Do you have any baby pictures?"

"I'm sure I do, some place. My mom isn't great at organizing that kind of stuff. You're so lucky to have these." I studied the photos on the page in front of me, trying to get a sense of who Lucy was.

"I thought it was a lame gift, and then when Lucy went missing, I was so glad to have these books. I took both of ours when I moved out."

"Do your parents still live in town?" I reached for another album from the stack.

"Yeah, they still live in the house we grew up in. It's just the street over from where you live."

"Really? I still can't believe I never knew about Lucy this whole time." My mouth fell open when I opened the next photo album. "How old is she in this one?"

"She was fourteen." Angie watched as I tried to digest what I was looking at. "Are you okay?"

"Yeah, I'm fine. It's just so sad to think about everything." I rubbed the tears out of my eye. "And it feels like I'm looking at myself in these pictures, especially these."

Angie rubbed my back. "It is sad, isn't it?"

"Am I just crazy? Or do I look like your sister?" I tried to blink away the tears.

"You're not crazy. I see it too." Angie pushed my hair out of my face. "I've never met anyone who looks like Lucy. She had a one-of-a-kind look."

"One-of-a-kind? What do you mean?"

"Well, I don't know, just her jet-black hair and her eyes..." Angie tilted her head back and smiled. "They were mystical, like the color of an emerald."

"Emerald green eyes. Jet-black hair and emerald green eyes; that's how I always describe myself. How can it be? I mean, we were practically neighbors."

Angie shrugged her shoulders. "I have no idea, but I'm just so glad I met you. You're a beautiful young woman."

I turned the page and saw more photos that could have been stolen from my life. The way she stood, her smile, all the little details that were too eerie to point out to her grieving sister. "This is going to sound crazy, but do you believe in reincarnation?"

"Reincarnation?" Angie tilted her head and scrunched up her nose. "I don't know. I guess I never thought about it."

"Yeah, it's stupid." I closed the book on my lap and set it with the rest of them.

"It's not stupid. Tell me about it." Angie took my hand. "Don't be so quick to dismiss things that are important to you."

"It just seems silly."

"Do you think Lucy was reincarnated into you?"

"I don't know what to think. I mean, my whole life I've felt like I didn't belong to my family. I don't look like anyone I know. And now, all these pictures, it's like I'm looking in the mirror."

"Have you ever seen your birth certificate?"

"Yeah, why?"

"Well, it's just that you said you felt like you didn't belong to your family."

"Yeah, I'm theirs. I guess that's all the proof I need and why I never questioned it. But now I don't even know who I am."

"Oh, Molly, I'm sorry. I didn't want to upset you. I just thought it would be fun to share my sister with you." Angie leaned over to give me a hug.

I fell against her chest and sobbed. "I don't know what is wrong with me. I know how hard this weekend is for you, and I'm just making it worse."

"No, that's not true. I like being with you. It's nice not being alone." She ran her hand over my hair.

"Maybe there's a reason we ran into each other." I rested my head on Angie's shoulder. "I've always wanted a big sister."

"And I've always wanted a little one. See, a perfect match."

"This isn't too weird for you?"

"What?"

"That I look like Lucy."

"No, not at all. I think it's nice, almost like she's back."

"I really want to help you find her. What can I do?"

"All any of us can do is just keep looking."

"Does anyone have any idea what happened?" I leaned into the couch to rest my head.

"Not really. There were some search parties, but nothing was ever found. The police have always told me they have no plans on doing any more searches, or spending any more time on it; that's why I put these searches together at the reunions. At least they are people who knew Lucy, so it's hard to say no to a day every ten years."

"Have you been doing it on you own all these years?"

"In the beginning my parents helped, but when the cops stopped cooperating, they gave up. My mom says she'll find out the truth when her time comes. Until then, she wants to enjoy the memories she has of her daughter."

"I don't think I could do that, but I have no room to talk. I have no idea how I'd act if my world was ripped apart like that."

"I was pretty pissed off when I heard her say it the first time. I didn't ... well, I still don't understand how you can just stop looking. I'll never be able to rest until I know where my sister is and what happened to her."

"Do you have any suspicions as to what happened?"

"I did, at least in the beginning, but after all these years I really don't know." Angie scooped up the photo albums and returned them to the bookcase. "Do you want to get back to the park? I'd hate for you to waste this beautiful day cooped up in here."

"I guess." I waited for her to expand on the last question but didn't want to push her. Something in my gut told me I didn't want to know who she thought did it. It would ruin me and all of the people I love, including this new friendship.

# CHAPTER ELEVEN

Marc's car was in the driveway when I arrived home. Guilt washed over me as I thought back to how I'd spent my morning. I wasn't sure how much longer I was going to be able to live a double life. But I liked Angie, and I wasn't not ready to give our friendship up.

Dad was in the kitchen sitting with Marc at the table when I walked in. "Hey, Molly." Marc stood and joined Mom on the deck.

"What was that about?" I took Marc's seat.

"Oh nothing." Dad folded the piece of paper that had been between them.

"What's that?" I squinted my eyes to get a better look.

"I said it was nothing." Dad stood and stuffed the paper into his back pocket before he left the room.

I slid open the screen door and stood between Marc and Mom. "What's going on?"

"Nothing, why?" Marc leaned back in his chair, the sun glaring in his eyes.

"Seriously, why won't anyone tell me what's going on? You and Dad stopped talking when I entered the house, then Dad stuffed something into his pocket and left. What were you talking about?"

"Molly, I said it was nothing. Don't make such a big deal out of this." Marc looked over at Mom. "I was just telling Mom the good news."

"Oh yeah?" I put my hands on my hips. "What good news is that?" My face tightened when I couldn't control my anger.

"That I'm moving back to Pine Grove." Marc shielded his eyes with his hand. "Molly, what's wrong? Why are you so upset?"

"It's nothing." I turned and slammed the screen door behind me. "It's nothing," I mumbled as I grabbed my car keys. "You can all kiss my ass," I yelled and walked out the front door. How could Marc go from hating Dad to keeping secrets from me?

My tires squealed as they peeled out of the driveway. My blood boiled as my accelerator hit the floor. I didn't know where I was going, only that I didn't want to be home. There was too much to digest from the pictures of Lucy to the secrets swarming around my house. I cranked the radio up and continued down the road, not knowing where it would take me or how far I'd get before I turned back.

When the anger subsided, I noticed I was right where Marc and I had been when we'd followed Mom. I turned my directional signal on and made the left turn onto the dirt road. My car stopped where Mom's had. A raindrop hit my windshield as if something was telling me to leave, but I didn't.

I grabbed my cell phone off my front seat and slipped it into my back pocket without checking to see if there were any missed messages and opened my trunk. I pulled out my yellow raincoat and put it on. "You're not going to tell me I can't be here." I slammed the hatch closed as I remembered Marc telling me to stay in the car. "I can do what I want."

A path worn in the tall grass at the edge of the parking area invited me to take a walk, the same one Mom was going to take a few days ago. The only purpose of this dead-end road was to get to this path. I needed to know why Mom was here. I pushed aside the thoughts of what might be slithering in the grass under me or clinging to the tress above me. My focus was on getting to the end of the trail.

Ten minutes of walking in the rain, and the path continued. Still nothing in sight. Could this be all there was out here? A dead-end road to a trail? No cabins or buildings of any sort. The worn passageway continued for as far as I could see. With each step I took the uneasy feeling I was trying to silence intensified.

"This is so stupid. I should just get out of here." The rain let up just as I was going to turn back. "You want me to keep going?" I didn't know who I was talking to, but I knew I had to follow this path until it ended. The clouds in the sky cleared out, and the sun returned.

I took off my raincoat and then looked up at the sky and smiled. I knew I was in the right spot. I just wasn't sure what that meant. I continued walking and let the sun warm my face. The smell of pine trees encased me. A peaceful feeling washed over me as I came to an opening. A few more steps led me to a meadow of dandelions. There were so many it looked like I was stepping on a yellow carpet. "Follow the yellow brick road." I giggled as I imagined spinning around in the flowers in a dress.

I held my arms out at my sides and did a twirl. When I stopped, something caught my attention through the trees. Curiosity propelled me in the direction of the unknown object. My heart danced under my shirt as I took slow, careful steps through the trees. I stopped when I saw it. A small, rundown, white house. It looked like a cottage you'd see in a fairy tale. Quaint and creepy.

I scanned the yard. There was no sign of movement, and the only thing filling the soundwaves was the squawking of crows. Last years dried leaves crunched under my feet as I made my way to the door. I pressed my face against the glass and peered through the dirty window. A table and four chairs filled the tiny kitchen. I couldn't see anything else. With a step back, I knocked on the door.

The throbbing of my pulse drowned out the birds circling the property. "Hello?" I jiggled the doorknob. The door opened. Frozen in disbelief that it was going to be this easy, I hesitated before I could push myself through the opening. "Hello? Is anyone home?"

When no one answered, I set my raincoat on the table and wiped the sweat off my hands. "Hello?" I took a step into the next room and saw a loveseat and rocking chair. A coffee table in the center of the room was covered in magazines. I ran my finger through the thick dust covering them before picking them up. The *People* magazines had the address labels removed, but the dates were intact. An assortment of years from the early 80s and 90s. I set them back where I'd found them and continued deeper into the house.

A door in the back of the room was jarred open. I pushed it open enough to look inside and saw a double bed neatly made. A dresser was pressed against the back wall across from an empty closet. A dirty pair of Sketchers were pushed under the nightstand.

When I walked back into the living room, I noticed a door. It looked like it should lead to the second floor. As I approached the door, I saw the padlock. I gave the handle a tug to see if there was any way to open it. It wouldn't budge.

It didn't appear that anyone had lived in this place in decades, if ever. There was no sign of life, yet someone was maintaining it. A hunting camp maybe. I took one last look around before leaving. There was no way of telling whose home I had been invading, and I didn't want to stick around to find out.

I picked up my pace as all of the *Dateline* episodes started playing on a loop in my mind. I wanted to get out of there before anyone else showed up. When I arrived back at my car, I let out the breath I had been holding. That peaceful feeling I felt earlier was gone. Replaced now by an impending sense of doom. I had to get out of here. I pulled my keys out of my pocket and unlocked the door as quickly as my fingers would allow me.

Once in my car, I locked my doors and drove out of the dirt road. My tires hit the pavement, and a sense of relief washed over me. It was like I was in an alternate universe, where time stood still. I glanced at the clock. It had been four hours since I'd left. I sat up and took my phone out of my back pocket and gave it a quick glance. No missed texts or calls. I tossed it onto the passenger's seat.

It'd been months since Dad hadn't blown up my phone

the minute he didn't know where I was. I hated it, but now I kind of missed it. No one even knew I was gone. It was like I was invisible to the people who were supposed to love me. Maybe Marc moving back to Pine Grove wasn't such a great idea after all.

# CHAPTER TWELVE

Marc's car was gone when I arrived back home. I rested my head against my seat as I tried to take in all of the events from the day. My once boring life was now too full to handle. Thankfully, school was out for the summer, and Dad agreed to pay me to keep track of Mom, so I had room for this new load of responsibility.

I took one last deep breath before I went inside. The house was quiet, and Mom and Dad were not in sight. I slipped into my room and locked the door behind me before falling onto my bed. I turned on my phone, still no messages. I closed my eyes and let the events from the day replay in my mind.

The vibration of my phone pushed the images out of my head. I opened one eye to see who was texting me. It was Angie. I rolled over so I could read the message. "Hey, Molly, I just wanted to make sure you were doing okay. I just want you to know I thought about what you said about reincarnation, and I'd like to talk more about it."

Something in me wanted to confess all of my hurt and

sorrows to my newfound best friend, but she had enough of her own. A tear rolled down my cheek as I stared at her message. *Maybe she really does care about me.* "It's been an interestingly shitty day. Thanks for checking on me. I'd love to talk more."

I held the phone, waiting for her response. "I'm sorry to hear that. Do you want to talk now?" My hand trembled at this simple question. I wanted to feel her warmth next to me while I cried, but I knew I shouldn't.

"I'm really tired right now. Actually, I'm about to take a nap. Maybe tomorrow?"

"Sweet dreams. Talk to you tomorrow."

I held my phone to my chest and imagined growing up as Angie's little sister. I had always wanted to have a sister to learn things from. Mom was too old to be fun. She was always a few blocks out of the neighborhood when it came to anything I wanted to talk about. And Marc wasn't a fixture in my life whatsoever. I was surprised I even know his name.

Angie's question about my birth certificate came back to me. What if she knew something I didn't? But what could she know? Visions of finding a new family forced a smile followed by immediate guilt. Mom was a good mother. Things were just hard because of the dementia. She still loved me.

But the dementia. What if that was just some ploy to keep me at home? I had planned to go away to school, but then she got sick. The timing seemed odd. She knew things she shouldn't, but maybe that was normal. Doubt filled me as I drifted off to sleep.

*The trees danced in the wind as I twirled around, my pink dress swishing in the wind. Angie took my hands and spun me in a circle. My giggles echoed off the mountains. "Faster!" I squealed as I began to slow down.*

*"One more time, silly girl." Angie's laugh matched mine. When she stopped, we fell to the ground, and the softness of the grass cushioned our fall. "Look up there, Molly." She pointed to the clouds. "Do you see it?"*

*"What?" I rested my head onto her chest and looked at the white pillows covering the sky.*

*"There." She pointed up again. "Can you see the angel?"*

*"I can, I can." I smiled as I watched the angel float over us. "She's pretty."*

*"She is." Angie kissed the top of my head. "I love you, Molly."*

*"I love you too." I nestled in closer, letting the safety of her embrace tighten around me. "Don't ever leave me, Angie." My squeaky voice shook with emotion.*

*"I won't, sweet girl. You're safe with me."*

*"I know. Don't ever leave. Don't let them take me."*

*"You're safe with me." Angie loosened her embrace, and she floated up to the clouds. She blew me a kiss before she vanished.*

*"Angie!" I jumped to my feet. "Come back."*

*"I will always be your angel, watching over you."*

My body jolted out of sleep; my pillow was moist from the tears. I pulled my blanket closer and hugged it. The rawness of the emotion from the dream settled around me. What did it all mean? Was Angie an angel sent to me? To save me? But from what? The questions from the day just kept multiplying.

I went to the attic to find the box of pictures stored up there. I needed to see my baby pictures. Did I look like Lucy then too? I rummaged around until I found a carboard box labeled "keep," tucked away in the corner of the room. When I opened it, I knew it was what I was looking for. It didn't look like the neat books of pictures that made up Lucy's life, but they held memories just the same. I pulled a handful of photos out and flipped through them.

I tossed the pile back in and tried again. The box was filled with all of the photos from my parents' married life, in no particular order. One picture was from Marc's grade school play, and the next was from my fifth birthday party. It was going to take forever to find what I was looking for. I stirred the contents of the box and took another handful.

A photo of Marc as a baby smiled back at me. His dimples even bigger back then. The photo stuck to the bottom was of me. My black curls covered my face as I chewed on my favorite teddy bear. I held the two photos side by side and did a comparison. We had the same nose, but nothing else stood out. Our eyes, hair, and smile were different.

I set the two photos to the side and took another scoop. I picked out the ones of me and added them to my pile. Memories from happier times flooded me. I missed the simpler times, when the only thing to worry about was if Mom bought more Lucky Charms for breakfast. I missed the old Mom, who was loving and remembered things about me. The one who was pushing me in this swing. The one who held my hand and made me feel safe.

I cleaned up my mess before I took the pictures back to my room. Why did our life have to be tucked away in a box? Why couldn't we display it like normal people? What were they hiding? The thought alone made me nauseous. I didn't want to think this way about the people I loved and trusted. Maybe they weren't hiding anything; maybe I just wanted too much.

# CHAPTER THIRTEEN

"Do you have time to get together today?" I sent the message to Angie before taking a pile of my clothes to the laundry room. I tossed my dirty clothes to the floor when I realized both the washer and dryer were full. "For fucks sake, does anyone do anything around here?" I found a basket and emptied the dryer so I could use the washing machine.

When I pulled the clothes out of the washer, I noticed Dad's jeans, the ones he was wearing yesterday. I stuck my hand in the back pocket. Jackpot. I pulled out the folded-up piece of paper that he and Marc had been looking at when I got home. It ripped apart as I unfolded it, but I could tell what it was. I'd seen it before. The flyer Angie had hung all over town, the ones Mom was taking down. "What the hell?" I looked over my shoulder before I threw the paper in the garbage and finished loading the washer.

When I was done, I checked to see if Angie had replied. She did. She was better at responding than anyone who was actually supposed to love me. "Yeah, do you want to go back to the park?"

"No, is it okay if I come over to your place? I have some stuff I want to show you."

"Sure, come on over anytime. I'll be here all day."

I went to my room and gathered the photos I found in the attic and a copy of my birth certificate before checking to see where Mom was. She was out on the deck with her coffee cup and magazine. I held my hand on the doorhandle before deciding not to disturb her. I didn't want the guilt of her being alone for the day to deter me from going. I didn't know where Marc was, and I didn't care if he saw me. It was no one's business where I was going or what I was doing. For the first time in my life, I was going to do what was best for me.

Marc's car wasn't at Shady Lane when I drove by. He never told me how long he was staying in town or when he needed to return home. He didn't say goodbye, so I assumed he was still around. I shook out the doubt and pulled in behind Angie's car. The front door swung open. "Hey there; that was quick."

"Sorry, I guess I forgot to tell you I was on my way." I shut my door and met her on the steps.

"Don't be sorry. I told you to come anytime." Angie held the door open as I walked past her. "Did Marc see you?"

"No, he's not at the motel. I'm not sure where he is." I tossed my purse onto the couch and collapsed next to it. "I don't know what's happening."

"What do you mean? Is everything alright?" Angie sat next to me.

"I don't know." I held my face. "I thought I knew my family, but they've been ... weird."

"Weird? How so?"

"Well, my mom has dementia, or at least that's what the doctor told us, and she's been running away, but then she seems normal. So I don't know if she's lying to us or if she's really sick."

"Oh, Molly, I'm sorry. That must be so hard to deal with." She took my hand.

"Yeah, but that's not all. Marc and Dad have been getting along, and that's just not normal. That's why he was staying at the Shady Lane. When I went home yesterday, they were sitting at the table together talking until I came in. Then they just stopped and scattered. They wouldn't tell me what they were talking about. They just kept telling me it was nothing."

Angie nodded as I continued.

"So I left, but no one even noticed I was gone. Not one text from any of them the whole time. And before you tell me that's normal, it's not. Dad usually needs to know where I am at all times. So why not yesterday?"

"I don't know, Molly. Do you think something could be going on with your mom that you don't know?"

"Maybe." I thought back to her pulling the flyers off the telephone poles. "She has been acting strange."

"You said she runs away. Do you know where she goes?"

"Funny you should ask. I think I figured it out yesterday." I thought back to the house in the woods. "But I don't know if she meant to go there, or if she was lost."

"Where?"

"You're going to think I'm crazy, but to this little house at the end of a dead-end road. We followed her there the other day, and then I went back yesterday. It's like from a fairy tale."

"How so?" Creases appeared on Angie's forehead.

"Well, for starters, I had to walk forever to get to it, and it was the only house, well building, on the road. It looked like someone hadn't lived there in years, but it also looked lived in. I don't know; it's hard to explain."

"Did you go inside?"

"Yeah, no one was around."

"And you were alone? In the woods? Molly, that's incredibly dangerous." Angie sighed. "Something could have happened to you."

"I know. I thought that as I was leaving. But before I felt this weird sense of peace. I can't even put it into words. It was like it was luring me in deeper."

"Where is this place? Do you know who owns it?"

"It's just outside of town. I have no idea who it belongs to or why my mom drove there."

"It sounds fascinating. I'd love to go with you sometime."

"I'd like that." I looked into Angie's eyes and remembered my dream. It was too embarrassing to share. "Oh, and I found something." I pulled the pictures out of my purse and handed them to her. "These were the only ones I could find but figured we could compare them."

"Aww, look at how cute you were." Angie's smile grew as she looked through the photos.

"Do you think I look like Lucy in them?"

She nodded. "I do." She went over to the bookcase and took out the same album we'd looked through yesterday. She flipped through the pages before she stopped and pulled out a picture. "Look at this." Angie held the two photos side by side.

"Oh my god." I covered my mouth. "We could be twins."

"I know; it's crazy, isn't it?"

"It is. I just don't understand. How is that possible?"

"I don't know." She slipped Lucy's photo back in its place. "Would it be alright if I took a picture of this one?" She held up my baby picture.

"Sure, what are you going to do with it?"

"I just want to keep it and show my mom. I think she would think it was neat." Angie smiled as she handed me the stack of photos.

"Oh yeah, I almost forgot." I took the folded piece of paper out and handed it to her. "I brought my birth certificate so you could look at it."

"Oh, you didn't have to do that." She unfolded the paper.

"Well, I just wanted you to see it." My cheeks blushed when I realized how absurd it was to bring it. "I don't know why; it's just that you asked about it."

"Thank you for this. It does put my mind at ease." Angie handed the document back to me.

"Why would it put your mind to ease?"

"Oh, I don't know. It's nothing."

"Please don't say that. I don't know how many more "it's nothings" I can take. Just tell me what you were thinking."

Angie sighed. "It's crazy. I don't want to put ideas into your head."

"But now I have all kinds of questions swirling through my mind. Just tell me, please."

"Well, you look so much like Lucy. I guess I wanted to believe you might be hers." Angie dropped her head. "See, it's crazy."

A knot began to grow in my stomach, and I started to sweat. "How?" Was the only word I could produce.

"I don't know. It's just that Marc and Lucy were dating

when she went missing, and Marc's so much older than you. And when you told me your birthday is in March, it just made sense." Angie pulled her bottom lip in as she bit it. "See, I told you—it's crazy."

"Why does March make sense? I don't understand."

"Well, you were born March 17, 2000. That's about nine months after Lucy went missing."

"So what are you saying?" Her words swirled around my head. "You think Lucy is my mother?"

"I'm not saying that. All I'm saying is it adds up. Coincidences happen all the time. It's obviously nothing. You have a birth certificate." Angie's smile eased some of the tension building inside me. "Don't worry about it. It's nothing."

"So you think Marc is my father?" Memories from the last few days flashed before my eyes. The flyers, all the secrets, the house in the woods. It all added up.

"Molly, please don't let my crazy ideas get you upset. I'm a grieving sister. I've been grabbing onto every clue I could find for the past twenty years."

"But she went missing in June, and I was born in March. Where was she that whole time?" I tried to connect the dots, unable to ignore the seeds that had been planted.

"Molly, please..."

"Oh my god." I covered my mouth to catch the vomit racing up my throat. "The house in the woods." The words came out in a whisper.

"What?" Angie leaned closer to me. "What did you say?"

"The house in the woods. Mom mentioned it before, she said it was where she went, and then I found it yesterday. It's theirs."

"The place you were going to take me to?"

I nodded, unable to find words.

"You think I'm right?"

I took a deep breath before the tears fell. "I don't know. It makes sense."

"Molly, it can't be, though. I just want answers, and I'm trying to make anything I can fit together. Please don't…"

"How can I find out? I'll never stop thinking about this."

Angie leaned back into the couch. "We could do one of those DNA things."

"Aren't those expensive? And don't we need a lab or something?" I brushed the tears away with the back of my hand.

"Not anymore. There are a few genealogy sites online that do it. We could both do it, and if it finds we're a match, then we have something to worry about, but don't let it drive you crazy until we know for sure." Angie took her phone off the coffee table and started scrolling. "Look, right here." She swiped her finger. "It says it will take six to eight weeks to get the results."

"That's a lifetime."

"Oh, honey, it's not that long. Trust me." Angie pushed closer to me and wrapped her arm around me. "I'll order them, and we can do them together; that way we can get our results at the same time."

"How am I supposed to go home without knowing? Or look at Marc?"

"We don't know anything yet. All we have is speculation."

"You watch crime shows too?" I nestled into her embrace and giggled.

"Yeah, I'm addicted to them. I watch to see if I can learn anything."

"Have you?"

"A few terms, but that's it really. I just love to know cases can be solved, and some of the best stories are when the families never give up."

"I like that part too."

"Can we keep this all between us?" Angie's attention was back on her phone. "Oh, it looks like I can expedite it and get the kits here by Wednesday." She set her phone down when she was finished. "There, all set. So can this be our little secret, at least until we figure it out?"

"Yeah."

"It's probably nothing." She tapped my knee. "Please don't worry."

"I can't stop thinking about things. If Lucy is my mom, where is she? Why didn't she want me?"

"If Lucy is your mom and she had a choice, I know she would be with you. Being a mom was one of her dreams. She didn't want to go to college; she just wanted to start a family and get married."

"That means..."

"No, don't think that. We don't know anything yet."

"Marc killed her." I buried my face in my hands.

"There are so many possibilities. Don't go to the worst one." Angie rubbed my back. "Molly, don't let your mind take you there. Marc loved Lucy. I know he did."

I tried to shake all of the questions out of my mind. I didn't know my brother well enough to know if he was capable of murder. Was that why he'd left? Mom and Dad knew too. They'd have to. They were all in on it? "That's why Mom was ripping down the flyers." I covered my mouth when my thoughts turned to words.

"Your mom was taking down the flyers?" Angie frowned.

"They all know, don't they? My whole life has been a lie." I stood and paced the living room, trying to quiet the thoughts pummeling me.

"Molly." Angie tried to be the voice of reason, but it was too late for that. There was no way out of the spiral I was falling down.

"Marc's moving back home; what if he knows I know?"

"Molly, you don't know anything, not yet. Are you afraid of Marc?"

"No, I wasn't, but maybe I don't know who he is. Maybe I should be."

"Why would he have any reason to believe you know anything? I mean, if you did? He doesn't know that you're here or that we've been talking, right?"

"No, he doesn't know." I snapped the hair elastic on my wrist, trying to pull myself out of the panic attack headed my way.

Angie came over and wrapped her arms around me. "I'm so sorry. I never should have said anything."

"No, I need to know the truth. What if I lived my whole life not knowing?" I let my head settle into Angie. "You could be my aunt."

"I'd love that job." She smoothed out my hair. "No matter what we find out, I want you to stay in my life, okay?" Angie took a step back to look at my face.

"I'd like that. I feel so alone most days."

"Me too. It's hard to trust people when you don't know what happened. I don't let people in, but you were different. I knew I could trust you."

"How?"

"Your eyes. I'd seen them before." She gave my hand a

squeeze. "Are you going to be alright? We have at least six weeks until we get an answer."

"I'll be okay. I'll just keep myself busy."

"That's a good idea. What will you do?" Angie pushed the hair out of my face.

"I'll read some of the books I've been meaning to."

"Lucy loved to read." Angie smiled. "Who's your favorite author?"

"Judy Blume, she has been since I was a kid. I just can't fall in love with anyone else's writing."

"Wait right here." Angie left me standing in the living room. When she returned, she handed me a box. "Open it."

Inside the box was a stack of Judy Blume books. "Are these yours?"

Angie took the box and placed it on the coffee table. She handed me *Tales of a Fourth Grade Nothing.* "Open it."

I opened the front cover and saw "This book belongs to Lucy" written inside. "Oh my god, really?" I covered my mouth.

"Yeah, she was Lucy's favorite author too. She read those books a hundred times each I bet. Mom bought her new books, but she wouldn't touch them. She said they just weren't the same."

"Wow, that's crazy. What are the chances of that?" I picked up another book and opened the cover to see the same inscription.

"I don't know; in a few weeks we'll know."

"Do you think reincarnation is still a possibility? That would explain our similarities." I set the books back in the box and took a seat on the couch.

"It could be. Let's go with that for now, okay? It's less scary and pretty cool." Angie joined me on the couch.

"It is pretty cool." I smiled at the thought of possibly sitting next to my sister. It was the only way I would be able to stay calm the next few weeks. "Have you ever been to a psychic medium?"

"No, I've thought about it, but part of me that hoped she was alive. I want to find Lucy, but until I do, I guess I don't want to know."

"That makes sense."

"Does it? It didn't when I said it. Have you ever been to one?"

"No, I've wanted to, but didn't really have a reason to. Some of my friends at school have been to one, and they couldn't stop talking about it." I snapped my hair tie on my wrist. "Maybe we should go, when you're ready."

"We could do that. It might give us some answers sooner than the DNA tests." Angie laughed. "It's pretty dumb I waited this long."

"I don't think it's dumb. It makes sense. You weren't ready. Besides, it's more fun to go with a friend."

"Do you know anyone we could go see?" Angie asked.

"I can ask my friends who they saw. I think it was someone right here in Pine Grove."

"Oh, I don't know about that. I think it'd be better if the person wasn't from here; that way they don't have any information about the case." Angie's attention went to the picture of Lucy on the wall. "I know it's been twenty years, but I'd like to at least imagine someone besides me remembers Lucy."

"No, that makes sense. I want the truth, not something made up."

"I'm not saying they wouldn't tell the truth. I just don't want anything to influence what is said."

"Okay, well, I'll figure this out since you got the DNA kits." The number of questions I had kept increasing. With every bit of information I uncovered, there was an uncertainty that followed. By the end of summer there should be answers to at least some of the questions. So much for a relaxing summer.

# CHAPTER FOURTEEN

"Hey, Molly." Marc set his coffee mug on the table. "I would have brought you one if I knew you were going to be here."

"Where else would I be?" I took a drink on orange juice to stop from rolling my eyes.

"I don't know; you never seem to be home anymore." Marc sat in the chair across from me, just like he did the few times he had dinner with us.

"Sorry if I have a life. I didn't know that wasn't allowed. Well, actually..."

"Are we okay, Molly? You've seemed mad at me ever since the reunion. Did I do something?"

"No." I drank the last of my juice, wishing I had left some in the glass for the next time I needed to avoid eye contact. "I have a lot on my mind."

"Anything you want to talk about?" Marc folded his hands on the table.

"No."

"Are you sure?"

"Yeah, I'm fine. Everything is fine." I smiled to make it convincing.

"Okay, well, if you want to talk, you can text or call me anytime. You know that, right?" Marc cleared his throat. "So you remember I said I was going to move back home?"

"Yeah."

"Well, I have to get back to Virginia. There's some stuff I have to do before I'll be able to make the move."

"I figured you couldn't just stay here. I know you have a life down there."

"I was wondering if you wanted to come back with me. I could bring you home in a week or two." Marc took a drink of coffee. "I think it would be good for you to get out of here for a

while."

"What about Mom? I can't just leave her here. That's the whole reason you're moving back here." There was nothing stopping me from rolling my eyes this time.

"Dad and I talked. He doesn't think Mom needs as much help as you do. He thinks she's doing better."

"Did you not listen to anything I said? He wants you to think that. He only agreed to pay me to watch out for Mom this summer so I'd shut up. He's never going to tell you the truth; he can't see it, or he doesn't want to." I shook my head in disgust. "Why are you even here?"

"Molly, that's not fair. I wanted you to have some time to be a kid. You've had to grow up so fast these last few years. I wanted you to have the chance to let loose and get some beach days in. Why are you mad at me?"

"It's not always about you. I just know Mom can't be alone. Someone needs to look out for her. Apparently, I'm the only one who gives a damn." I pushed myself away from the table. "You can go now."

"I'm sorry. I guess I just feel guilty for making you do everything for so long." Marc dropped his head. "In a few months you won't have to. I'll be back, and we can share the responsibility."

"Yeah, okay. See you then." I got up and put my glass in the sink.

Marc was behind me when I turned around. "Come on, Molly. Don't be like that."

Frozen in place by the fear pulsating through my body, I closed my eyes to try to get the memories of my brother back, the ones from before. Before I thought he was my dad, and before I thought he had killed my mom.

He placed his hand on my shoulder. "Molly."

The hair on the back of my neck stood from his touch. I took a step to get away.

"What's going on? Why won't you talk to me?"

"I just have a lot on my mind. I..." I closed my eyes to try to pull myself together. "I'm not feeling well. I have this killer headache."

"Okay, well, why didn't you just say that? I would have shut up." Marc laughed. "I'm going to miss you. I wished we'd had more time together."

"Yeah, maybe next time." I put my hand to my head to go along with my story.

"Thank you for making me go to my reunion. It was nice talking to old friends. I didn't know how much I'd missed it." Marc leaned against the counter. "Beth and James are getting a divorce. At least that's what she said last night."

"Wait, last night?" I raised my brow, forgetting about my fake headache.

"It's not how it sounds. We went out for dinner and caught up. She's a great woman. I didn't realize how much I'd missed her, missed my life back here." Marc's eyes lit up.

"Are you two dating? Already?"

"No, we're just friends."

"With benefits?" I squinted my eyes, not wanting the answer.

"Gross, no. She's not gross; this is. Don't ask me about that stuff."

"Yeah, it is gross; you're old." I stuck out my tongue.

"Oh, stop it. Old people can have a good time."

"Double gross."

"Knock it off." Marc blushed. "It's just nice having a friend."

"They have kids, right?"

"Yeah, they're teenagers, though. Why?"

"Do you even like kids?" I crossed my arms as I tried to figure out who this man standing in front of me was.

"Yeah, I don't hate them. I just never thought I'd have any."

"Why not? You're still young enough to have a couple. A few if you bag yourself a younger woman." I tossed my head back as an evil laugh emerged.

"Looks like someone is feeling better, you jackass."

It was so easy to fall back into believing Marc was my older brother I looked up to. I didn't want to think all the awful things about him. It didn't add up; he was too sweet to be scary. "I love you. I know I don't say it enough, but I do, and I want to get to know you better. I'm looking forward to spending more time with you; that is until Beth and your new babies take it all."

"You have nothing to worry about. I don't think I'll ever be a dad, not without Lucy." Marc hung his head. "We'd talked about having kids together, after we got married. I can't imagine having a family with anyone else."

"It's okay to live your life. Don't you think Lucy would want you to be happy? If she loved you as much as you love her, she'd want you to be happy."

"Maybe, but I can't think about that. Beth and I are just friends. She's not even divorced yet. I don't think I need to worry about having kids right now. Besides, we're almost forty. There's no way she'd want to start over, not when her kids are almost grown." Marc put his hands in his pockets and rocked on the heels of his feet. "Oh, and, Molly?"

"Yeah?"

"I love you too."

The headache I had faked earlier came crashing down on me. I didn't know if I wanted to know if Marc was my dad, or if Lucy was my mom. I definitely didn't want to know if Marc was a killer. And if I was reincarnated, I didn't want to be in love with my brother. All of the options I had to choose from made my stomach hurt. I guessed they weren't kidding when they said ignorance is bliss.

# CHAPTER FIFTEEN

Mom and I stood in the driveway as we watched Marc head back to Virginia. "I hate when he leaves." Mom blew her nose.

"Yeah, but it's going to be one of the last times he leaves." When Marc's car was out of sight, I took Mom's hand and led her to the backyard to enjoy the beautiful day. "Your flowers are so vibrant this year."

"They are pretty, aren't they?" Mom bent down and picked a red tulip. She put it to her nose before she handed it to me. "A pretty flower for a pretty girl."

"Thanks, Mom." I put the flower behind my ear and sat in the Adirondack chair facing the garden. She sat in the chair next to me. "Hey, Mom, can I ask you a question?"

"You know you can." Mom rested her head against the back of her chair, letting the sun beat down on her face.

"Did you like being pregnant?"

She sat up to look at me. "Is there something you need to tell me?"

"No, I was just thinking I've never asked you any questions about my birth or about any of that stuff."

"Are you sure? You've never been interested before." Mom blocked the sun from her eyes. "Are you trying to tell me something?"

"No, I promise. I just don't want to miss the chance to have this talk with you." I looked away before she could look into my eyes. She always used to be able to tell when I was lying; although I wasn't not really lying, just switching up the truth.

"Hmm. Okay, well, you know you can talk to me about anything, right? I know you're old enough to get on birth control, but if you want my help, all you have to do is ask."

"I know that, Mom. It's just that I'm curious about your life when you were younger, and I don't want to run out of time to ask questions. None of us are going to live forever."

"So this is just because you don't think I'm going to remember you?" She shook her head and laughed. "You got me all excited over this nonsense."

"It's not nonsense. You're not getting any younger, and I want to know these things." I slid back into my chair. "I've never even seen any pictures of you pregnant. How am I supposed to know what to expect?"

"Molly, for god's sakes, I was fat and round. What more do you want to know? I looked like every other pregnant woman." Mom crossed her arms.

"Do you have any pictures? I'd love to have them."

"You know where we keep the photos; if you want them that bad, you're going to have to dig for them."

"Mom, I don't want to make you mad. I just wanted to

talk. I love you and want to talk to you while we have time. No one ever knows what tomorrow will bring. I just want to learn about you."

"I'm sorry, Molly, it's just hard for me." She frowned as she closed her eyes. "I hate what is happening to me."

"I'm sorry, Mom." I couldn't tell if she was being sincere or trying to change the subject. "Do you remember the other day when Marc and I followed you down that dirt road?"

Mom's face showed no expression. "No, I'm sorry. I can't remember."

"The dirt road, just out of town? The dead-end?"

"No, sorry. I don't have any idea where that is." She sank deeper into her seat. "Why do you ask?" She turned to look at me.

"I was just wondering what brought you there or if you'd been there before. It's so pretty I thought maybe we could go back and take a walk."

Mom bit at the inside of her mouth as she fidgeted in her chair. "Why would we go there when there's plenty of beautiful landscape around here?"

"Because this place is different. There's nothing around, no people or cars, just nature." I watched to see if she reacted. She did not.

"Why not; that sounds lovely." Mom smiled before she leaned back.

"Okay, do you want to go now? It's such a gorgeous day." I stood and held my hand out for her to take.

"No, I'm tired today. Let's just take it easy today and relax." She closed her eyes again.

"Okay, well if you're going to nap, I think I'll just go." I turned and hesitated to walk away, waiting for her to call my bluff.

"Be safe, honey." She didn't even try to stop me. Maybe she really didn't have anything to hide.

I went inside and poured a glass of lemonade before going to my room. A nap sounded like just what I needed after the emotional roller-coaster I'd been on the last few days. I sprawled out on my bed and waited for my thoughts to quiet long enough to get some rest. As soon as silence was near, the events of the last week played on a reel inside my head.

The picture of Lucy took up the most real estate. Her smiling face made me want answers. This whole thing started so I could help Marc, and now I'd been sucked in for myself. Things were more complicated than I ever could have imagined. Never in my wildest dreams did I think my life would be suitable for a Lifetime movie; now it seemed to be turning into a miniseries.

Finding a medium might be just what I needed to ease some of the confusion. I wanted to at least know who I should trust and who I needed to stay away from. I really wanted to hear that there was nothing to report. It would be the best money I ever wasted. I opened a search window on my phone and looked for a medium within driving distance from Pine Grove. Angie was right about finding someone who wouldn't know anything about the case. That would be next to impossible in this town.

Everyone knew everyone's business here. I didn't think I could make a move that the neighbors didn't know about. That was why none of this made sense. Why hadn't anyone said anything to me about Lucy before. How could she still be missing, and no one had even mentioned her name?

The results populated my screen. Surprisingly there were three psychic mediums within an hour from here. I sent a screenshot of the names to Angie to make sure she didn't know who they were. While I waited for her response, I tried to find more information about each of them. I was able to find one of their websites and hoped Angie would agree to go to that one. She looked nice and welcoming. I needed both. I also needed someone who wasn't going to judge me or report what they'd find out.

The ringing of my phone startled me. "Hey, Angie."

"Hi, Molly. I got your text. Wow, who knew there are so many options around here! I don't know any of them; you pick."

"What's your schedule like?" I realized I didn't even know what Angie did for work. "I can book it around what you have going on. I'm wide open until school starts."

"Me too. I'm wide open."

"Really? You're in school?"

"Kind of. I'm a teacher."

"That's so cool. We need to spend more time getting to know each other!"

Angie laughed. "I agree."

"I liked Sara the best. I'm going to try to schedule something with her. I'll let you know. Talk to you soon."

I hung up the phone and clicked on the link on Sara's website to book our appointment. It was way easier than I had anticipated. "We're set for this Saturday at 1:00."

"Great! I'm looking forward to it! By the way, our kits will be here tomorrow."

"I can't wait!" I put my phone down and rested my head on my pillow. Part of me wanted this over, and part of me didn't want to know. Either way I guessed I'd have a family. One I knew, or one I'd have to.

CHAPTER SIXTEEN

Angie greeted me at the door with the DNA kits. "I saved mine so we could do it together."

"What exactly are we doing?"

"We just have to spit in a tube thingy. That's it." She handed me a box.

"That's gross." I turned the box over to examine it.

"It's just spit. It's not that bad. At least there aren't any needles involved."

"True. I hate blood. Mine or anyone else's."

"What are you going to school for? I guess I just assumed you were in nursing." Angie pulled a chair out from the table and tore the plastic off her package.

"Nursing, no; where did you get that from?" I joined her at the table.

"I guess because you said your mom is sick. I don't know." She shrugged.

"I'm studying early childhood ed. I want to be a first-grade teacher."

"That's the grade I started out with. They were a lot of

fun." Angie pulled out the directions. "What do we need these for? How hard is it to spit?"

"What grade do you teach now?" I opened my box to catch up with Angie.

"Sixth grade. It's the worst. Don't ever do it. Middle school will age you a hundred years. The drama is awful. I miss the sweet little kids."

"Why did you change?"

"The school was so small they didn't need two first grade teachers, so I had to take what they offered or move out of town. Since I'll never leave Pine Grove, at least not until I find Lucy, I took the offer."

"That must be awful. I don't think I could survive that. Preteen drama is the worst." I pulled out my tube and unscrewed it. "Are we ready for answers?" I held the plastic tube up before I put it to my lips.

"Here goes nothing." Angie toasted my tube. "Cheers."

We filled our containers with spit and sealed them before packing them in their envelopes. "Do you want to take a walk to the post office? It's such a nice day; it might feel nice to get some fresh air."

"Won't Marc see us?" Angie asked as she cleaned up our mess.

"No, he went back to Virginia yesterday. He's going home to get things in order before he moves back here."

"Did he tell you when he plans on coming back?"

"No, but he did try to get me to go with him. He told me he'd bring me home in a week or two." I stood by the door and waited for Angie to join me.

"He wanted you to go with him? Have you ever done that before?" Angie raised her eyebrow.

"No, he's never invited me to his place before."

"Why do you think he did this time?" Angie asked.

"I've been trying to figure that out. I have no idea."

"Do you think he knows we're talking?" Angie picked up her envelope and followed me out the door.

"I don't think so, and even if he knew, what would taking me to Virginia do? It's not like I wouldn't be back." I covered my mouth to hide the gasp. "Unless…"

"Don't go there, Molly. We don't have any reason to think he'd want to hurt you." Angie gave my back a pat. "I'm sure that's not why."

"Unless he knows about the house in the woods, and he knows I know. What if he knows I know?" I spun around in an attempt to find an answer. "I didn't even think about that. Do you think he…"

"Molly, take a deep breath." Angie took my hand. "Try to relax. You didn't go. You're safe."

I tried to calm my thoughts. "You're right. Maybe he just wanted to be nice. He knows I've never been anywhere."

"Okay, see, so maybe that's all it was. Don't let things you don't even know about take control of your life." She held up her envelope. "Not until we get answers."

"Yeah, I guess my mind plays tricks on me. I just can't stop thinking about Lucy. I want to know what happened to her."

"You and me both." Angie put her arm around me as we walked. "But you didn't even know about her until last week, so don't let this get to you. Not yet, and maybe not ever. Looking for Lucy has stolen so much of my life. I don't want to see it do the same thing to you."

"No matter what we find out, I want to help you. You shouldn't have to do this alone."

"You can help; just don't put your life on hold to do it."

"I won't." But that was a promise I couldn't make. I needed to know where Lucy was. I wasn't sure there was anything that could stop me now.

Angie held the door of the blue mailbox open so I could toss in my spit sample. "Does it feel weird to be mailing your bodily fluids?"

"A little, I guess, but at least it's just spit. It could be a lot worse. Can you imagine the guys who open this thing up? Now that's a job I don't want." I laughed at the thought of our packages arriving in some laboratory across the country.

"I don't know. I bet it's a fascinating job. I loved science class and the labs we had to do."

"You must be smart. I hated science. Writing was my favorite class."

"Reading and writing, you really do remind me of Lucy. She always wanted to write children's books. She loved little kids, probably older ones too." Angie smiled at the memory. "She had quite the imagination, she always did."

"Me too. I've wanted to write a book since before I knew what they were. I never really thought about children's books, but I've always wanted to see my name on the cover of a book."

"What do you write?"

"I don't. I used to write poetry, before Mom got sick, but now I can't find my creativity. It's like it dried up." I sighed at the thought of a wasted dream.

"It's not too late. You're still so young; you have your whole life ahead of you. Did you want to write a book of poetry or a novel?"

"A novel. I had the perfect storyline; I even have the book

outlined." I looked up and saw a flash of red. A cardinal flew onto the branch above me. "I haven't seen a cardinal in years."

"Me either. He's gorgeous." Angie looked up to admire the bird with me.

"You know they say cardinals are signs from heaven." I watched as the bird flew off. "Maybe it was Lucy coming to say hi."

"That would be nice." Angie looked to the cloudless blue sky. "I've asked her to send me a sign since I thought she was dead. I've never noticed any before, but maybe I just wasn't paying attention."

I took Angie's hand in mine. "Or maybe you were, and you just didn't want to admit she might be gone."

"You're probably right. The only sign that will really get my attention is when I'm able to bring her home." Angie turned to me and held my face. "Or maybe I'm looking at the biggest sign of all. Maybe I get to have my sister back in my life through you."

"As nice as that would be, I kind of hope that's not true." I dropped my head. "I'm sorry."

"Don't be sorry. I can't even imagine how difficult this must be for you. I've had twenty years to get used to all of this; you haven't even had ten days."

"I don't even know what to think. One minute I'm sure we have it figured out, and the next I can't even go there. I don't know what I'll do with the answers. I'm actually scared to death. But I have to know."

"Your world has been rocked, just like mine was all those years ago. I'm so sorry. I feel like such a jerk." Angie began to cry. "I can't believe I did this to you."

"Angie, you didn't do anything to me. The truth is I was going to look for you at the reunion. After I saw how you looked at me the night of the search, I needed to ask you questions. At first I thought it was because I wanted to help my brother, but now it's because something in my gut is telling me I can't stop until I have answers."

Angie covered her face. "I'm so selfish. I just wanted my sister back so badly I was willing to do anything. I didn't think what consequences there would be."

"Don't blame yourself. I'd do what you did if it were my sister. You love Lucy; there's no fault in that." I pulled Angie into a hug. "I love you." I melted into her arms. "I'm sorry. I don't know why I said that."

"I love you too. I know it's weird, but there's just something special about you. Sisters no matter what. Unless I'm your aunt, but you get the idea." Angie laughed as she gave me a tight squeeze. "My god, this is exhausting."

"I know. We're on one hell of an emotional roller-coaster."

"We sure are, and I hate those things."

"So do I. See, this is meant to be, no matter what." Still holding Angie close, I smiled. "I think I have a new novel to write."

"Will you at least make me look younger?" Angie snorted. "Geeze, I haven't laughed that hard since I was a kid. See what you do to me?"

"You are the absolute best friend I've ever had."

"That's what Lucy used to say to me. Word for word."

Goose bumps covered my body. "Maybe we didn't need those tests after all."

CHAPTER SEVENTEEN

I brought the box of pictures down from the attic and dumped the contents onto the living room floor. I hadn't thought about the mess it would make until it was too late. Two generations of memories coated the floor. A rug made out of our life.

"What on earth are you doing?" Mom stood in the doorway with her hands on her hips.

"You told me if I wanted to find those pictures they'd be in here." I pushed the stacks down into a single layer.

"What pictures?"

"The ones from when you were pregnant with me. I want to see what I looked like on the inside."

"Look at the mess you've made. You should pick this up before your father gets home." Mom shot me a look of disgust.

"Where is he?" I held up a picture. "Look, it's when I lost all of my top teeth."

"That was awful. You looked like an old woman trapped in a little girl's body."

"I'm so glad you didn't tell me that then." I tossed the memory back into the pile. "Do you want to help?"

Mom crossed her arms and leaned against the wall. "No, I don't like reminiscing."

"Why not? We had a good life. Why not relive some of those memories?"

"Because we'll never get them back. It's a waste of time living in the past." Mom walked away. I heard the screen door open.

"Mom?" The door closed without a response. I sorted the pictures into piles. Marc's, mine, and my parents. When I got to the last picture, I noticed there was not one of my mom with a pregnant belly. Not from when she had Marc or me. I went back through my pile and started to organize them by age.

I picked up the rest of the photos and put them back in the box. Mom was right; I didn't want to have this mess out when Dad got home. He was the last person I wanted to talk about the past with. There was not one good memory that I could pull up with him in it. If he didn't have a Budweiser in his hand, he had a shitty attitude. As a kid, I didn't know he was an alcoholic, or that not every dad drank in order to tolerate being home. It was just how it was. Mom and he got into their fair share of fights about his drinking throughout the years. Now, no one even spoke of it.

If Marc hadn't told me Dad was just as much of an asshole when he was growing up, I would have taken it personal. Knowing I wasn't the only kid he was trying to avoid made it a little easier to bare. Like they say, misery loves company.

I returned the box to the attic, keeping my pictures out.

No one else wanted them. Like Mom said, she didn't like to live in the past. I wasn't sure how many moms didn't want to look at old baby pictures. I thought it was something everyone did. I guess not in this family. The list of 'not in this family' seemed to get longer every year.

I went outside to find Mom, but the backyard was empty. I felt my heart drop to the pit of my stomach. I raced back inside to look out the front door. Her car was gone. Dad was going to kill me. I scrambled to find my phone and keys and rushed out the door. "Where in the hell could she have gone now?"

I took the usual route and slowly circled through town. And then I remembered. The dirt road, the dead-end, the house in the woods. I turned my car around at the gas station and headed out of town. I hadn't called anyone else to tell them Mom was gone yet. I could be wasting valuable time without telling Dad, but I didn't want to deal with his crap right now.

I turned the radio on and tried to let go of the worries. She was safe; she had to be. I danced along to Taylor Swift before noticing the dirt road on my right. I turned my directional signal on and made the turn. I pushed out all of the tension I was holding and inched my way to the end of the road.

Her car was there. I tightened my grip on the steering wheel and sat up straight. This couldn't be an accident. The possibility that this was her house was too big to be a coincidence. She knew right where she was going. I pulled my car in next to hers and turned to look. Her head was leaned back on the seat.

"Mom?" I jumped out of my car, leaving the door open.

She still hadn't moved when I approached her. "Mom!" I knocked on her window. She turned to look at me. I let out the breath I had been holding. "Mom." I sank into my body as I tried to open her door. "Come on; let me in."

Mom shook her head and motioned for me to leave before she put her head back against her seat.

"Mom, what the hell? What's wrong? Let me in." I pulled at her door handle. She kept her eyes closed, as if she couldn't hear me. I looked over and saw the passenger side door was unlocked and walked around the back so she couldn't see me. When I reached the door handle, Mom's eyes fluttered open, and she stretched to reach the lock.

I was quick enough to pull the door open. "What's going on, Mom?" I slid into the open seat and closed the door before she could kick me out. "Mom, why aren't you talking to me?"

"You shouldn't be here." Her cheeks were moist and her eyes red.

"Why are you here? Why do you keep coming back?" I noticed a pistol in her lap. Unsure what to do, I sat as still as possible.

"You need to go." She returned to resting her head and closed her eyes.

"Mom, are you okay? Do you need help?" Part of me wanted to go, to get as far away from here as possible, but part of me wanted to save my mom.

"You need to go."

"I'm not leaving you here, Mom. I love you."

"You're a foolish girl." Mom smiled and started to cry.

"Mom, just tell me what's wrong. I want to help you." I leaned in slowly and gave her a hug. When she put her arms around me, I felt for the gun. I rested my hand on it and waited for the perfect time.

"I don't know what's happening to me. I can't remember anything. I don't know why I'm here." Before she let go of me, I slowly pulled the gun out of her lap and set it on the floor next to my door. Her hand went to her empty lap. "Give that back to me."

"No, Mom. We have to get out of here. You can't have that." I looked in the back seat to see if there was anything else that might cause her harm. It was empty, not even an empty soda bottle.

"Molly, give it back to me now." Her voice was sharp, and the tears were gone.

"I can't. It's not safe." I studied her face to see if I could figure out what was going on. Desperation was the only thing staring back at me. "What were you doing?"

"I can't tell you." Mom turned her head away from me. "But you need to go. You're not safe."

"What do you mean?" I put my hand down to try to locate the gun. The cold metal met my fingertips. Knowing it was there didn't help chase the impending doom away.

"Molly, please promise me you'll never come back here." She whipped her head around to make eye contact.

I couldn't make that promise. I needed to come back, now more than ever. "Why can't you tell me what's going on?"

"You need to promise." Mom's eyes bugged out of her face. "Do you understand?"

"Will you come home with me?" I reached for her hand, leaving my other hand on the pistol.

She rubbed her eyes before putting her hand in mine. "Please don't let your father know we were here."

"I won't tell him, Mom. I promise." That was the only promise I could make her. "Are you alright to drive?"

"Yes."

"I'm going to follow behind you. If it looks like you need help, I'm going to call the police, okay?"

"I understand." Mom straightened herself in her seat. "Molly?"

"Yeah, Mom?"

"Can I have the gun back?" She held her hand out.

"No, I'm sorry. I can't give that back to you."

Her grip tightened on the steering wheel. "It's not mine. Your father will notice that it's missing."

"I'll put it back when we get home." I picked up the gun and held it pointing toward the ground. I'd never held one before, and not knowing anything about them made it even more terrifying. I set the gun on the floor of the passenger side of my car and waited for Mom to drive out. I pulled out right behind her, making sure I would be able to keep up with her.

Mom went there to kill herself. The reality behind that thought took my breath away. If I hadn't found her when I did, there was no telling if she would be alive. But why there? Why now? The weight of every thought and worry crashed down on me. I shook my head to clear it and focused my attention on Mom's taillights. I needed to make sure she made it home alive. She was acting strange, but was it just depression?

The drive home felt like an eternity. Hyper focused on every move I saw Mom make made my shoulders tense. When we finally arrived at home, I rolled my neck to ease the stiffness. Mom got out of her car and walked into the house.

She didn't wait for me, or even look at me. Dad still wasn't here, and I wasn't sure if that was a good thing yet.

I looked down at the gun, not sure what to do with it. Mom knew where Dad kept them obviously. I didn't want her to get it again, but I also didn't want Dad to know she'd taken it, and I sure as hell did'n't want him to think I touched it. He had others, so even if I didn't put this one back, she could still get another one. "Shit." I reached for the gun and brought it inside, being careful not to let anyone see me with it.

"Mom?" I went through the house and found her in her bed. "Mom, I need to do something with this." I held the pistol up. "Before Dad gets home."

Mom sat up and swung her legs off the bed. "Give it to me." She held her hand out.

"Will you promise me you won't take it again?"

"No." Mom walked over to where I was and took the gun out of my hand. "But I won't hurt myself with it."

"What were you doing? Do you want to talk? Are you okay?" I watched as she put the gun back in the gun safe. "I didn't even think you had a key to that thing."

"I didn't, but your father left his on the nightstand the other day, so I made a copy of it." She locked the safe and tucked the key into her pocket.

"Why?" I sat on her bed and waited for her to join me.

"Why shouldn't I be able to get into it whenever I want to? Why is he the only one who should feel safe in this house?" Mom stood by the door. "Molly, I'm tired. We can talk about this later?"

"No, Mom, this needs to be talked about now. You had a gun. You were going to kill yourself. That's not something that can wait."

"Why do you think I was going to kill myself? Why would I do that?"

"Why did you have that gun with you? And you were acting weird, not like yourself." I snapped the elastic on my wrist. "You scared me."

"I don't even know who I am anymore, so how can I act like myself?" She stayed by the door. It didn't appear she had any intention of having the conversation I wanted. "I'm tired. I just want to take a nap."

"But, Mom, why? Why did you take the gun with you? Why were you sitting in your car at that place?" I got off her bed and walked past her.

"Molly, it would be best if you just drop it."

"I'll drop it when you tell me what's going on."

"It's safer if you don't know. You can't tell anyone about today; do you understand me?" Mom crossed her arms, and her eyes dropped.

"Do you promise me you're not going to do anything to hurt yourself?"

"I promise." Mom shut the door, leaving me on the opposite side.

"Mom, I love you." I put my hand on the wall.

"I love you too, Molly."

# CHAPTER EIGHTEEN

"Are you ready for this?" Angie took the keys out of the ignition and held her hand out.

"Yeah, I need to know. It's all I can think about. I know you told me to try not to think about it until we know for sure, but the more I try to push it out, the more it fills my head."

"Well, I hope Sara can answer some of these questions then."

"Me too." I cracked my knuckles before opening my door. "Sorry, I do that when I'm nervous."

"So did Lucy." Angie gave a half smile. "Okay, here goes nothing."

I followed behind Angie and tried to calm my racing heart. I was sure it was loud enough for her to hear. "Are you scared?"

"I'm more excited to be able to hear from Lucy." Angie turned around and looked at me. "Oh my god, Molly, you look awful." She took my hand and gave it a squeeze.

"Remember, no matter what, I love you. You're forever my girl."

I couldn't contain my laughter. "What's with you nineties kids always talking in song lyrics?"

"Oops, I did it again." Angie held her stomach and laughed. "I honestly didn't mean to do that. There was just so many great songs, and I guess they make their way into conversations."

"I guess it's cute." My nerves began to settle. A woman with a big smile met us at the door. Sara did not look how I had pictured her, or even like the picture on her website.

"Hello, you must be Molly and Angie. Come on in." Sara held the door open with her back. "I expected you'd be early. I could feel you were really looking forward to our visit."

Angie and I gave each other a quick look before either one of us spoke. "Yeah, we are excited, I guess you could say." Angie took my hand as we waited for Sara to show us to our seats.

"Right this way." Sara motioned for us to follow her. She moved a curtain of beads that clacked together as they closed behind her. "Just push right through." Sara stood behind a small table. "You ladies can have a seat."

I pushed my chair closer to Angie and sat. I rubbed my sweaty palms on the knees of my jeans. "I really liked your website." I cracked a knuckle before I straightened out my hands.

"There's nothing to be afraid of." Sara crossed her legs and sat back in her chair. "I take it this is your first time visiting a psychic."

"It is for me." I looked over to Angie. "For both of us."

"Well, there's nothing to worry about. Every psychic does

things a little different, so let me tell you how I do things." Sara held up a stack of cards. "These are my tarot cards. I use them as a guide, but I get most of the messages from the spirit. You see, not all psychics are mediums, but all mediums are psychic. The difference is we will be able to communicate with your loved ones who have passed, as long as they are here and are willing to participate."

"Wait, so you mean they don't have to talk to us?" My shoulders fell with a sigh.

"They don't have to do anything. Most of the time, though, they do come through and give messages. If there is someone you are hoping to hear from it's helpful to talk to them in your mind, and let them know you would like them to join us. I just ask that you don't tell me anything about them, unless I ask you a question. The less information, the better. That way there's no way I can influence what comes through."

Sara shuffled the cards in her hands as she continued to talk. "It's okay to tell me if I'm wrong too. The spirits send me pictures and sometimes smells or tastes to help communicate what they want to share. I do hear them as well, but it all depends on the spirit we are working with. You can ask anything you want, but I can't promise you an answer. Sometimes spirits are not ready to talk about the things you want to talk about. How I do this is I will spread out a few cards and listen for guidance from the spirit. If after they start communicating with us, we need more clarity, I will pull another card. Do you have any questions?"

"No." Angie and I answered together.

"Okay, let's begin then." Sara shuffled the cards some more before she set some cards down in front of us. She closed her eyes. "It seems we have a spirit here that is very eager to talk to you. She said she doesn't want to mess around with these silly cards."

Angie laughed and began to cry. "She's here."

Sara handed her a box of tissues. "I forgot to mention you may need these."

"She's a feisty one." Sara held her hand up. "But not in a destructive way. She knows what she wants. A no nonsense kind of gal."

Angie nodded. "That sounds like her."

"Sister." Sara smiled. "She wants you to know that's what she called you."

Angie covered her mouth and nodded. "Sissy, that's what I called her."

"She's giving me an L name. Lacey, Lucky, Lucy."

"Lucy." Angie dabbed at her eyes. "So she's dead."

Sara closed her eyes. "She said you didn't know what happened to her. She has been trying to get your attention, but you weren't listening."

"How?"

"She's been coming to you in your dreams. She wants you to pay attention because she's really there."

"How did she die? Where is she?"

"She won't say. She said it's not important."

"It is important. I need to know." Angie slapped the table. "That's not fair."

"She said you'll understand why soon enough. The answers will come."

"What about Molly? Can she tell us about that?" Angie took my hand.

"She can't. She keeps saying the answers will come. She is

glad you two have each other. It's good to have a friend; you've been alone too long." Sara closed her eyes and placed her hand on her chest. "She's circling you with love. She wants you to know she can hear you when you talk to her."

"Really?" Angie sniffled. "I always feel crazy when I talk to her."

"Don't stop. It helps keep her connected to you." Sara nodded. "She loves you very much. She's sorry she can't give you the answers you're looking for."

"Why? Why can't she? I need proof that she's dead. I need closure. I need to know who did this to her." Angie's voice raised with her desperation.

"You have what you need. She wants you to trust her."

"What does that even mean?" Angie held her hands up. "What do I have? I need answers. Who took you? Where are you?"

Sara shook her head. "She told you to trust her. That's all she can offer you right now."

"Does she have anything to say to me?" I snapped the hair elastic on my wrist.

Sara opened her mouth to answer and then shut it just as quickly. "No."

"What were you going to say?" I fidgeted in my chair.

"She doesn't have anything to say. I'm sorry."

"But you were going to say something. I saw you open your mouth." I crossed my arms and squinted my eyes. "I wanted some answers."

"I'm sorry. Sometimes there aren't any. Even in death there isn't always an answer to everything. She might not know what you are looking for, or you might not be ready to hear the truth. It's not my job to report the latter."

"So you're holding back information? How can you do that?" I looked to Angie to see if she was as outraged as I was. She was picking at her fingernail, and I couldn't pull her attention away.

"Look, I work for both of you. If she's telling me you're not ready to hear something, I have to respect her wishes no matter how badly you want answers." Sara gave me a sympathetic smile and leaned forward. "I can tell you things will become clearer very soon."

"Are we safe?" Angie continued to pick at her finger. "Should we be worried?"

"I don't know, but I do know if there was something your sister knew about your safety, she'd tell you. She's not saying anything, so that tells me there's no imminent danger."

I pulled at my shorts. "Does she know anything about the house in the woods?"

Sara's eyes widened. "It's not safe. You need to stay away from there."

"Why?" Angie and I asked at the same time.

"She doesn't want to talk about it, but she's begging you to listen to her." Sara closed her eyes. "Please stay away."

"Is that where she is?" Angie asked.

"She said she's done for now. She's getting tired." Sara folded her hands in front of her.

"Can't she just answer that one last question before she goes?" Angie leaned forward.

"No, I'm sorry. Once I lose connection, I'm afraid I can't get it back. It takes a great deal of energy to communicate as much as she did today. You should be grateful for how clear her messages came across."

"I need to know. Can't you tell me? The cards?" Angie pointed to the tarot spread on the table.

Sara piled the cards and added them to the stack. "I'm sorry. She asked me not to use them."

"But I'm asking you to. I just need that one answer. Where is my sister? I just want to be able to bring her home, for my parents. I want this nightmare to be over." Angie held her head in her hands.

"I really don't know what I can say. I don't know where she is, she didn't tell me, and I'm not getting anything. My guess would be there's a reason she doesn't want you to go to that house you were talking about. You can do what you want with what she told you. If I were you and it were my sister, I'd be at that house right now." Sara shrugged. "But that's just me. Readings are just for guidance; you can take what you want and leave what you don't."

"So you think we should go?" Angie bit at her nail.

"I'm not saying what I think you should do. I'm just telling you what I would do." Sara looked at the clock. "I'm sorry, but our time is up. I have another appointment soon."

"No last pieces of advice or words of wisdom?" Angie stood and pushed her hair off her shoulders.

"Just know that your sister loves you very much. She wants what is best for you, and she is only withholding information to save you." Sara stood to walk us back to the door.

"Thank you." Angie nodded as she opened the door. "You've been very helpful."

## CHAPTER NINETEEN

"We have to go." Angie started the car and backed out of the parking lot.

"Go where?" I asked, already knowing the answer.

"To that house in the woods you were telling me about. Where is it?"

"It's just outside of Pine Grove, but we shouldn't go. Lucy said so." I sat on my hands to keep from cracking my knuckles. "It could be dangerous."

"You don't have to go; just tell me where it is. I need to go. You heard Sara. She said she'd go if it were her sister. She knows something she's not telling us." Angie impatiently tapped her thumb on the steering wheel.

I sighed and looked out the window. "I wasn't going to say anything before, but I really need to tell someone."

"What's wrong?" Angie looked over at me before returning her eyes to the road.

"The other day my mom took off again. Something told me to go check the dead-end road she had gone to before, where the house in the woods is." I closed my eyes, pulling up the fear from that day. "And she was there, but she was in her car still."

"Okay, what's wrong with that? You already knew she knew about the place."

"She had a gun in her lap. I think she went there to kill herself. She made me promise not to tell anyone, but I think it's important for you to know if you really want to go there."

"Why would she kill herself?" Angie pulled the car over at a gas station. "Why would she do it there?"

"I don't know. She said she wasn't going to hurt herself, but she wouldn't tell me anything really. She just told me it wasn't safe there. I don't know if we should go back, not after hearing Lucy say that today too."

"But what if she is there? We'd have answers. I'd have my sister back. My parents could say goodbye to their child. I think it's worth it." Angie held out her hand. "It's okay if you don't want to go with me. I'll go alone, but I have to go. There is no way I'll be able to sleep until I've at least been there and looked around."

"Okay." I dropped my head in defeat. "I'll go with you, but can we at least drive by my house to make sure my parents are home before we go?"

"Alright, but wouldn't we see their cars if they were there?" Angie pulled back onto the road.

"Maybe, but I'd feel safer knowing for sure. It's on the way anyway."

"Okay." Angie held her hand out for me to take. "You know I love you, right? I'm not going to ditch you if your family had something to do with this."

"I know." But I didn't. Part of me that wondered if the truth came out if Angie would ever be able to look at me again. I could possibly love the monsters who took her sister's life, and I wasn't sure I'd be able to stop even if I knew.

The drive back to Pine Grove seemed to take forever. Silence filled the void between us. It seemed we both had too much on our minds to keep the conversation going. Angie drove down our street. "Looks like both cars are there." Angie smiled. "Are you ready?"

"Yeah, okay, let's go. Just follow Main Street until you leave town." I pointed out the window. Beads of sweat rolled down my back as I thought about what we might find.

"Do you think we should have a gun?" Angie slowed down at the Shady Lane.

"I don't know. I don't think anyone will be there." My heart raced at the thought.

"Okay, here we go." Angie turned on the radio. "How about something to dance to?" She hit buttons until an upbeat song came on. "Oh, this one will work. Show me your moves."

"You're literally looking at them." I stayed still in my seat. "That's right, I am the life of the party."

"You're such a goofball." Angie moved her shoulders to the music. "Come on; it's like this."

"Yeah, no thanks. I'll just watch you." I was grateful for the distraction and the laugh.

"You don't like to dance?"

"Not really. I wasn't allowed to go to school dances; you know, on count of boys being there." I shrugged.

"Well, that's lame. You need some excitement in your life."

"I think I've met that quota these last couple weeks." We both laughed, and Angie finished with a snort.

"Good point. But you know what I mean. You need to have some fun. Life's too short." She went back to bobbing her head to the music.

"Just up here you'll want to turn left onto the dirt road. There isn't a sign, so I'm not even sure what it's called." I put my hands under my thighs so I wouldn't snap, crackle, and pop my knuckles. "Right there."

Angie turned onto the road and followed it to the place Mom's car had been parked. "This is the place?" She scanned the area. "It's kind of out in the open. How did the cops miss this?"

"The house is deep in the woods. If you didn't know it was there, you wouldn't look for it. Besides, my dad was the sheriff. I'm sure he kept people away from here." The words cut on their way out. I didn't want to even think about what Marc, Dad, or even Mom had done.

"Okay, let's go." Angie reached under her seat and pulled something out. "In case we need it." She opened a bag and took out a handgun.

"You just drive around with that thing?" My hand was on the door handle, but I couldn't take my eyes off the shiny black metal.

"Yeah, ever since I started searching for Lucy and was old enough, I bought it. I didn't know what or who I was going to run into." Angie got out of the car and slipped the gun into the back of her jeans.

"Whoa, you're a natural." I crossed my arms tight around my waist, trying to calm my nerves.

Angie laughed. "Well, to be a hundred percent honest, I have had some practice." Her smile grew. "Russ, one of the

FBI agents who's been working on Lucy's case from the beginning, took me out shooting a few times."

"Oh, looks like someone has a crush on Russ." I loosened the grip on myself and took a deep breath.

"Well, he is cute and nice, and he has been super helpful all these years." Angie opened her car door and bent down. "I guess I should bring this in case we find anything."

"I don't think there's service out there." I felt my back pocket to make sure my phone was in there. "I didn't check, but my guess would be there isn't."

"We can at least take pictures of anything we find." Angie bent down and tied her shoe. "Alright, are you ready?"

"I guess." I stepped in front of her and led the way. "Don't you think you should call your friend? Maybe he could come out here with us."

"I'll call him if we find anything. I don't want to send him on a wild goose chase. He's busy, and I don't want to look crazy."

"Why would you look crazy? You're trying to find your sister." I pushed a branch out of my face, holding it so it didn't slap Angie.

"Because I don't think he believes in psychics. I want him to take this seriously, so I want to have something concrete before I ask him to come."

"I liked him too." I laughed and kept walking along the path.

"What?" Angie followed behind me, taking extra steps to keep up.

"He doesn't sound very openminded. If he's worth being in love with, he should at least respect your beliefs."

"Jesus, Molly, we're not dating; he's just easy on the eyes. I don't even know if he's single. I just like working with him. I don't plan on marrying him." Angie stopped and blew out air. "Can we slow down a little? You're practically running."

I stopped and looked around. "I'm sorry. I guess I just want to get there as quickly as I can and get this over with. I'm a little freaked out."

"Why are you freaked out?" Angie caught up with me and took my hand.

"Because I don't know what we're going to find, and if we find anything I'm not sure what to think. I mean, this is potentially my whole family. Then what happens?"

Angie took my hand. "Molly, I'm sorry. I didn't even stop to think how this must be for you. I'm so focused on finding Lucy, I wasn't thinking about how this might affect you."

"It's okay. I understand. It's just hard for me. I don't know what to think."

"I know where I'm going now. Do you want me to bring you home and come back on my own?" Angie turned to go back to her car.

I pulled her hand. "No. I don't want you going there alone, and if it is my family, they'd be less likely to hurt you if I'm with you." I didn't know if that were true. I didn't know if they would hurt me too, if they thought I knew something. I didn't know anything anymore.

"Thank you." Angie squeezed my hand.

We walked the rest of the way to the house in the woods in silence. Only the sound of the birds chirping and bugs buzzing filled the air. The sun beat down on us as we entered the opening to the house. "There it is."

"It really is out of the way, isn't it?" Angie put her hands on her hips and caught her breath. "Should we start inside?"

Her question crashed down on top of me. We were looking for a dead body, possibly of my mother. And if we found it, found her, my life would be over as I knew it. This ending would only lead to another. "Okay." The only word I could press through my lips. I walked to the front door and turned the doorknob. I looked back at Angie. "It's locked."

"How did you get in last time?" Angie pushed past me and tried the door, and it opened with an eerie squeak. She stepped aside for me to enter.

"That's strange." My body stiffened as my feet hit the floor. "I could have sworn it was locked."

Angie put her hand on my shoulder. "Are you okay?"

I nodded and took another step inside. The sun lit up the house, making it feel like a normal house. Not one tucked away in the forest used for god only knows. "Yeah." I made the same loop I did the first time. This time I felt more uneasy, knowing that this could belong to my family. Somehow not knowing who was here before made me less on edge. The stakes were higher. Why couldn't Mom just be having an affair like Marc said. I'd give anything for adultery right now.

An overwhelming sense of sadness washed over me as I stood in the bedroom doorway. Seeing the bed neatly made brought on images of Lucy tied to the headboard. I shook the image out of my mind and jumped out of my skin when I felt something touch my neck.

"Molly, are you alright?" Angie's voice snapped me out of the panic I was trapped in and sent me into another when I turned to look at her.

"Oh my god." I fell against the door frame and covered my mouth.

"What is it?" Angie's eyes widened.

I pointed to the front door. "I left my raincoat here last time. Someone moved it." My yellow jacket hung on a hook by the door. "They know I was here."

"Molly, how could they know it's you?"

"It's my raincoat."

"Yeah, there are lots of yellow raincoats. You don't own the only one. Maybe they don't know it's yours." Angie stepped into the room past me and started picking things up.

"But they'd know. My mom bought it for me."

"Did they say anything to you?" Angie opened the top drawer of the bureau.

"No." I peeled my eyes off the front door and stood next to Angie. "But why would they?"

"I don't know. If they were pissed about you being here, don't you think you would have heard something by now?" Angie continued on, opening each drawer. "This thing is empty." She reached her arm in the opening and felt around. "Nothing here."

"Yeah, I guess you're right." But someone had been here. That meant they could come back at any time. "I think we should get out of here."

"I want to look through the whole place first. We can't leave yet." Angie walked over to the other side of the room and got on her hands and knees, feeling the floor.

"What are you looking for?"

"Anything." She knocked on the rug and angled her head down. "I'm looking to see if there are any secret passages in here."

"Secret passages?" I scrunched my nose. "This isn't Narnia."

"I make my students read that book." She laughed. "I take it you haven't?"

"What?"

"Narnia isn't in the floor; it's in the closet." Angie bowed her head and snorted as she crawled along the room.

"Actually, it's a wardrobe." I put my hands on my hips and smirked. "That's one of my favorite books."

Angie held her hand out. "Help me up. There's nothing in here."

"I could have told you that." I pulled her to her feet.

"Well, I needed to be sure. I've waited twenty years to find Lucy. I need to make sure I leave nothing unturned." Angie brushed her hands on her pants and went into the living room. She picked up the stack of magazines. "Did you see the dates on these?"

"Yeah, there's some from the 80s and 90s."

"But look, this one is from the same week Lucy went missing, June 5, 1999."

"Whoa, I guess I missed that before." I took the rest of the stack from Angie and went through the dates. "But it doesn't make sense. This one is from October 18, 1980. Why is there such a range in the dates? They're like twenty years apart."

"I have no idea." Angie flipped through the pages, studying it before moving on. She folded it up and stuck it in her back pocket. "I want to look at this more closely later."

"What are you looking for?"

"I don't know. If Lucy were here, maybe she wrote something in there." Angie got on her knees, like in the bedroom, and started feeling around the carpet.

I got down and did the same on the other side of the room. I peeled at the carpet in the corner. Brown painted wood was the only thing under the dark blue rug. I pushed it back down and crawled over to the couch. I took out my phone, turned on the flashlight, and lit up the darkness. I reached my hand under and pulled out a clump of something. In the light, I knew what it was. "Oh my god, Angie, look at this." I held up the strands of black hair.

"Where did you find that?" Angie crawled over to me and took it out of my hand. "Oh my god, it's Lucy's."

"I mean, it could be mine." My body heated at the thought of the discovery we were going to make.

"Molly, when was the last time you were here?" Angie held the hair up close to her face to examine it. "This has been here for a while."

"Last week."

"And that's the only time you've been here?"

"That I can remember." The weight of sadness closed my eyes.

"Then this can't be yours. This has to be Lucy's. She had to have been here." Angie held the hair to her nose and inhaled. The dust caused her to sneeze.

"It could be anything, though. Besides, how long does hair last?" I reached back under the couch and found another clump of dust. "Why doesn't anyone vacuum in here?"

"I'm glad they didn't." Angie put the hair into her pocket and stuck her hand under the couch, her head pressed against the side.

"Do you want to flip it over?" I got on my knees and waited for Angie to appear.

"That's a good idea." Angie leaned on the couch and pushed herself up. "I'm getting too old for this."

"Me too." Once on my feet, I took one end of the sofa, and Angie had the other. We flipped it onto its back.

Angie bent down and examined the underside. She ran her hands over the fabric and then got back on her knees and searched the area it had been sitting. "There's nothing here. That was a good find, Molly."

"How will you know if it's Lucy's?"

"I'll send it to Russ and ask him to take a look." She got back on her feet and helped me replace the couch.

"Shouldn't we have left it there? So he could have found it?" I wiped sweat off of my forehead.

"Maybe." She shrugged. "But hopefully there's more here, somewhere."

"The only place left is upstairs, but it's locked." I went over to the door and pointed. "Wait, the padlock is gone." I turned the handle, and a steep flight of stairs greeted me. "There was a lock here last time."

"Let's go have a look." Angie held the flashlight on her phone to light up the stairs. "Looks safe enough." The wood creaked under her feet as she climbed to the top.

I followed behind her, holding onto the railing at the side. "What do you see?"

"Looks like another bedroom." Angie turned into the room on her left. "It's empty." Her voice echoed.

"Empty? Like completely?" I joined her in the large, vacant space. "Why would the door be locked?" My thought became words.

"I don't know, maybe it wasn't before." Angie walked the perimeter of the room before going into the next room. "There's a bed in this one."

"Is that all?" I went to the window and pulled the curtain back. "Wait, Angie, come here."

"What is it? Did you find something?" Angie rushed back in.

"No, but look." I held the curtain open. "You can see the trail perfectly. Maybe this is the lookout room."

Angie held the other side open and pressed her face to the window. "Yeah, you're right. You can see pretty far down the path too."

"Was there anything else in the other room?" I let the curtain fall closed.

"Not that I saw. I didn't really have a chance to look around." Angie followed me to check out the other room.

"Did you open the closet?" I stood in the doorway, afraid what might be behind the door.

"Not yet." Angie walked over to the door and pulled it open. "Some hangers and an empty box." She stood on her tippytoes and reached up to the top shelf. "Nothing."

"I don't understand why we didn't find anything. A whole house full of nothing. It doesn't make sense." I put my hand on the wall. "If this is my parents' house, why didn't we use it? I never knew about this place. There's obviously nothing here, so why couldn't we have spent time here? It would have been fun."

"We found a couple things." Angie tapped her back pocket. "The magazine has to mean something. And the hair. That might be all we need to prove she was here."

"But what if Marc knew about this place and brought Lucy here? You know, to fool around? That would explain the hair."

"It could." Angie put her hand on my back. "You're right;

we still don't know anything. I want to look around outside before we head back."

"What would we be looking for out there?"

"I don't know. Anything out of the ordinary." Angie shrugged and held her hand out. "Let's go."

I took her hand and followed her down the stairs. I paused to look around one last time. "Alright." I swallowed the ball forming in my throat. "I don't understand why Lucy and my mom said it was dangerous. What did we miss?"

"I don't know, but if that door was locked before, and someone knew you had been here, they might have gotten rid of evidence. Besides, whoever it is had over twenty years to dispose of anything. We still don't really know who owns this place. It could be anyone."

"Yeah, it could be, but that doesn't explain why I look like this." I wanted answers as much as I didn't. The longer I didn't know anything the better.

"Come on; let's get out there." Angie gave my hand a tug and pulled me through the open door. "Let's at least walk around the house and see if there is anything that catches our eye."

We circled the house and didn't see anything. "Wait, look over there." I pointed to a path headed into the woods, behind the house. I spread open the trees hanging over the path. "Do you smell that?" The fallen branches and dead leaves crunched under our feet.

"Yeah, what is it?" Angie's nose turned up before her hand covered it. "It's a firepit." Angie pointed to a burnt pile in the ground.

We walked closer to the blackened hole in the ground. I kicked at the edges. "It looks like it's pretty fresh."

"It does, and also like it's been here for a while."

"What did they burn?" I covered my nose, now unable to stand the smell any longer.

"It must have been whatever they took out of the house."

"But what would smell like that?" My gag reflex made my stomach wretch.

"I have no idea. It smells toxic, like chemicals or something." Angie took a photo of the hole and quickly covered her nose again. "Okay, I think we can get out of here. I'll send this to Russ and see if he wants to take a look. Maybe he can at least figure out who owns this place."

"That's a good place to start; maybe he can answer a few questions." I took one last look around before we took the trail through the woods back to Angie's car. The uneasy, sinking feeling I had experienced last time returned. Whatever was in this forest did not want us here, or maybe they didn't want us to leave.

## CHAPTER TWENTY

"Where have you been all day?" Dad asked as soon as the door opened.

"I was with some friends." I kept my hand on the door, remembering the rain jacket I had forgotten at the house in the woods.

"Friends? Like who?" Dad set the newspaper down on the table. "Do I know these friends?"

"Why does it matter? I'm nineteen; I'm not a child." I folded my arms in protest.

"I know, but the world is a scary, dangerous place." He looked over his glasses at me. "Isn't that right?"

"What? How would I know? I never get to go anywhere."

"Except today. You were gone all day, out having fun with friends."

"Yeah, true." I nodded and gave him a smile. "Where's Mom?"

"Funny you should ask, since it's your job to take care of her." Dad tapped his fingers on the table, impatiently waiting for me to fight back.

"Well, funny thing is I thought I had weekends off." I opened the fridge and pulled out a ginger ale. "Besides, she doesn't want me babysitting her."

"I don't give a damn what she wants. I need you to keep your eye on her and make sure she doesn't get lost again."

"I will." The pop of the can pulled my attention away from him. "Have you heard from Marc? When's he coming home?"

"He'll be here next weekend. I'm going down to help him pack. I'll need you to watch your mother for me. I hope that's not too big of an inconvenience."

"He's moving back already? I thought he had stuff to take care of. What's the hurry?" I put the cold can to my mouth to avoid eye contact.

"He wants to be home. Who cares how fast it is? Don't you want your brother around?" Dad raised his brow.

"Of course, I do. It's just that he said he had some stuff to do. It just seems fast." I set my can on the counter. "Where is he staying?"

"He'll stay here with us until he gets an apartment." Dad picked the paper back up, letting me know he was done talking.

I saw Mom outside sitting on the patio. The sliding of the glass door made her jump. "So you must have heard, Marc's coming back home."

"Yes, how nice." Her smile grew, and she set down her magazine.

"What are you reading?" I picked it up and turned it over. It was a *People's* magazine, the same as the ones at the house in the woods.

I felt the blood drain from my face. One more thing that

pointed the finger at my family. I was running out of options to cast the blame elsewhere. "Mom?"

"Yes, honey?" She tilted her head in my direction.

"Do you what happened to Lucy Minor?"

She closed her eyes and pushed out a breath. "You really shouldn't get involved in this sort of stuff."

"What does that mean?" I set the magazine back on the table.

"It means you need to keep your nose out of people's business. You have no idea what kind of monsters are out there."

"I saw you taking down Lucy's posters. Why would you do that? Are you trying to protect someone?" I felt my heart pound against my chest so loud I was sure she heard it too.

"Molly, this is not something you should be mixed up in. Do you understand me?" She lowered her voice and leaned in closer. "Do not mention this to anyone else."

"Why, though? What happened to her?" My unwillingness to drop the issue ruffled her feathers.

"Some questions don't have answers."

"Mom, I look like her. You must see it."

"Drop it." She picked the magazine up and stuck her nose in it. "Do not bring this up again."

I went back inside and locked myself in my bedroom. Mom's reaction was all the answer I needed. She knew something, and she wasn't talking. Her dementia seemed to be nonexistent today too. How did that even work? How was it that she could be forgetful and get lost one day and then be back to normal the next. The lack of consistency was beginning to make me feel crazy, like I was living in Neverland.

I threw myself on my bed and hid my head under my

pillow. I should have gone away to college when I had the chance. Now I was stuck in Pine Grove until I'd graduate. That was two more years. I took my phone out of my pocket and sent a text to Marc. "Hey, you're moving back fast. What happened?" I tossed the phone and put the pillow over my mouth and then screamed into it.

The ding alerted me of a new message. "Dad said I should hurry. He said Mom's not doing good. I want as much time with her as I can have before anything happens to her."

"What? Mom's fine. I literally just had one of the most lucid conversations with her I've ever had."

"Really?" The phone rang. "Molly?"

"Yeah?" I twisted my shirt around my finger.

"What's going on? Mom's okay? Why would Dad lie to me?"

"I have no idea. Why does anyone lie?"

"That's pretty rotten, though. If she's okay and he's lying just to get me to come home sooner…"

"Well, that's Dad for you." The frustration in my voice oozed off of me.

"I had to leave my job without notice, and I've been busting my ass packing up my crap since Dad called. I thought this was urgent." Marc sighed. "What the hell is going on up there? You're sure Mom's not sicker than you think?"

"She's outside right now reading a magazine. She was driving the other day. She's fine."

"Are you okay? Are you still mad at me?" Marc cleared his throat. "I hate when you're mad at me."

"I'm not mad. I just…" A sigh replaced the words I wanted to say. "Hey?"

"What?"

"There is something you can do to make it up to me." I twirled a strand of my hair.

"What do you need?"

"If I buy you a test to check your ancestry, would you do it for me? It's for extra credit for school."

"Sure, but I already did one of those things a while ago. Do you want me to do another one?"

"Why did you do one?"

"My ex-girlfriend bought it for me for Christmas last year. I had actually forgotten about it."

"Really? That's a weird gift. What did you find out?"

"We're part Irish, French, and Scottish, I think. It was pretty boring. There weren't any close matches, just a bunch of third and fourth cousins I think."

"Hmm. That's odd."

"What is?"

"That you're Irish. You don't look like a leprechaun."

"Funny." I could almost hear him roll his eyes. "Hey, Molly, just don't tell Dad, okay?"

"Tell Dad what? That you're a leprechaun?" I snorted.

"No, jackass, that I took the test. He gave me a long lecture about never doing anything like that. Something about people selling my DNA or something crazy like that. I just don't want to hear his shit."

"Sell your DNA? Is that even a thing?"

"I don't know. It's some conspiracy bullshit he believes. Just please, don't tell him I did it, and if you do it, don't tell him. Unless you want the lecture. In that case, tell him all you want." Marc laughed.

"Yeah, I think I'll pass. Dad's a real dick most days." I dug at my fingernail while I got enough courage to ask. "Marc?"

"What now?"

"What do you remember about Lucy? What was she like?" I closed my eyes to fight back the tears.

"Aw, Molly, shit." He sighed. "She was amazing. I loved her so much. I told you all this when I was there. Are you okay?"

I sniffled. "Yeah, I guess it's just hard to imagine being in her shoes. I mean, no one even knows where she is. How do you think her family is able to live every day not knowing? I'd die if something happened like that to someone I loved."

"I don't know. I imagine they're suffering. I try not to think about them. I know that makes me sound like an asshole, but I just can't bring myself to think about that. My pain is so deep, I don't have room for theirs; if that makes sense."

"It does." I laid back on my bed. "She must have been so afraid."

"Yeah, probably. I really don't want to talk about this, about her." Marc cleared his throat. "Shit, I don't know if I'm ready to be back there."

"I'm sorry. I didn't want to upset you. It's just that I have so many questions."

"So Dad lied to me to get me to move back home next week. That really pisses me off. Why would he do that?" Marc grunted. "I should have known he would've needed to be in control of this."

"He does have to be in control, of everything. I hate being here. I can't believe you have the chance to be there, and you're moving back here." I couldn't hold back the laughter. "You're a dumbass."

"Hey, I'm only coming back to help with Mom. It's not my fault Dad made shit up to get me there sooner. It was the plan anyway, so what's a rushed, panic move? At least I have less time to think about it."

"Oh yeah, and you'll be able to see Beth. That's got to be worth something."

"You're such a pain in the ass. One thing at a time. Make sure you make my bed for me. I'm going to be exhausted after I have to hang out with Dad for a weekend."

"The weekend? He's going to be gone for a weekend?"

"Yeah, you're welcome. But you better be home when I get there and do something stupid so you can give me a break." Marc yawned. "Hey, kid, I have to get some sleep. I have a long day tomorrow. I have a house to pack."

"See you soon. I love you."

"Love you too, Molly. Stay out of trouble, at least until I get home."

How could it be possible Marc could be so evil. I do love him. Even without being in my life much, he was the one person I could count on. He knew what I was up against; he'd been here before. Dad wasn't an easy person to live with, and it wasn't nice to compare notes. Us against him. That was how it had always been. Now, I didn't know who was against who. Or even who anyone was anymore.

CHAPTER TWENTY-ONE

Dad left before I woke up. A whole weekend without him. I didn't think I'd ever had so much freedom without him around, not at home anyway. Mom was at the table drinking her coffee. "Good morning, sleepyhead. You don't want to waste the beautiful day."

"It is nice." I looked out the window and stretched. "How about we go for a walk?"

"That sounds nice. Where do you want to go?" Mom drank the last of her coffee before she got up to take care of her cup.

"I don't know." My skin itched at the thought. I did know, but I didn't know how to ask. "How about we see where the road takes us?"

"Okay, that sounds fun. Let me go get my sneakers on." Mom left me alone in the kitchen. I poured myself a bowl of Frosted Flakes and enjoyed my breakfast without Dad breathing down my neck, judging my poor choice of breakfast food.

When I was finished with breakfast, I went to my room

to get ready. I noticed Mom on the floor in her closet. I stood by her room and watched. She took out a large carboard box. When that was out of the way, she took out a shoe box that was under a pile of clothes. She opened and took a deep breath before pulling out the contents. She spread what looked like newspaper clippings on the floor around her. She placed her hand on the papers and looked down at them.

"Mom?"

She jumped and gathered all of the clippings off the floor. "Molly, you scared me. I didn't know you were there."

"What are you looking at?" I took a few steps toward her.

"It's nothing." Mom stuffed everything back into the box and buried it in her closet. "So where are we going?"

"I don't know yet. I have to get dressed, and then we can go." I left her alone in her room and went to mine. I tried to figure out what she could be hiding from me, or what else.

Mom was waiting for me in the kitchen, in the same spot I'd found her when I woke up. "Are you ready? Did you take your medicine?"

"Yes, Mother." Mom got up and took her purse off the table. "Your Dad sure has you brainwashed, huh?"

"What do you mean? Don't you want to feel better? That's what your pills are for."

"No, it's not. They're to make me sick. That's what he wants. You know how against it I was. But it was the only way to shut your father up."

"If you don't think they're helping, then why are you taking them? If they make you sicker, it doesn't make sense. Why don't you just tell him no?"

"You know how your father is. I can't just tell him no; not

and live to hear about it." Mom opened the door. "Come on; let's go."

"What did you just say?" I waited in the kitchen for her to answer me, but she was already outside. I followed her to the car. "Mom? Are you afraid of Dad?"

"Molly, let's just have a nice day, okay? I don't want to talk about your father today, or ever." She laughed. "Wouldn't life be great if it were just the two of us?"

"What about Marc? I mean, I'm all for getting rid of Dad, but what about the three of us?"

"Okay, he can stay too." Mom rolled down the window and put her arm on the door. "I just want to be free."

"Have you ever talked about getting divorced? Why stay somewhere you're not happy?" I looked in the rearview as I backed the car out of the driveway.

"If it were only that easy."

"But it is. Why does it have to be hard? You shouldn't stay with someone you don't love. Life's too short for that. You and I could get a place."

"Molly, it doesn't work like that."

"Yeah, it does. If you're not happy, you should leave him. I'll help you. And when Marc gets home, I'm sure he'll help too. Mom, life's too short to be miserable. Don't you want to live?"

"My life is almost over. It's too late for me, but you have your whole life ahead of you. Don't get messed up with anyone who will hurt you. Take your advice and find something or someone who makes you happy. You can make up for what I missed out on." Mom put her hand on my leg. "Get as far away from this town as you can, and don't look back. Don't worry about me."

"Mom, I can't leave you here, not when I know how unhappy you are. I can help you. We can leave together."

"Where are we going?" Mom pulled her hand away. "Molly, we can't go there."

"Where?" I knew the answer; I just wanted to see if she did.

"Don't play games with me, Molly. I don't want to go there. Not today, and not ever."

"What place? What are you talking about?" I glanced over at Mom as I drove past the dirt road.

"Molly, I know you've been there. I found your jacket."

I pulled my car over and caught my breath. "You found my jacket?"

"Yes. I knew it was yours, but your father didn't. He just figured a hunter stumbled across the house. I couldn't bring it home and let him know it was yours." Mom looked out the window to avoid eye contact.

"What is that place? How come I didn't know about it?"

"You don't need to know about it." Mom sighed. "Just don't ever go back there, okay?"

"Why not? If it's our house, why can't I go there?"

"It's not our house. I hate it there." Mom closed her eyes, keeping her head turned away from me. "He can't know you know."

"Does Marc know? Has he been there?" I tried to get Mom to turn her head by staring at her. It didn't work.

"No one can know. Do not speak of it again; do you understand me?" She squinted her eyes to look into mine. "You need to promise me to stay away from there."

"Why can't you just answer my questions? I wouldn't want to go so badly if you would talk to me."

"There are some things I don't want to talk about. Some things are better left unsaid. Don't go poking sleeping bears."

"Why were you there the other day? Who are you afraid of?" The questions kept coming, even when I tried to stop them. They flowed out of me like a dam had let lose.

"Drop it, Molly." Mom crossed her arms. "Are we going to enjoy the day, or are you going to keep needling me?"

"I'll drop it." I pulled onto the road and headed back to Pine Grove. "Can I ask you one more thing?"

"Would you take me home?" She rested her head against the headrest.

"Never mind. Let's just walk around the park in town. It's so pretty there, then we can get lunch."

"Okay, that sounds lovely. It's been a while since we've had a girls' day, just for fun." She was right; it had been years since we'd spent time together just because. When I was little, we would go to the movies or the lake for the day. "I can't even remember the last time we had a day together like this."

Mom reached her hand over. "Let's make the most of it, okay?"

"Okay, Mom. I love you."

"I love you too, Molly."

"If you ever change your mind, and you want help, the offer stands. Just say the word, and we can pack up and head out of town." I pretended to zip my lips. "But enough about that; let's go have some fun."

# CHAPTER TWENTY-TWO

"They received my sample. Check and see if they got yours." Angie's text lit up my screen. Marc was sitting in the chair across the room and didn't even notice I was on my phone.

I signed into the account I'd made when we mailed out the samples and saw the green check mark had moved down the list. "Mine too!" I hadn't had time to let Angie know anything since we were last together. It seemed like so much had happened in such a short amount of time, and now with Marc back it was going to be harder to slip away.

"Hey, have you talked to Beth yet?"

"No, not yet. I've been kind of busy." Marc didn't peel his eyes off the TV, staring aimlessly at the commercials for dog food and Viagra.

"What are you waiting for? You're not getting any younger. Don't you want to go out with her before you need to use that stuff?" I pointed at the TV.

Marc threw a pillow at me. "Shut up, you sicko."

"What? You're almost forty. Isn't that the time you start to need that stuff?" I shrugged and put the pillow behind my back. "Ahh, thank you; it was just what I needed."

"You're such an ass. I don't want to talk about this stuff with my sister. Gross."

"What, we're both adults. Why is it gross?"

"I don't want to know about your sex life, and I don't want you to know about mine." Marc looked at his phone screen. "I guess it couldn't hurt to at least tell her I'm back."

Perfect, soon Beth could fill his attention, and he'd never even notice I was missing. I really needed to see Angie. There were so many things I needed to talk through, and she was the only person I could trust right now. At least, I thought I could trust her. Who even knew anymore? For all I knew she could be setting me up.

"Can I come over tomorrow?" I sent the text and waited for Angie's reply.

"Yeah! I miss you! Russ will be here tomorrow."

"Oh, I can wait. You two should have some alone time." I ended the message with a wink emoji. Why was everyone else finding love, and I was stuck in my room with a pile of books?

"No, don't be gross. I want you to meet him."

"Are you sure?"

"Yes, he'll be here around 1:00, so come over anytime. See you then."

"See you tomorrow." I put my phone down and noticed a smile growing on Marc's face.

"Oh, looks like someone is glad they listened to their annoying sister." I tossed the pillow back at him.

"You were right; she's happy I'm back. We're going to hang out tomorrow."

"That's great."

"Do you want to come? We could go to the movies or out to lunch or something."

"No way. I don't want to get in the middle of that." I stuck my tongue out.

"Oh, knock it off. We're both respectable adults."

"Yeah, until you get liquored up. I saw Beth at the reunion when she had one too many."

"To be fair, that was like five too many, and she had just found out her husband was having an affair." Marc's attention went back to his phone screen.

"I'll leave you two alone." I made kissing faces when I left the room. Mom and Dad's bedroom door was closed, and I heard the faint murmurs of talking. I pressed my head to the door to try to hear what they were talking about. I couldn't make out anything they were saying, but I thought Mom was crying.

I went to my room and imagined life with only Mom. What would it have looked like if it were just the two of us? Then my mind wandered even further. What would my life have been like if Lucy were my mom? What if she were? What was she like? She would be thirty-nine now. Would I have had more brothers and sisters? Would we live in Pine Grove? Would I have had grandparents?

Mom and Dad's parents were all dead when I was born. When all of my friends were talking about spending the weekend with their grandparents, I could never join in. I never knew what it was like to have fun old people to spend time with. My parents were the same ages as my friends' grandparents. Because they *were* my grandparents. The idea flooded me with emotions. I wanted to talk to someone about the possibility. Someone to tell me what kind of mother Lucy would have been. I guessed that was why it was so nice to have Angie. She could probably answer all of my questions.

I fell asleep with thoughts of how life could have been. Lucy's life was taken from her, but so was mine. A prisoner in a life that was not even mine. The pit of my stomach burned from not knowing.

*Her black hair fell in my face as she sang a lullaby. "Hush little baby." Her kiss warmed my forehead. I was a baby. I couldn't talk, only stare back into her emerald green eyes. My little hand wrapped around her finger, and her smile lit up the room. "I love you, Molly."*

*Her love warmed my tiny body as she held me close.*

*"Give me the baby." The voice pulled me out of my trance, and my happy coos turned to screams.*

*"No, please, no." Lucy's tears fell on my face and mixed with mine. "Don't take my baby."*

*Everything went black, and the warmth I had been wrapped in went cold. Ice cold. The shrill screams filled the room. They grew louder and louder until the bubble we were in popped.*

I jumped as I woke up, my eyes still wet from tears and my throat sore. "Lucy, was that you?" I rolled over and saw my dad standing over my bed.

"What did you just say?" His hands were on his hips as he looked down at me.

I rubbed the sleep from my eyes and tried to get my vision into focus. "Huh?"

"What's all the goddamn screaming? I'm trying to sleep."

"Sorry." I sat up and squinted my eyes. "I must have been having a bad dream."

"About what? Aren't you a little too old to be having bad dreams?"

"You're never too old to have bad dreams." I pulled my blanket over me. "Sorry I woke you up."

"Grow up, would you. My god, you're not a toddler anymore." Dad slammed my door behind him.

What the hell did he mean? And why did he think he could waltz into my room? I got out of bed and locked my door. I got back into bed and pulled the covers up to my chin and thought about the dream. Did that really happen?

A light knock at my door pulled my attention out of my head. Marc appeared in the doorway. "Are you alright?"

I motioned for him to come in. "No. Shut the door."

Marc closed the door and stood next to my bed. "Will you sit with me?"

"Okay." He sat on the edge of my bed. "I heard you screaming. Are you okay?"

I shook my head and started to cry. "No."

"I heard Dad in here. He's such a dick." Marc put his hand on my knee. "I didn't think you had nightmares anymore."

"Anymore? What do you mean?"

"Mom used to tell me about them. She'd called them night terrors. I guess I'd thought you'd stopped."

"I don't remember any of that. When?"

Marc scratched his head. "I don't know. You were pretty little. Three or four maybe."

"Did she say why?"

"No, she was just scared, I guess. If you screamed like that when you were little, I would have been scared too. That's horrifying."

"Why would Mom tell you?" I pulled the blanket tighter around me.

"I don't know. Maybe she didn't have much else to talk about." Marc shrugged. "She wasn't making fun of you. I think she was just afraid."

"But why? She was a nurse; nothing should shake her."

"She hasn't been a nurse since before I was born."

"What? I thought she was working when you were little."

"Nope, not that I can remember anyway. Maybe she did when I was little, but I never remember her working outside of the house. I guess I was enough to keep her busy."

"Is everything in my life a lie? How come no one told me about these night terrors? I should know. What if I was at a friend's house or something and started screaming?"

Marc rubbed my knee. "Molly, don't worry about it right now. Try to get some sleep. I can sit with you until you fall asleep, if you want."

"No, I'm fine." My body trembled under the sheets.

"You don't seem fine. Are you sure? I don't mind. I can sleep on your floor, if you want."

"No, I want to be alone." I closed my eyes in an attempt to get rid of him.

"Okay, well, if you change your mind, text me. I'll come back if you need me."

"Thanks." I closed my eyes tight and tried to drown out the memories. The ones I could remember and the ones just coming back to me. All these years and part of me always knew. If only I had listened sooner.

# CHAPTER TWENTY-THREE

I managed to leave the house without anyone noticing. I had rehearsed what I was going to say if anyone asked me where I was going. *Just going to the library to get some extra credit work in.* Looked like I could save it for next time, or at least for when I would come back. I backed out of the driveway and made my way to Angie's. I wanted to talk to her and slip out before Russ got there. The last thing I wanted to do was be a third wheel.

Angie was waiting outside, sitting on her front porch when I pulled in. "Hey, it feels like forever since I saw you." She wrapped me in a hug as soon as I got out of my car.

"I know. I was thinking the same thing." I rested my head on her shoulder before pulling away. "I've missed you."

"Me too." Angie took my hand. "I thought I did something to upset you last time. I'm really sorry about being so self-absorbed."

"You're not self-absorbed; you're looking for answers, and so am I. It's just hard to change my view of the people I've loved my whole life."

"I don't want you to hate your family. The last thing I want to do is isolate you from them." Angie put her hand to her heart. "But I can feel it. I know you're Lucy's. I knew the first time I saw you, and every second we spend together confirms it."

"I know ... I know she's my mom." I sat on the stairs and dropped my head. "Now all we need to do is find her. I need to know what happened to her."

Angie joined me on the stairs. "You know?"

"Yeah, I had this dream about her last night, and Marc said I've been having night terrors since I was a little kid."

"What did you dream?"

"She was holding me, and I felt so loved and warm. She was a good mom; I could feel it." I closed my eyes to pull back the memory. "But someone took me out of her arms. We were both screaming." I brushed the tears off my cheek. "That's all I remember. I don't know who took me, or what happened to her."

"Was it at the house?" Angie placed her hand on my leg. "Did you see what it happened?"

I closed my eyes. "I think we were in a bed, but I don't know."

"But you don't know where?" Angie's desperation soaked into my skin. I wanted to give her more answers, but it was all I had.

"No, I'm sorry."

"It's okay." Angie put her arm around my back and pulled me closer. "We'll figure this out. I know we'll find her."

"I hope so." Except only part of me hoped so. I didn't want Marc to get in trouble, but if he'd killed my mother, why shouldn't he? He had twenty years of freedom, and what did Lucy have? Twenty years of silence.

"Russ is excited to meet you." Angie gave me a squeeze.

"I was thinking I'd get out of here before he gets here. I don't want to intrude."

"Don't be silly. I want you here. Besides, I think it would be good for you to talk over a safety plan with him."

"What do you mean?"

"Well, if anyone at your house figures out what you know, you could be in danger. Russ is an expert in this stuff. He'll give you tips on how to read your surroundings and ideas for how to stay safe."

"You think I'm in danger?" I leaned into her and closed my eyes. "This is all so exhausting."

"I know. I'm sorry, but at least you don't have to do this alone. I'm right here anytime you need me. Day or night."

"But doesn't that put you in danger too?"

"I'm already there. I've never been quiet about my search efforts. I've never given up, and I never will. People around here know that. I probably have a huge target on my back."

"My mom knows I was at the house. She told me never to go back." I cracked my knuckles. "I asked her straight out if she knew where Lucy was, but she wouldn't answer me. She told me to drop it."

"You told her?"

"I didn't tell her what I know, only asked her what happened to Lucy. My dad was gone, and I wanted to see what she'd tell me. She told me nothing. Just gave me a warning to stay out of it."

"Holy crap, Molly, that's not good."

"She said my dad didn't know it was my raincoat, but she

did. She said he just thought a hunter was passing through. So as far as I know he doesn't know, only her."

"What about Marc? Does he know you know anything?" Angie rubbed her forehead.

"Not unless Mom told him. But get this—I asked Marc to take one of those tests we took, and he said he'd already taken one."

"He took a DNA test? His results are public?"

"I guess. He said they were pretty boring and didn't tell him much. But he didn't seem freaked out that I took one. All he said was not to tell Dad. If he had something to hide, why wouldn't he be worried?"

"I don't know. But that's huge. His results will give us our answer. You're pretty smart, Molly. Good work."

"But I didn't do anything; he already did it." I stood and stretched. "That's what I don't understand. If he has a secret daughter, why would he go out of his way to be found out?"

"I don't know. People do stupid shit. He's gotten away with it for twenty years; he probably figures he's out of the woods." Angie went to the door. "Let's go get out of the sun for a while. I need a drink."

"Isn't it too early for that?" I tilted my head and laughed.

"A drink, like lemonade or orange juice. I'm not a day drinker, even though it might help with this anxiety." Angie put her hand on her hip and smiled. "And no naughty drinks for you, missy."

"I don't drink. I'm a good girl." I pulled out my phone. "Looks like Russy-poo will be here soon. Shouldn't you go get freshened up?" I wiggled my eyebrows at her.

"Oh my god, you're terrible. Please don't tell him I think

he's the bee's knees." Angie took two glasses out and opened the refrigerator.

"Did you just say bee's knees? How old are you? A hundred?"

"Oh, knock it off; you've never said that before?" Angie set the bottles of orange juice and lemonade next to the glasses.

"Yeah, never, at least not until a minute ago. Who the hell says that?" I poured the juice into my glass.

"Well, whatever you call it, don't tell him I think he's cute. I don't want to make things weird between us. It's strictly business."

"I don't get you people. If you like someone, tell them. Who cares? Life's too short to worry about the little stuff."

"You sure are wise beyond your years." Angie took a drink of her lemonade. "I wish I could live as freely as you."

"Yeah, well, I don't live as free when it's my life. It's way easier to give advice than it is to take it. I've never had anything except a book boyfriend or two."

Angie spit out her drink. "You're too funny. I think we should work on changing that."

"No thanks. I have too much to focus on with school and taking care of my mom. Oh yeah, don't forget to add finding a killer slash finding my birth mother to the list."

"Well, you need some fun on your list."

"And so do you." I held my glass and looked out the window. "Oh, and looks like your fun just arrived."

"Oh my god, Molly. Please, don't say anything." Angie ran her fingers through her hair. "How do I look?" She adjusted her shirt before she opened the door.

"You look beautiful." I watched out the window and saw the smile grow on Russ' face when he saw Angie.

"Hey there." Angie giggled, causing me to do the same.

I covered my mouth and noticed Angie shot me daggers. "Sorry." I sat at the table with my back to her so I could laugh without being noticed.

"It's so nice to see you, Angie." Russ' deep voice sent chills down my spine. "Oh, this must be Molly."

I turned around in my chair and gave him a smile. "Hi." Angie was right—he was cute.

"It's nice to meet you, Molly. I've heard a lot about you." Russ leaned against the counter and crossed his arms. His biceps bulged out of his t-shirt.

"That's strange. I haven't heard much about you." My lips curled up in a smile I couldn't hide.

"I've told her about you." Angie's cheeks blushed. "She's kidding. Isn't that right, Molly?"

"Yeah, she did tell me about you. I'm just messing around. It's nice to meet you." I stood and reached out my hand. "Thanks for coming by today."

His massive hand encased mine. "It's my pleasure. I'll do anything to help Angie."

Flustered, Angie choked on her drink. She dried her mouth with her arm. "Sorry."

"You okay?" Russ turned his attention to Angie.

"Yeah, I'm fine." Angie picked up a plastic bag and handed it to Russ. "This is the hair we found at that house I was telling you about."

Russ took the bag and examined the contents. "Hmm, we could probably run some tests on this, but since you took it out of the house, it won't help the case at all."

"But if we know for sure it's Lucy's, then isn't that enough to prove she was there?" Angie pushed her hair behind her ear.

"Well, yeah, but she was dating Marc at the time of her disappearance, so it wouldn't be unusual for her hair to be in the house of his parents." Russ held the bag up to the window to get a better look.

"Are you sure the house belongs to my parents?" I asked, not wanting the answer.

"I'm not sure. Angie didn't have the address, so I wasn't able to check. I was hoping you could bring me out there today so I could take a look." Russ' blue eyes danced in the sunlight.

"I don't know if that's a good idea." I looked over to Angie for support, but she was no help. Russ had her complete attention.

"Well, if you're not up to going, would it be alright if Angie brings me? I want to get a look around and see if there is anything that pops out." Russ looked at his watch. "We still have plenty of daylight."

"It'd probably be better if you two went alone. I just... I'm not sure I'm ready to go back there right now." The headache was growing, stealing any chance of having a constructive conversation. "Angie, would it be okay if I go sit in the living room?"

"Yeah, sure. Are you okay?" She followed behind me.

"I'm not feeling well." I squinted my eyes to squeeze out the pain.

"Can I get you anything?" Angie hovered over me.

"No, I think I'm just tired." I pressed my cold hand against my hot forehead.

"Maybe I should stay with you. We can give Russ directions to the house. Is that okay, Russ?"

"Yeah, that would be fine." Russ nodded as he joined us in the living room.

"No, don't be silly. I need to rest. You two should go check things out. I'll be fine after a nap. Would it be okay if I stayed here? I really don't want to go home right now." I curled up on the couch and closed my eyes.

"Of course, you can." Angie covered me up with the throw blanket she'd pulled off the back of the chair. "I told you you're always welcome here."

"Are you up to a few more questions? Or should we go?" Russ bent down in an attempt to make eye contact.

"Come on; we can talk with her when we get back." Angie pulled him out of the living room. "Are you sure you don't need anything?" Angie paused in the doorway.

"No, I'm just tired. I don't know what came over me, but I don't think I can keep my eyes open."

"Okay, well, we'll be back in a while." Angie blew me a kiss. "Feel better, kiddo."

With Angie and Russ gone, I had more time to think. It seemed like it was all I'd been doing, but I hadn't been able to amount to anything. The quiet of Angie's house was what I needed to gather my thoughts. There was a lot to catch up with from the last few weeks. I let my body settle into the softness of the sofa and drifted off to sleep. Safe and alone.

CHAPTER TWENTY-FOUR

The room was dark when the vibrating of my phone pulled me out of sleep. Unsure where I was in the first few moments, my heart raced as I took in my surroundings. Angie's living room. My breathing slowed when I figured it out. My phone started to vibrate again, reminding me what had woke me up in the first place.

I took my phone out of my back pocket and squinted to see who was calling. It was Dad. The panic I had shaken off covered me like a blanket. I let the call go to voicemail as I tried to decide what I would tell him. I had ten missed calls, all from Dad, and twice as many texts from Marc. I hadn't told anyone where I was going when I left this morning. I didn't expect to be gone all day and had hoped no one would have noticed I was missing.

"Angie?" A new set of worries washed over me. "Angie, are you there?" I turned the lamp on and walked down the hall to her bedroom. The room was empty. I went to the window and saw her car was there, but Russ' was not. They must still be at the house in the woods, but there was no way they could see anything. It would be pitch black there at this time.

*Oh my god.* I should have gone with them. What if something happened to them? The questions came out faster than my racing heart. *What have I done?* I stared at my phone screen paralyzed by the incoming call. I couldn't go home, not now; not without knowing where Angie was. And if I answered the phone, Dad would demand I get my ass home. I could already hear his voice barking the order.

When the call ended, I sent Marc a text. "Cover for me?"

"Where in the hell are you? Dad is going bat-shit crazy."

"I'm at a friend's house. I'm fine, but I'm not sure when I'll be back. Please tell Dad you knew where I was, you just forgot."

"OMG! He'll kill me! Why should I cover for you?"

"It's a long story. PLEASE?? I'm begging you."

"You owe me. BIG TIME!"

"You're a lifesaver. I love you."

"Love you too."

"Hey, have you guys been home all day?"

"Yeah, why?"

"No reason." I could only hope he was telling the truth, and that Angie and Russ would walk through the door any minute. I pressed my nose against the window in the front door as I scanned the street. The breath from my mouth fogged up the glass. "Come on, Angie; where are you?" The beating of my heart filled the room around me as I thought about every possible scenario.

Maybe someone else was at the house. What if a bear attacked them? Or they got in a car accident? Every story I told myself became a little less hopeful and a lot more tragic.

They were dead. They had to be. I turned my phone on to search for accidents in the area when a text from Angie appeared on the screen. "Be home soon."

I collapsed on the floor next to the door and sobbed. They were okay. My relief turned to anger as I thought about the worry that had nearly drown me. They'd been gone for hours. What could have possibly taken this long? Images of them curled up together in the house in the woods fueled my anger. They'd left me here all this time without letting me know they were okay.

Outraged by their selfishness, I got to my feet to let myself out. The headlights from Russ' pickup nearly blinded me. I shielded my eyes while I waited for him to turn off his truck. "Molly, we found her." Angie ran over to me without closing her door. "We found Lucy."

Russ got out of the truck. "We don't know what we found, but we're going to check it out in the morning."

"You found her?" I lowered my arm to look at Angie's face. It was covered in streaks of dirt.

"Yeah, it has to be her." Angie put her arm around me and pulled me close. "It's almost over."

"Angie, I told you we don't really know what we found yet. You can't go telling everyone until we know. It could jeopardize the case."

"You found a body? At the house?" I looked between Russ and Angie to see if they'd divulge any more information.

Angie nodded. "She's coming home."

Russ sighed. "We don't know what we found." He rubbed his face. "There's a cop keeping watch tonight, and we'll go back in the morning. This can't get out, though. No one is supposed to know."

"I won't say anything." I crossed my arms to try to keep warm in the night air. "You're going back tomorrow?"

"I am, but you girls can't go back. We have to keep the integrity of the scene. The less people there the better. We'll have answers soon enough." Russ yawned. "I need to get home and get some rest. Tomorrow's going to be a long day."

"Why don't you stay here?" I looked at Angie, waiting for her to extend the offer herself.

Russ ran his hand through his hair. "I don't think that's a good idea. Not while the investigation is going on."

"Who's going to know? Besides, I have to get home before my family suspects anything. I don't think Angie should be here alone tonight. I think it's your duty to make sure she's okay." I unlocked my car. "I'll be back in the morning."

"You can't go, not yet. I have to tell you what we found." Angie followed me to my car.

"Russ said we can't talk about it yet. Why don't you get some sleep, and you can tell me all about it when he's not here?" I opened my door. "I hope this is what you think it is."

"Me too. I've never wanted anything more." Angie reached over and gave me a kiss. "Be back first thing tomorrow morning?"

"I'll be here as soon as I wake up." I backed out of Angie's driveway and made the short drive home. The lights in the house were still on, and I didn't know if I wanted to go in. What if they knew something was going on? For the first time, I genuinely questioned my safety. If it was Lucy they'd found tonight, someone in this house was the reason she was there. Someone was a murderer.

## CHAPTER TWENTY-FIVE

"Look what the cat dragged in." Marc put the Bud Lite bottle to his lips and tipped his head back.

"What are you doing up? And why the hell are you drinking that? If you're going to drink alone, you should at least drink something respectable." I set my phone on the table and sat next to him.

"You'll get to ask questions after you pay me back for the wrath of hell you made me endure." He took another drink. "This was all there was in the fridge, and there was no way I was going to leave with Dad in such a rage. Jesus, is he always like that?"

"Rage? What did he do? Is Mom okay?" I looked around the house to see if there was any aftermath left behind. There was nothing out of place.

"Why wouldn't she be?" Marc twisted the cap off another beer. "Nothing quite as good as warm piss."

"What the hell, Marc. Don't drink it if you don't like it." I grabbed for the bottle.

He swatted at my hand. "Get outta here. I need this."

"You don't need it. What did I miss today?" I went to the fridge and poured a glass of orange juice.

"Oh, I don't know, just Dad storming around in a complete rage. What the fuck is up with him these days? Why didn't you tell me how controlling he is?"

"I guess I didn't notice." I shrugged and thought back to some of the stuff Dad had done. "You know, now that you put a name to it, I can see it. I didn't really think much of it before."

"You're a grown ass woman; why does he have to know where you are or what you're doing every second of the day? I made the mistake of telling him to calm down." Marc shook his head. "Do yourself a favor and never do that."

"What did he do?"

"He tore me a new asshole. Told me to stay out of his business and to get the fuck out. Like dude, I just got back here because you invited me." Marc finished the second beer and put it next to the other four.

I picked up one of the empties. "Did you drink all of these?"

"Yup, and those too." He squinted his eyes and pointed to another empty six pack.

"Jesus, Marc. What the hell? You're going to be sick."

"Maybe." He threw his hands up. "We have to get out of here." His voice dropped to a whisper as he scanned our surroundings.

I leaned in to hear what he was saying. "Why? What happened?"

Marc held his finger to his lips. "He's crazy."

"Who? Dad?"

Marc nodded. "Come back to Virginia with me, or let's go

somewhere else. I can't be here, and you shouldn't stay here either."

"What about Mom? I can't leave her here. You see how he is; she shouldn't have to stay here with him." The discovery of Lucy, or whoever Russ and Angie had found at the house in the woods fell back in my lap. I couldn't push it away any longer.

"So, she can come too. We have to get out of here. He's snapped or something. I don't remember him being like this when I was younger." Marc opened the refrigerator door and started pushing stuff around. "There has to be some more in here somewhere."

I picked up my phone and keys and went over to Marc. "Knock it off. You don't need anymore. Come on; let's go for a ride." I pulled my brother away from his quest for more alcohol and guided him to the door.

Surprisingly, he didn't protest the idea. "You better drive." He burped and then giggled. "Where are we going?"

I reached over and buckled his seat belt. "For a ride." I backed into the road and turned toward town. I wanted to take him to the house in the woods, but I wasn't sure why. Did I want to remove the body and get the blame off my brother, or did I want him to admit to what he did? The swirl of emotions brewing inside of me took my breath away. Something made me take the turn to the high school. I put my car in park and looked over at Marc.

"What are we doing here?"

"Come with me." I got out of the car and walked over to his door and opened it for him. "Come on." I reached over him and unbuckled his seat belt.

"This is weird. Why are we here?" Marc dug his heels into the dirt parking lot.

"Just come on." I took his hand and led him to the bulletin board. I pulled down a flyer of Lucy and walked him to the bleachers.

Marc rubbed his eyes as he plopped on the bench next to me. "What's going on?"

I handed him the picture of Lucy and watched his expression change from questioning to sadness. His eyes filled with tears as he stared at her. "Why are you doing this?"

"What happened to Lucy?" I watched as he drifted further away from me.

"I don't know." He covered his mouth and focused on her picture. "I loved you so much, Lucy." He held the photo to his chest and closed his eyes. "I'm so sorry for letting you down."

"Why are you sorry?"

Marc opened one eye and looked at me. "I told you what I did."

"No, you didn't. Tell me what happened." I pushed closer to him so he couldn't make eye contact with me and had to focus his attention on Lucy.

"We got into a fight, and I left her. I fucking left her."

"What were you fighting about?"

"I told you." His tears fell on the paper.

"I don't remember, so tell me again."

"She wanted to tell me something, but I just wanted to have a good time. I didn't want to talk about anything. I just wanted to party."

"What did she want to tell you?"

"How would I know? I never saw her again." Marc rubbed his hand across his nose.

"Was it that she was pregnant?"

The crinkling of the paper became louder as Marc crunched it between his hands. "No. She wasn't pregnant." Marc smoothed out the paper. "Is that what you wanted to tell me, Lucy? Were you pregnant?"

"Marc, you know the answer to that." I swallowed the lump in my throat. "You knew she was pregnant."

Marc hung his head and began to sob. "That's what I always thought. I lost my girl and my baby."

"Is that really what you thought? That you lost her? You lost them?"

"Yeah, that's why I had to get out of here. It was bad enough that I'd lost her, but then she took my baby from me." Marc balled up his fist. "She took my baby from me."

"Who did?"

"That fucking bitch. She stole everything from me." Marc punched the metal under us, sending a shockwave of noise through the quietness of the night. "Why couldn't she have just told me she didn't want to be with me? Why did she have to do this to me?"

"What did she do to you?"

"She left me. She crushed me. I couldn't live like that."

"Is that why you killed her?" The words spilled out of my mouth before I knew what I had said.

Marc spun his head around to look at me. Rage radiated off of him. "What did you just say?"

"Did you kill Lucy so she wouldn't leave you?" I inched away from him and spun my legs off the side of the bleachers so I could start running if I needed to.

"No. Why would you even say that?" Marc jumped off the bench.

"I don't know." I choked on my words on their way out. "Someone killed her."

"How do you know that? Maybe she ran away. Started a new life. How the hell does anyone really know?" Marc crumpled up the flier and threw it at my face.

"You promise me, you didn't kill her?"

"Why are you even asking me that? What the hell is wrong with you? I thought it was us against them? I thought you had my back. Why are you doing this to me?" Marc took a step closer to me. "I thought we were family."

"I just want to understand. I want to know why I look like her. I want to know what happened to my mother."

Marc's mouth dropped open. "Are you fucking saying what I think you're saying? You think Lucy is your mom?" He shook his head. "What kind of drugs are you on?" He punched his fist into his hand as he paced the grass in front of me. "It's that bitch Angie, isn't it? She's always had it in for me."

"Why would she have it in for you? Why would you even mention her?"

"Oh, I don't know? Beth told me the two of you were talking at the reunion." Marc folded his arms. "I should have fucking known."

"Should have known what? That Angie would see me and know that her sister is my mother?" I jumped off the bleachers and got into his face. "You should have known you couldn't keep me a secret forever."

"What in the actual fuck are you talking about? You're not my kid."

"Oh yeah? Well, when my results come back, I think

you'll be singing a different song. You won't be able to hide it then, will you?"

"You're as crazy as Dad. I don't know why I came back. I thought you were different, but obviously you're unhinged. Just like your fucking father."

"Yeah, just like him." I shoved Marc's chest. "You're the definition of unhinged. At least Angie is a decent person. At least she wants to help me."

"So, I was right— that bitch is involved. She's feeding you bullshit stories to make you turn on me. Just like everyone else in this goddamn town."

"She's not feeding me bullshit; she's helping me."

"Jesus fucking Christ. Think what you want, but I know that bitch. Her own sister didn't like her." Marc turned to walk away. "I can't wait until you get your fucking results, and you can see what kind of a nut job you really are. Fucking unbelievable. And to think I actually gave a shit about you."

"Marc, wait." I ran after him. This wasn't how I wanted the night to turn out. It might be the last time I'd get to see my brother outside of jail. It was probably our last night to be together before his secrets were unable to be covered up. "Marc, I'm sorry."

"Go to Hell."

"No, Marc, wait. I'm sorry. I didn't mean anything I just said. I'm confused. I want answers too. I'm sorry."

"Why are you doing this to me? Don't you know me better than that? Do you really think I could kill someone? Someone I loved?"

"No, I don't. I guess you're right; I let Angie get into my head. I wanted to help her find her sister. I didn't mean to start all this." I pulled on his arm to make him stop. "Please, let's go home and forget about this. Okay?"

"Molly, I don't understand how you could see me like that. You actually think I'm evil? Or that I'm your father? If I were your dad, why would I leave you with Dad? He's a fucking psychopath. I wouldn't even leave my dog with him."

"I don't know. I got caught up in everything. I wanted you to tell me it was an accident or something. I don't think you're evil. I love you, Marc. Please, understand I'm so confused."

Marc's body softened when he saw my tears. "Molly, I don't know why you look like Lucy. It breaks my heart every time I look at you. All I see is the future Lucy and I could have had together. It's like the universe's sick, twisted joke. You can't have your girl, but your little sister looks just like the baby you could have had. Ha-ha, better luck next time."

"I wish you were my dad. You're way better than Dad." I elbowed Marc in the ribs. "I'm sorry."

"It's fine. You're not the first person to accuse me of killing Lucy, and you probably won't be the last. God, I fucking hate small towns."

"Come on; let's go before anyone notices we're gone."

Marc stumbled into me and hugged me. "I love you, Lucy." He picked up my hair and started to smell it.

"What are you doing?" I took a step back to get out of his embrace. "Marc?"

"I'm tired. Let's go home."

"Yeah, that's a great idea."

# CHAPTER TWENTY-SIX

When I came out of my room, Dad was at the table with the newspaper, an empty mug in front of him. "Nice to see you remember where you live." He didn't lower the paper.

I rolled my eyes on my way to the refrigerator. "Sorry if I have a life." The bottles in the door rattled when I slammed it shut.

"As long as you live in my house, you follow my rules." He folded the paper and tossed it onto the table.

"Yeah, well, what if I don't want to live here? Then what? Are you going to tell me what to do then?" I slammed the milk on the counter and crossed my arms. "When are you going to realize that I'm not a baby anymore?"

"You need to watch yourself, young lady." Dad stood and took his glasses off.

"What's going on out here?" Marc came into the kitchen, his eyes squinting to block the sun.

"Dad told me I have to follow his rules if I want to live here, so I told him I'm leaving. I don't need to live here and be treated like a child. I'm nineteen fucking years old." I took a step behind Marc to put him closer to Dad.

"Whoa, whoa, whoa." Marc's hand went to his head. "Why don't you sit back down."

"Don't tell me what to do, and don't use that language in my house." Dad's face grew red. "Get the hell out of my way." Dad pushed Marc.

"Hands off, old man." Marc held his arms out to block me. "Molly, go to your room."

"Don't get involved. Get the hell out of my way."

I ran down the hall to my room and unplugged my phone and grabbed a sweatshirt out of my closet. With a quick look around, I knew I needed to get out of the house while Dad was this angry. There wasn't going to be anything I could do or say to get him to calm down, and I knew it was going to get worse as the day went on.

Dad and Marc were still yelling in the kitchen. I needed to get past them to get my keys so I could leave. I opened my door to hear what they were screaming about. They were standing right where I needed to be. I couldn't nonchalantly walk past them and slip out. I closed my bedroom door and locked it and then opened my window. I found a backpack in my closet and stuffed some clothes into it before putting it on my back and crawled out my window.

I ran to the road and kept running. Angie's house was too far to walk to without risking being found. At the end of the street, I found some trees to hide in and sent Angie a text. "Can you please come get me?"

"Are you okay?"

"No, just come get me ASAP. I'm by Mrs. Nelson's house."

"On my way."

I waited in the bushes, crouching so no one could see me until I heard a car slow down. I stood and pushed the branches out of my face. Angie was driving slowly on the other side of the road. I waved my arms to get her attention.

"What's going on?" Angie looked in her rearview mirror while she waited for me to get in.

"It's my dad; he's being impossible. He's mad I was gone all day yesterday. Him and Marc are fighting right now." I put my backpack on the floor and fastened my seat belt. "I had to get out of there."

"Where's your car? Are you sure you're okay?" Angie turned to look at me before she started to drive.

"My keys were in the kitchen, and I didn't want them to see me. It's a long story." I rested my head against the seat. "Can we go back to your place."

Angie nodded. "Yeah, of course." She placed her hand on my leg and gave me a tap. "Russ is already at the house."

"Already? They're not messing around, huh?"

"No. I couldn't sleep last night thinking about it. Lucy's coming home." Angie brushed a tear off her cheek.

"You're sure it was…"

"No, we can't be sure. Russ said it could take a while to know for sure. We don't even know if it's a body. It could be bones." Angie took her keys out of the ignition. "But I know in my heart it's her." She clutched her hand to her chest. "I just know it."

"I couldn't really sleep either." I thought back to the night at the school with Marc. There was no sense to be made from it. I didn't know any more now than I did before we went. I just loved my brother a little more.

"I know how hard this must be for you. You know I want

what's best for you too. I need these answers. You understand that, right?"

"I know. And I want what's best for you and your family. It's hard to wrap my head around all of the lies. You know?"

Angie nodded. "I can't even imagine what that's like. All I know is how to have this unbearable hole inside of me. One that will never be filled ever again. Even if it is Lucy, I know it's not going to magically fix everything. I know it's going to hurt all over because I'll know now. Without having her body, part of me that likes to pretend that she ran away and started a new life someplace else."

"She wouldn't do that to you, though." I held my hand out for Angie to hold. "I know she's my mom. I know she wouldn't have left me, left us. I know someone took her from us."

"Russ thinks you're her daughter too. After he met you, he said there's no mistaking it."

"I wonder how many other people think that. My whole life in this town and no one ever mentioned I looked like a missing girl. They're up in everyone's business about everything, but they can't give me a heads-up?"

We laughed together. "I can honestly say I never saw you around town, and you live next to my parents' house. They've never said a word about you either."

"I guess I was always a homebody. I'd rather be home than out on the town."

"Well, whatever the reason our paths crossed now, I'm grateful." Angie got out of the car and watched me. "You are beautiful."

"So are you." I winked. "So how was last night? Was there another reason you didn't get any sleep?"

"No." Angie lowered her head and blushed. "We're just friends. But it was nice having him here."

"Did you at least sleep together?"

"No, he stayed in the guest room." She pointed at my backpack. "Should I make the bed up for you? Do you want to stay with me for a while?"

"Could I? I mean, if it's not too much trouble."

"Molly, I told you before—you're always welcome here." Angie put her hand on my back and led me inside.

"Thank you. I didn't know where I was going to go." I put my bag down and hugged her. "I love you."

"I love you too. Thank you for spending the day with me. I'm not sure how much longer I'll be able to wait to hear the news."

"Tell me what happened yesterday. You guys were gone forever." I sat on the couch I had napped on the night before.

"Well, on the drive there I mentioned something about cadaver dogs."

"How romantic."

"He said something similar." Angie snorted. "What can I say, I'm going to need some practice."

"I'm just messing around. I know that wasn't the purpose of your outing."

"Right, so I wanted to get as much accomplished as we could, so I asked about the dogs. Russ said he had a connection who owed him a favor, so they came by the house. His friend Mickey brought the dog into the house, but it didn't find anything in there. I don't know if I was relieved or annoyed when there wasn't a hit." She shrugged. "Anyway, Mickey let the dog roam the area, and Pluto got a hit."

"Wait a minute, Mickey and Pluto?"

"Yeah, we had that joke too. So Pluto sat on a spot, and Russ started to dig. He found something that looked like bones to me, but he stopped. He said he didn't want to compromise the investigation. So I don't even know what Pluto found. Mickey said he's never been wrong before." Angie pulled at the threads on the hem of her jeans.

"Where was the spot?"

"It was through those trees, kind of near the firepit."

"Was Russ able to figure out who owns the house?" I snapped the elastic on my wrist.

"If he did, he hasn't told me. He hasn't really told me much. He did say he could get the results to our DNA quicker, though, if that's something you want to do."

"How? Is he going to call the company and make them hurry up?" I bit at the inside of my cheek.

"No, he can run the test for us. If you're interested, he said he could do it for us."

"What are we waiting for? You know there's no way I can wait."

"Okay, when he gets back, I'll tell him." Angie turned over her phone. "I don't know how much longer I can wait until he calls me."

"Did he say he was going to call you? If it's an investigation, how is he able to share anything with you? I mean, couldn't that hurt the investigation?"

"I didn't think about that. You're probably right. Russ won't be able to tell me anything, not unless they know it's Lucy." Angie picked at her pant leg. "Damn it. I was really thinking I'd know something today."

"Maybe he'll tell you. I mean, you are involved. You were

there when you guys made the discovery. Mickey knows you know."

"You're right." She stared at her phone. "I really wish I could have been there today."

"Do you, though? I mean, if they do find Lucy, do you really want to remember her like that? I don't think I'd want to. It's one thing to want to know where she is and another to see her skeleton."

"Her skeleton." Angie covered her mouth. "You know I was so excited to think we'd found her, and I didn't really think past that. You're right. I don't want to see her like that."

"Did Russ say anything about the house or the set-up of it?" My attempt to change the subject to pull her out of her thoughts.

"He didn't say much. He thought it could be someone's hunting camp, until we found the bones, or whatever it is we were going to leave."

"Really? He didn't get any vibes from that place?" I looked out the window. "At least they have a nice day to be outside."

"What if it was nothing, and we don't have any answers? I didn't even think of that as a possibility. What if it's a dead-end? Then what am I going to do? I'm running out of options."

"Why don't you wait until they're done before you give up. We'll either get answers or we'll keep looking. Besides, if Russ is offering a quicker DNA test, we'll know something pretty soon, right?"

"That's true." Angie nodded. "Unless that's a dead-end too." Angie sighed.

"Hey, calm down; one thing at a time." I pulled a pillow

off the couch and hugged it. "Did you ever accuse Marc of killing Lucy before? Like when it all first happened?"

"Yeah, I think most of Pine Grove did. And when he fell off the face of the earth, it made us all think we were on to something. Why?"

"He said something about people thinking he'd killed Lucy, but I wasn't sure if it was just in his head or if it had really happened."

"No, it really happened. Honestly, I still believe he did it. And finding her body at that house confirmed it for me."

"But there's a chance it's not her, and we don't even know who owns the house. So..."

"Molly, I know you love your brother, but I love my sister. Blaming Marc is all I've ever had. I needed someone to be angry with. I needed some sort of answer in order to keep looking. Marc was the only piece of the puzzle that fit, and he still fits. I really wish I was wrong."

"Me too. I'm having a hard time with this. I can get on board with Lucy being my mom, I guess, but the idea that my older brother killed her isn't something I can get behind. Couldn't there be someone else? Some other person who could have hurt Lucy?"

"If there is, then how do you think she could be your mom? Marc was the last boyfriend she had. It's the only thing that adds up." Angie looked at her phone. "Let's talk about something else. How's your mom doing?"

"That's not the best subject to change to. I have no idea who she is either."

"How about school? Tell me about your favorite class." Angie pulled her leg under her.

"I love English; I guess because I get an excuse to

read when I should be doing homework. Except, I hate to read what people tell me to. I want to get lost in a book of my choosing. I was thinking I should take summer classes to speed up the process, and then I think about having to get a real job, and I'm glad I took the summer off."

"If you want my advice, take the summers off. Enjoy the time you have in school because once you're out life gets complicated."

"Great! Just what I need, life to get more complicated."

"You know what I mean. Enjoy the ride now because once you get on the freeway, there's no turning back."

"But you get your summers off, right? That's pretty cool. You get to work at a job you love and get your summers off. That's the best of both worlds."

"It was, when I was working with the grade I wanted to, but now that I'm with a bunch of preteens, I'd rather poke my eyes out." Angie yawned. "I think not sleeping has caught up with me. Do you mind if I go lay down?"

"No, go ahead. I think I'll take a nap too. These last few days have been brutal. I might have gotten on that freeway you were speaking of."

"Want to nap together? Or is that weird?" Angie stood and stretched. "Strange, right?"

"No, I'd like that. I don't think my mind will let me be alone right now." I got off the couch and followed her to her room. "Our first sleepover, but for old people."

"Hey, watch who you're calling old, missy." Angie kicked off her sandals and crawled into bed. "It's been a long time since I've slept with anyone."

"I'm pretty sure I hold that record. This will be the first

time for me." I crawled under the covers and let my head fall onto the pillow.

"Not even sleepovers with girlfriends?"

"No, I was a homebody." I rolled closer to Angie, and she put her arm around me. "Sweet dreams."

"Back atcha, kiddo."

I snuggled into the arms of the woman who may be my aunt. I'd have my answer much sooner than I anticipated. For now, it was time to let the worries of the world drift away.

## CHAPTER TWENTY-SEVEN

The loud banging sounded like it was in my dreams, but it kept coming when I opened my eyes. "Angie, do you hear that?" I gave her a shove, but she didn't budge. "Angie."

She rolled over, taking the blankets with her.

I pushed on her back, my heart now racing. "Angie, I think someone's at the door."

"Hmm." She stretched and looked at me through one eye. "Huh?"

"I think someone's here." The banging stopped, but the sound from Angie's phone drifted down the hall.

Angie jumped out of bed, tripping on the sheet laced between her legs. "Jesus Christ." Back on her feet, she ran to the ringing. "Hello?"

I met her in the living room, where she was on her way to the front door. "Who is it?" I stood behind the wall in an attempt to stay hidden.

Russ was on the doorstep when the door opened. "I was about to bust your door down." Out of breath, Russ had his hands on his thighs as he tried to catch his breath.

Angie tossed her hair off her shoulder. "I'm sorry; we were napping." She covered the yawn she couldn't chase away.

"Can I come in?" Russ took a step inside before finishing his question.

"Yeah, of course. Is everything alright?" Angie pulled her shirt down and folded her arms.

I came out of hiding and stood next to Angie, mimicking her earlier moves in an attempt to look put together. "Hey."

"Hi, Molly. I'm glad you're here." Russ motioned to the living room with his muscular arm. "Why don't we go in there so we can talk?"

"It was her, wasn't it?" Angie's voice was a cross between chipper and melancholy.

"Have a seat so we can talk." Russ stood in the entrance of the living room with his hands on his hips. He paced the room while and lowered his head. "Here's the thing." Russ clapped his hands and then dropped them to his side and blew out a burst of air.

"Would you just spit it out?" Angie snapped before she started biting her fingernail.

Russ ran his hand through his hair. "So we did find a body today, but there's no way of knowing who it is, at least not right away. We're going to have to run some tests to find out. It gets complicated because the remains are so old. We're working with bones and teeth."

"How long before we know? Can I tell my parents? Should I call the funeral home?" Angie stopped gnawing on her finger long enough to spit out her questions in rapid fire.

"I don't know. It depends on a lot of factors. I've requested the process be streamlined, but there's no way of telling. I wouldn't tell your parents yet, and I'd most definitely hold off on the funeral home." Russ sat in the chair by the window and pulled the curtains open. "Whoever it is, we'll need to do our tests and investigate before we can release the remains. From what we can tell from what we've seen is it was an adult female. But there's no guarantee until further testing is completed."

I cleared my throat. "Were you able to find out who owns the property?"

Russ dropped his head. "Yeah." He rubbed his hand over his face. "Molly, Wesley and Catherine Jackson own the property."

"You're sure?" I looked over at Angie, already knowing the answer.

"Yeah." He nodded. "They're at the station being questioned right now."

My heart dropped to the pit of my stomach. "My mom too? Why her? What about Marc?"

"Her name is on the property, so she has to be questioned. We don't have any proof or evidence that links Marc to that house yet, so we can't question him." Russ looked out the window again, pulling his attention away from us. "Ah, so I also need to ask if you'd be open to giving us a DNA sample." Russ looked into my eyes.

"Yeah, of course." I gave the elastic on my wrist a snap, so hard it broke. "Is this to tell if I'm related to the person you found?"

"Yes, I think it will help with the investigation." Russ walked over to the door. "I have someone here who has offered to take your sample and get it back to the lab as soon as possible." He opened the door and motioned for someone to come in.

A short, curvy woman with big rimmed black glasses stepped into the kitchen. Her red curls were a mess on her head. She set what looked like a tackle box on the table and started pulling things out.

"Betty, this is Molly." Russ put his hand on my back. "And this is Angie."

"Are you going to take mine too?" Angie stepped forward.

"Yes, that would be helpful. I'd like to get Marc's too, but we can wait until we get a warrant, unless that's something you can help with, Molly?"

"Does he know what's going on?" I took a deep breath to try to push out the headache taking up residency in my head.

"He was home when your parents were taken into custody, so I believe he's aware. I don't know how much he knows." Russ held onto the back of the kitchen chair as we waited for Betty.

"Should I call him?" I took my phone off the counter where I had left it before our nap. "I should, shouldn't I?"

"If you want. I don't see how it could hurt. It might be helpful to see where his head is at." Russ looked at his watch. "Do you want to call him now and see if you can get him here before Betty has to go?"

"Okay, I'll give him a call." A wave of sadness crashed around me when I saw the five missed calls from Marc. "He's been trying to call me too. No one knows where I am." I dialed his number and waited for him to answer.

"Molly? I've been trying to find you all afternoon. Where are you?"

"Hi, Marc. Sorry I left this morning. I had to get out of there." I looked up at Russ and closed my eyes to hold off the tears.

"You have to get home. I need to talk to you. Where are you? I'll come get you." I couldn't tell how he was doing by the sound of his voice. He seemed remarkably calm for the situation.

"I ... ah ... I'm at Angie's house. Would you…"

"Goddamn it, Molly! What the hell are you doing there? Where does she live? I'm coming to get you."

"Marc, I'm here with the detective. I know what happened." I cleared my throat to get the words to come. "Can you come over here and talk to him?"

"To who?" I heard Marc's keys in the background.

"Russ, the detective. I'm giving them my DNA. Would you be willing to give them yours too?"

"Yeah, text me the address, and I'll be right there." His car door closed before he hung up.

I sent Angie's address to Marc and slipped my phone into my back pocket. "He's on his way."

"And he's going to cooperate?" Angie asked before she crossed her arms.

"Yeah." I placed my hand on my head and braced myself on the counter.

"Perfect." Russ clapped his hands. "Are you about ready, Betty?"

Betty pushed her glassed up on her nose. "Ready whenever you are, sir."

"Molly, why don't you get yours done before Marc gets here, in case he changes his mind." Russ held his hand out to guide me to the chair by Betty.

"Okay." I took the seat and rested my head in my hands. My body trembled as I waited for instruction.

"It's super simple; no need to worry." Betty's smile helped

ease my nerves. "I'm just going to put this inside your mouth and move it around. It won't hurt at all." She held up a long white swab. "Open wide."

I opened my mouth and tilted my head back.

"All done. See, it wasn't that bad." Betty put the swab into a plastic bag and sealed it.

"That's it?" I stood and let Angie have the chair so I could wait for Marc.

"Your turn." Betty changed her gloves and opened a new swab.

I stepped outside to wait for Marc just as he pulled in behind Betty's car. I walked toward him, unsure if I should be cautious or not. I wasn't sure who he was anymore. The world felt like it was slipping by in slow motion. "Hey."

Marc ran to me and hugged me. "I was so worried about you. I had no idea where you were." His voice cracked. "What the hell is happening? No one has told me anything. They came and took Mom and Dad."

"They didn't tell you why?" My face was still pressed into my brother's body.

"No, I asked, but they told me to get back in the house."

"Did you see it happen? Did they cuff Mom?"

Marc pulled away. "Yeah. She stood there and let them. She didn't give them any fight. Neither did Dad. It was like an episode of the Twilight Zone."

"Dad didn't fight? Even after the mood he was in earlier?"

"No, he was calmer than I've ever seen him." Marc ran his hands through his hair and pulled. "What the hell is going on?"

"They found a body." My voice barely left my mouth.

"What?" Marc leaned in to hear me.

"They found a body on their property."

"A body? At the house? When?" Marc jerked his head away.

"Not at the house, at their property in the woods." I crossed my arms to help ease my stomachache.

"What house in the woods?"

"Their house in the woods, the place we followed Mom to."

"They have another house? How the hell did I not know that?" Marc tossed his head back and sighed. "A body? Whose?"

"They don't know yet." I looked at my feet to avoid eye contact. "It might be Lucy."

"What?" Marc's jaw dropped. "No, no, no. How?" He took steps backward.

"Who else could it be?"

"They think I did it, don't they?" Marc bent over like he was going to vomit. "Oh my fucking god."

"If you don't have anything to hide, come inside and let them have your DNA. It's the only way to prove you're innocent."

"You don't believe me, do you? And Angie. Fuck." Marc threw his hands in the air. "Well, come on; let's get it over with."

I walked back to the house, not waiting for Marc. I wasn't sure I could look at him. I wasn't sure I'd ever be able to. "Are you ready?"

"As ready as I'll ever be."

"Hey, guys. Marc's here." I held the door open for him to come inside.

"Hi, Marc." Russ reached out his hand. "Thank you for

your willingness to cooperate. Just so we're clear, you're doing this on your own free will. Correct?"

"Yeah." Marc dropped his hand to his side. "What do you want me to do?"

"Betty will help you over there." Russ pointed to the open chair. "She'll explain the process for you."

"What are you hoping to find out from this? What is it going to prove?" Marc cracked his knuckles as he stared at Russ, not acknowledging Angie who was also in the room.

"Well, I'm not really sure. We're looking to rule some stuff out." Russ smiled and pointed to Betty again.

"What the hell." Marc took the seat in front of Betty.

She explained the process to him, like she had to me earlier. I couldn't help but feel like I had led my brother to his horrible fate. Something was telling me I should have let him run. But here I was protecting a dead woman who might be nothing to me. I covered my mouth and left the kitchen where I collapsed on the floor in the bathroom.

"Molly, are you alright?" Angie tapped on the door. "Honey, let me in."

On my knees on the cold floor, I let the floodgates open. Every emotion I had been holding onto fell out of me onto the floor. My body heaved between sobs. I couldn't have stood to let Angie in if I'd wanted to. Thoughts of my mom and dad being driven away in a police car made my insides feel hollow. Images of Lucy's last moments pushed those thoughts out. My dream came back to me. I watched someone rip me out of Lucy's arms. But who? I closed my eyes tighter to try to pull the image up, but nothing came.

"Molly, come on; let me in." Angie's voice made me want to go to her, but I couldn't.

"Mol, come on; let us in." The uncomfortableness in Marc's voice made my heart hurt even more. He was here for me.

"I can't." The room started to spin, and everything went black.

# CHAPTER TWENTY-EIGHT

I woke up to my head in Angie's lap and Marc kneeling over me with a cold washcloth. "What happened?"

"You passed out." Marc pushed the hair out of my eyes. "You really scared us."

I looked up at Angie who was rocking me. "I'm sorry. I didn't mean…"

"Don't be sorry. You've been through a lot today; we all have." Angie looked at Marc. "I don't know what to think right now, but I want to make sure you're safe." Angie rubbed my cheek.

"Look, I know what you're thinking, but you have to believe me. I have no idea what is going on. I'm on the same page as all the rest of you." Marc stood and brushed his knees off.

"It seems funny." Angie stopped and sighed. "No, this isn't the time or place for this. We've waited this long, so what's a few more days?"

"I don't know what my DNA is going to prove, but when it

proves you wrong, I hope you can see I'm hurting too. I loved Lucy more than anything. Don't you think I want to know what happened to her?"

"Marc, it's not the time or place. Let's get through the next days for Molly. She's the one who needs us right now. And us fighting isn't going to help." Angie held her hand up for Marc. "Truce? At least for now?"

Marc shook her hand. "Truce, as long as you mean it."

"Where's Russ and Betty?" I tried to sit up, but Angie hadn't let go of me yet.

"Betty took the samples back to the lab to get the process started, and Russ is around here somewhere."

"How long before we know anything?" I wiggled my way free from Angie's grip.

"I'm not sure. Russ?" Angie pulled herself off the bathroom floor. "Russ?"

"I think he's outside. I heard the door close a while ago." Marc gave me his hand to pull me to my feet. "I want to ask him a couple questions too."

We filed out of the bathroom, Angie leading the way, and Marc following close behind. "Russ?" Angie opened the front door and stuck her head out.

Russ held up his finger and then pointed to his phone. We all went inside and sat around the kitchen table. "So now what?" I looked over at Marc.

"I have no idea. I don't know if they can keep Mom and Dad, or if they've been appointed a lawyer. There must be some sort of mistake. Like, how long have they had the house in question?"

"Forty-five years." Russ closed the door behind him. "The

records indicate that the house has belonged to your father since 1976."

"Then how come Mom was taken in too? They weren't married until 1979." Marc turned his attention to Russ. "What if the body has been there since 1975? Then there's no way it could be our parents. You're all just assuming. Assuming it's Lucy. Assuming it's someone in our family."

"You're right. We don't have an exact way to know how long the body has been there; at least not until we figure some more stuff out." Russ put his hands in his pockets. "Your parents have been released for now. They called their attorney, and there was nothing they could be held on. Not yet."

"So they're back at the house?" I massaged the pain out of my forehead. "Dad's going to be furious. We should get home."

"Molly, you don't have to go home. You can stay with me, as long as you want." Angie put her hand on mine. "I'm worried about you."

"Look, it's nice you're concerned, but she'll be fine. She was fine before, and she'll be fine now. But Molly's right—we should get home and see what's going on."

"How long before we know the results of our testing today?" I asked Russ.

"Betty is going to try to get it expedited, but it could be a couple of days. I'll give you a call when it comes back." Russ gave me a pat on the back. "You have my number; call me anytime."

"Come on, Molly. Let's go see what's going on." Marc reached for my hand. "Thank you for taking care of her." He nodded in Angie's direction. "She's a good kid. I just want to make sure she's okay."

"Me too, Marc. I don't want to see anything happen to her. I know all too well how bad it hurts to lose someone I love." Angie placed her hand on her chest.

"Yeah, so do I." With his hand on the doorknob, Marc turned to Russ. "I trust you'll let me know as well?"

"Of course." Russ smiled. "I'll be in touch."

I dropped into Marc's car and turned my head to look out the window.

"What is happening?" Marc screamed. "Dad is going to be a complete asshole. Are you sure you want to go home? Maybe it would be best if you stay with Angie."

"No, I want to go home. I want to see Mom. I kind of wish they would have kept Dad."

"But he didn't do anything, aside from being a dick." Marc sighed.

"Marc, are you sure, like a hundred percent certain that you had no idea about that house?"

"Molly, I promise you I had no idea. I've never been there. Don't you think I would have used something like that to my advantage as a teenager? Partying in a house would have been way cooler than the quarry. And if I knew about that house, Lucy might still be here. We would have gone there that night. She'd still be with me."

"Who do you think they found then?" I didn't pry my eyes off the window, watching everything that had been familiar fade into surroundings I didn't recognize.

"I have no idea. It could be anyone. If that house is deep in the woods, it is the perfect place to hide a body. Anyone could have done it. Just because it was found on their land doesn't mean anything." Marc tapped my knee. "This is all going to blow over; don't you worry."

"You're probably right." I tightened my grip around my seat belt and closed my eyes. I knew he wasn't right. I couldn't understand how he could keep lying to me.

CHAPTER TWENTY-NINE

The arguing could be heard from the driveway. Mom and Dad were screaming at each other. "Should we go?" Marc asked before we reached the door.

"No, come on; we need to make sure Mom's okay." I increased my stride to get inside faster.

"Guys, guys, stop it," Marc shouted over them.

Dad whipped his head around. "What the fuck did you just say?"

"I asked you to stop it. People can hear you from outside. Don't you think the neighborhood has had enough of a show for one day?" Marc went to the fridge.

"Keep your hands off my beer." Dad's face was red with fury.

"Calm down; you're going to have a heart attack." Marc put his hands up. "Why don't you tell us what happened?"

"It's none of your goddamn business. It seems someone is trying to fuck with us. That's all. I know this is just some game one of those morons is playing. I haven't even been retired a year. They want to get back at me for something." Dad's mood turned on a dime.

"Wait, so you think this is some practical joke or revenge plan?" Marc leaned against the counter. "You think a dead body found on your land is a joke?"

"You never know. Stranger things have happened." Dad reached into the refrigerator and took out two beers, handing one to Marc.

Mom stormed out of the kitchen. I followed her to her room and slipped in behind her before she could keep me out. "Mom?"

"Not now, Molly." She shooed me away.

"But, Mom." I sat on her bed and waited for her to join me.

"Molly, now is not a good time."

"I want to know what happened. What's going on?"

She held her finger to her lips.

"Mom."

"Not now." She mouthed the words.

"Are you okay at least?"

"Yes, I'm fine." She shook her head, letting me know there was more to the story. "Later," she whispered and sat next to me.

The door flung open, and Dad stood in the entrance. "What's going on in here?"

"I wanted to make sure Mom was okay."

"Why wouldn't she be?" Dad tipped the beer bottle back.

"You're right; she's fine. We're just resting now. Maybe watch a movie, Mom?"

"No, Molly, I'm tired. Maybe tomorrow." She got off the

bed and went to her bureau and took out a nightgown. "I'm going to bed."

I left her room, knowing there was way more to the story. Something she wasn't telling me. Did she know the answers? She must. She was probably in on the whole thing. I didn't understand how Marc was so good at pretending. It was scary, really.

I went to my room to try to let the events from the day fall out of my head. I stared at the ceiling, trying to figure out the truth. Two days before we'd know anything. I already knew the hours were going to move at a snail's pace. I rolled onto my side and tried to get some rest. The fastest way to move time was to sleep it away.

When my eyes closed, all I saw was dirt being thrown on top of me. I gasped to catch my breath and sat up. The images that came were never enough to show me anything. It was probably all my imagination anyway. I blew the panic out of my lungs and put my head back on the pillow. "Come on, Lucy, just show me."

I floated off to sleep, letting the weight of the worries from the day go. As I got lighter, so did the air around me. Crickets chirped, playing the soundtrack of the night. Peaceful bliss.

*"Hush little baby." The silkiness of her lips lingered on my forehead. "Mommy loves you, little one."*

*My eyes became heavy. I couldn't keep them open any longer. The warmth of my mother's love turned colder than ice. My tiny body trembled without her touch. I tried to pry my eyes open to see what was happening. Where was my mother? Something overpowered my desire to know. I silenced my screams to try to hear hers.*

*"No, please, no."*

*"It'll only hurt for a second." Sinister laughter filled the emptiness. A voice I had heard before, but whose?*

*"No, you can't do this to me. No, please, no. Don't hurt my baby." The pleas became quieter with each passing second. "Please, no."*

*"Hush little baby." A different voice this time. A different touch.*

*"No." Just a whisper now.*

*My eyes wouldn't open, no matter how hard I tried. I couldn't see what was happening. The screaming stopped.*

"Molly? Molly?" Marc's voice pulled me out of my dream.

I opened my eyes and squinted. "What do you want?"

"It sounded like you were having a bad dream. I didn't want Dad to come in and yell at you." Marc sat on the edge of my bed.

"It did? How could you tell?" I sat up and looked around the room to try to orient myself.

"I don't know; you were sort of crying and talking."

"What did I say?" I pushed the hair out of my eyes.

"No, or something like that." Marc shrugged. "I couldn't really make it out. Are you okay?"

"I guess so. I'm exhausted. I don't know what's gotten into me."

"It's stress. That always keeps me up too. When I was in boot camp, it took me weeks before I was able to feel rested."

"Boot camp? When were you in boot camp?"

"That's how I got out of here. I didn't have enough money saved up to go away to school, so I joined the Air Force."

"You were in the Air Force? How come I didn't know about that?" I scratched my head and looked up at the ceiling. "What else don't I know?"

"I don't know. I guess I didn't think it was important. You were still kind of young when I was discharged."

"You were discharged? From the Air Force? Isn't that bad?"

Marc laughed. "I guess, sometimes it is, but I was discharged because of my mental health. The whole thing with Lucy really got to me. I was struggling too much to be of use to anyone, so they let me go."

"Because you were mentally unstable?"

"Well, that doesn't sound very good when you say it like that." Marc dropped his head. "There are some things in my life that I'm not proud of, but they make me who I am today."

"Are you still? Mentally unstable?" I asked, wishing I hadn't the second I heard my own question.

"Are you really asking me that? Jesus, Molly." Marc hung his head. "I thought you knew who I was. Why would you ask such a bullshit question?"

"Marc, I'm barely awake. Don't be mad at me for that."

"I don't know what to think, Molly. I don't know who to trust anymore. I thought you were my baby sister. I would have done anything for you." He walked out of my room, shutting the door behind him.

"Marc, wait. Marc." I laid back and tried to connect the dots. I hadn't ever known any of the information Marc had just shared. A mentally unstable person could have murdered someone and then went on with their life. It did explain some of the holes I couldn't fill. And maybe he had multiple personalities. That could be why he didn't remember, and why he'd given his DNA without protesting.

Who was talking in my dream? Did Marc hear more than he'd told me? I got up and locked my bedroom door. I didn't want anyone walking in on me again, not when I could be talking in my sleep. Back in bed, I closed my eyes and tried to pull back the images from the dreams I kept having. Why couldn't I keep my eyes open?

My heavy eyes returned and whisked me back to sleep.

# CHAPTER THIRTY

The ding from an incoming text woke me. "Russ is coming over. Can you get over here alone?" Angie didn't wait for me to reply before sending a second message. "Don't tell anyone where you're going, okay?"

"What's going on?" I stared at my phone, knowing the answer.

"He has some information. Just get here ASAP."

I threw the covers off of me and pulled on some jeans and a t-shirt. I remembered I had a bag at Angie's, so I wouldn't need to waste time getting ready. I slipped on my flip flops and shut my door quietly.

No one was in the kitchen, or anywhere that I could see. The coast was clear. I took my keys off the counter and headed for the door. My car was the only one in the driveway. I couldn't worry about where Mom was now, or what was happening in the house of secrets, I was off to have my own.

I felt like I was fleeing to my mistress' house, not wanting to be found by my current family; like I was trading my old life in for a new one. Except it sucked. This one and that one.

There were no winners here. Not in what was and not in what might be.

Angie was sitting on her steps when I pulled in. "Hey, that was quick."

"You said get here ASAP." I shut the door and ran into Angie's arms. "What's going on? Where's Russ?"

"He's on his way. He wouldn't tell me anything over the phone; he told me to get you here as soon as I could." Angie brushed her shirt and looked down. "This is crazy, huh?"

"Yeah, my nerves are shot. I have no idea who anyone in my life is anymore. I had to lock my bedroom door last night in order to try to get some sleep." I sat next to Angie on the stairs.

"I didn't know what to expect, you know? I've wanted this day to come since I got the news that Lucy was missing. But now..." She held her hands up. "I don't know what I want. I hate seeing how this is affecting you."

I leaned into Angie. "Don't worry about me. I'm sorry. For everything."

"Don't you dare be sorry. You didn't do anything. You didn't ask to be involved." Angie put her arm around me and pulled me close.

"But it's my family that hurt yours. How can you not be upset with me?"

"Molly, you had nothing to do with any of this. It's not your fault that you love your family. I mean, why wouldn't you?"

"Because they're awful?" I snickered at the thought, trying to take the pain out of the reality. "Except my mom. I don't think she has anything to do with it."

"No? But she raised you. You don't think she knew where

you came from?" Angie shrugged. "I guess we'll find out soon enough."

Mom must have known. Angie was right—she raised me as her own. I closed my eyes and shook the thought out of my mind. There was still a possibility that Mom was my mom. Until I knew for sure, I couldn't let my mind go there. "I really wish Russ would hurry up."

"Me too. He should be here soon." Angie turned her phone over. "He hasn't tried to call."

The sun on my face was the only thing that made me feel real. The waiting was more tortuous than anything I had ever experienced. The fate of my future was minutes away.

Angie gave me a shake. "He's here." She stood, reaching out her hand to help me up.

Russ pulled in behind my car. I couldn't see his face clearly, but it didn't look like he was happy. Time stood still as I waited for him to exit his truck. His door swung open, and Angie's body jittered with energy. Russ dropped his head and walked over to us. "Hi, guys. Can we go inside to talk?"

"Okay." Angie gulped loud enough for me to hear. "Is something wrong?"

"Let's just go inside." Russ followed behind us, his hands stuffed into his pockets.

We gathered in the kitchen, each standing behind a chair. "Okay, we're inside. Now tell us what's going on." Angie sighed with impatience.

"Why don't we sit first." Russ cleared his throat.

"For god's sake, just spit it out." Angie pulled out a chair and plopped into it.

Russ sat and rubbed his face. "So, ah, I don't really know how to say this."

"Just say it." Angie leaned into the table.

"It's not Lucy. The body we found isn't your sister." Russ held his hand to his face.

"Then who is it?" Angie stared Russ in the eyes. "Who else could it be?"

"I don't know. We're still trying to figure it out." Russ turned his attention to me. "I think you may be in danger."

"Why? If it's not Lucy, then there's no way my family is involved." My mouth went dry. "I'm fine."

"Molly, we have reason to believe your family is involved. Until we have more information, I don't feel comfortable having you around them." Russ folded his hands in front of him and leaned back. "Angie, would you be able to get away for a while with Molly?"

"They'd never hurt me." I interrupted him before Angie could respond. "You're wrong about them. I'm safe."

"Molly, I can't tell you what I know yet, but I need you to understand I'm doing this for your best interest. I'm not trying to be a jerk. Desperate people do desperate things."

"Why would they be desperate. They know they didn't do anything. They know this is all a mistake, just like you'll know soon too." My body shook from the anger coursing through my veins. "Tell him this is crazy."

"Molly, I think you should listen to him. Let's get away for a little while. It'll be fun." Angie reached for my hand.

I pulled away. "No, this is so unnecessary. It wasn't Lucy. That means I'm not who you think I am. You don't have to take care of me anymore."

"Molly, come on. You know I love you, no matter what. Let's just hear Russ out. How long do you think we'd need to be away?" Angie's calmness triggered my rage.

"Why are you letting him tell us what to do? He didn't find your sister. Why are you going to give up so easily?" I pushed away from the table.

"In the next few days, we should know more. I can't make you do anything, but if you were my daughter, I wouldn't want you in that house when things are about to explode." Russ cleared his throat. "I can't say much, but I can tell you we have reason to believe your family is involved with the murder of the woman we found on their property."

"Just tell me what you know. Why should I believe you?" I crossed my arms and paced the kitchen.

"Molly, I can't tell you. I am hopeful we will have the results soon from the DNA samples that were taken. That should give us more insight and help us move forward." Russ dropped his head. "If you agree to leave with Angie for a while, I can tell you something. But you have to promise you will not contact your family until we give the okay."

"Just tell me."

"Not until you make me that promise." Russ folded his arms to mimic mine.

"Fine, I promise."

"Molly, your father is not Wesley Jackson."

"What? What does that even mean?" I rolled my eyes.

"Molly, he's been impersonating a dead man for the past five decades. When we ran his prints, they came back as Jonathan Rivers. Jonathan Rivers has been on the run since 1968." Russ folded his hands together and stretched them out in front of him.

"What? On the run? For what?" I asked the questions before my brain had time to process what Russ had said.

"Why did you let him go?" Angie snapped.

"We didn't know, not until after we'd released him. The guys were on their way to pick him up this morning, but I wanted to make sure Molly was some place safe first." Russ rolled his neck.

"Why me? What about my mom or Marc?"

"We have reason to believe they're involved as well. I really can't give any more details. I need you as far away from Pine Grove as possible while we find your father."

"But what about my mom? She was acting funny last night." Cold sweat gathered under my bangs. "She knows, doesn't she?"

"Look, Molly, I don't know." Russ looked at his watch. "I need to get you someplace safe. Now. Are you willing to get out of here for a few days?"

"I don't have anything with me." I fought back the urge to throw up. "I have to go back home first."

Russ shook his head. "No, I'm sorry, but you need to leave now. You can buy what you need when you get there."

"What is he wanted for?" I asked the question I didn't want the answer to.

"Molly." Russ ran his hand through his hair. "It's better if I don't say."

"You have to tell her. You can't leave her hanging like that. She needs to ... no, we need to know who we're hiding from." Angie stood behind me and put her hand on my back.

"For murder."

"Oh my god, he did it, didn't he?" My shoulders dropped. "Okay, I'll go. But under one condition."

"What's that, Molly?"

"Make sure my mom is safe. Get her away from him as soon as you can. Please?"

Russ nodded. "I'll do my best."

"That's not good enough. I need you to promise me."

"I promise I'll do my best to keep your mom safe." Russ handed Angie an envelope. "Everything you need is in there." He held out his hand. "Molly, I'm going to need your phone."

"Why?"

"In case you're being tracked. I need to make sure no one will be able to find you. A new phone is in the package." He pointed to Angie's hand. "Do not call anyone from your family. Do not let anyone know where you are."

"Why exactly do you think I'm in danger now? Why do you think he'll hurt me now?" I braced myself on the counter as I took in everything that was unfolding around me.

"Because you may be evidence."

"Lucy." My knees started to buckle.

"Maybe. We don't know yet, but he does." Russ gave me a forced smile. "We're going to do everything we can to get the answers as soon as possible. It shouldn't be long."

Angie came back to the kitchen with two packed bags. "Here." She handed me a duffle bag. "I put some stuff I thought might work for you."

"Thanks." My head felt like it tripled in weight. I could barely hold it up.

"Come on; let's get out of here." Angie picked her keys up and turned off the lights.

"I'm going to follow you guys until you get to the next town. I want to make sure I cover your tracks. I'll call you, Angie, as soon as I know anything."

"I don't understand." It was the only thought I could form into words.

"I know, honey. It's a lot to take in." Angie took my hand

as she followed the prompts from her GPS. "But look at it this way, we get a girls' getaway."

"I don't think that's what this is. I won't be able to enjoy anything. Not until I know what the hell is going on." Everything Russ had said circled around me, settling onto my chest. I couldn't breathe.

"I understand." Angie tapped her thumb against the steering wheel. "How about some music?" She turned on the radio and started bobbing her head along. "I love Tom Petty."

"So does Marc." Tears pushed their way through my closed eyes. Everything in my life was right down to my brother's favorite band.

"Tom makes everything better. Come on; sing along." Angie reached over and turned the volume up.

"I don't think he'll be able to fix this mess." I sank into the seat and closed my eyes.

"We're here." Angie's announcement jerked me out of my nap. "Already?" I sat up and looked around. "Where are we?"

"Murray, New Hampshire. It's a lake town." Angie unbuckled her seat belt and pushed back against her seat.

"Where's the lake?" Visions of the paradise we were whisked away to fizzled out fast. "This doesn't look relaxing, or even very hidden."

"Well, we are about an hour away from home. Besides, who even knows where Murray, New Hampshire is? I think we're safe."

"An hour away doesn't seem very safe. Why couldn't we have stayed at your place?" I blew out the morning's frustration before I unbuckled.

"Marc knows where I live."

"So, I thought I'm on the run from my dad, not Marc." I

raised my brow.

"Molly, I thought you understood." Angie frowned. "Honey, it's not only your dad we're hiding from, but your mom and Marc too."

"Why? They're not the ones wanted for murder. I don't get it, any of it."

"Russ couldn't tell us everything, remember. We're supposed to trust him and wait." Angie opened her door. "Come on; let's go check out our room."

"Isn't that weird? That Russ gave you the key to our room? Like we don't even have to go into the lobby and check-in? Something seems fishy."

"Nah, I'm sure Russ and his team have connections. I know we're safe. Try to get some rest. Maybe there's a pool we can go lounge by." Angie got out of the car and reached her arms over her head in a stretch.

I followed behind her to the back side of the cabin. "This place is creepy." I shook my shoulders to get the chill that had settled over me out.

"Aw, no, I think it's cute. Maybe there's a great book inside." Angie winked.

"I doubt the people who stay here even know how to read." I scowled as I waited for her to unlock our door.

"That's not very nice." Angie let the door swing open. "See, it's cute."

"Silence of the Lambs cute." I closed the door behind me and fell face-first onto the bed.

Angie rummaged through her purse and tapped my leg. "Hey, catch." She tossed a book at me.

"*Tiger Eyes*? How'd you know this is my favorite Judy Blume book?" I sat up and held it to my chest.

"I had a feeling. It was Lucy's favorite too." Angie sat on the bed next to mine and gave it a bounce. "The beds are comfy."

I flipped through the pages and smiled. "Thank you. This is just what I needed."

"I know." Angie checked her phone. "No messages. I guess that means we have time to at least settle in."

"That's good because I'm going to be busy the next few hours."

"I'm glad I thought to bring it with us. I didn't think to bring any books for me, but I could use a few good games of Solitaire. It's been a while since I vegged out."

"They think they're going to find Lucy, don't they?" I rolled onto my side.

"I think so. Russ didn't say, but I think so. If Jonathan Rivers has murdered before, chances are pretty good he'll do it again. Or he's involved somehow. But let's try not to worry about that right now. Let's get our minds lost in something else for a little while and worry later. We don't really know anything yet, so let's enjoy the blissfulness of ignorance."

"Am I going to have to talk like that when I'm a teacher?" I laughed. "Time to sharpen my vocabulary." I opened the cover and saw *This book belongs to Lucy Minor. This is the best book ever. Return when finished. Or else.*

The feistiness of her words brought a smile to my face. She was a fighter. The thought of her having to fight for her life was too much to bear. No matter who had taken Lucy's life, I wouldn't ever find forgiveness, even if she wasn't my mother. It would take an absolute monster to dim a spark like Lucy's. Whoever stole her from this world wasn't someone I wanted in my life.

# CHAPTER THIRTY-ONE

A knock on the cabin door made the hair on the back of my neck stand up. I looked over and saw Angie hadn't heard it. I pulled the covers over my head and hoped it would go away. Louder this time, I heard movement from Angie's direction.

"Molly, go get in the bathroom. Someone is at the door." Angie pulled the covers off of my face. She held her finger to her lips and waited for me to hide.

In the bathroom, I stood in the shower and pulled the curtain shut. My heart drummed against my chest, echoing in my ears. The thumping noise was soon the only thing I could focus on. I closed my eyes as I tried to make myself invisible, wishing away my existence.

"Molly, you can come out; it's just Russ." Angie's voice sounded far away. I wasn't sure I should believe her.

"Just Russ? Nice." His familiar voice filled the room. I pulled the curtain open and went back to my bed. "What's going on?"

"I told her to hide. I didn't know it was you." Angie pulled the covers up on her bed before she sat down.

"Oh." Russ put his hands in his pockets. "Great job taking care of her."

"Why are you here? What's going on?" I pulled the blankets up to my neck and sat against the headboard.

"We have the results back from the DNA tests." Russ ran his hand down his face before he sat on the edge of Angie's bed.

"And?" Angie got off her bed and joined me on mine.

"And you and Molly are related." Russ hung his head. "And..."

"What about Marc?" I couldn't let the news settle without knowing.

"Molly, Marc is your father. But..."

Angie pulled me close. "I knew it."

"But what I've been trying to say is when we ran the other tests, it doesn't appear that Marc shares DNA with your mom or dad." Russ sat up and pulled an envelope out of his back pocket.

"How is that possible? So Marc's my dad, but we're not related to our mom and dad? I don't understand."

"We're trying to figure it out. Good news is we found your father, or ah Jonathan Rivers, and he is currently in custody. We've brought Marc in for questioning as well as your mom."

"Is Marc in trouble?" I pulled the blanket closer to me as I tried to see my brother, or my father in this new light.

"Most likely, yes. We have proof that you are his child and Lucy is your mother. You were born after she went missing. It's not looking good for him." Russ handed the paper to me. "This shows the results."

"What did Marc say? When you told him?" The paper

crinkled in my hands. I couldn't bring myself to look at it. I wasn't ready to see the truth yet.

"He's denying everything. He said there's no way it could be possible." Russ shrugged. "But you see the proof is right there. Lies can't hold up to a test with a 99.9 percentage accuracy rate.

"There's no way this could be a mistake?" My fingernails dug into the palm of my hand as my grip on the sheet tightened.

"No, Molly, I'm afraid not." Russ frowned. "The good news is you can come home. You're no longer in any immediate danger."

"Home. I don't even know where that is." A wave of sadness crashed down on me as I tried to grasp what was happening.

"Molly, you have a home with me." Angie put her arm around me. "And my parents will be so excited to meet you. Your grandparents."

"Thanks." I dropped my shoulders in defeat. I didn't even know who I was. Who anyone was.

"Your mom, or ah... Catherine is in custody too." Russ paused. "She's being charged with kidnapping."

"But what if she didn't know? What if..."

"Molly, she'll get a chance to tell us her side of the story."

"But her dementia? How will she remember anything? How will she..."

"She asked to talk with you." Russ locked eyes with me. "I told her that would have to be up to you."

"Can I?"

"If you want to, but you don't have to. It's totally up to you."

"I want to. When can I see her?"

"I can bring you there right now, or Angie can bring you." Russ stood and stretched his hands out in front of him. "If you want to come with me, I have to get back soon. I wanted to tell you the news in person."

"Did she tell you what she wanted to say to me?" I closed my eyes to blink away the tears.

"No, just that she wanted to talk to you before she would tell us anything."

"I want to go now." I grabbed Angie's hand. "Will you come with me?"

"Of course." Angie got off the bed and started putting her belongings into her bag.

"Okay, well, I have to get back to the station. I'll see you shortly." Russ nodded. "I can't begin to imagine what either one of you are feeling right now. Take your time and let the information sink in. It's a lot."

"Do you think I could see Marc too?" I bit my lip to hold the emotion back.

"I don't see why not. As long as you're sure that's what you want." Russ opened the door. "I don't think there's any way I'd be able to let you talk with your dad, though. He's too dangerous."

"I don't ever want to see him again." The hate I had for him multiplied with every thought that came back to me. He was never who he said he was. I could deal with that. I wasn't sure if I'd ever be okay with losing the rest of my family. Or whoever they were. The guilt of loving my brother was stronger than anything I had ever experienced. I knew I had to hold him accountable for what he did to Lucy, but something in me wouldn't let me.

# CHAPTER THIRTY-TWO

"Are you ready?" Angie held her hand out. "You can change your mind if you want to."

"No, I want to do this. I want to see what she has to say." I put my hand on the door handle. "Is it okay if I go in alone?"

"Yes, of course. I'll wait out here for you."

I reached into the backseat and unzipped the duffle bag Angie had packed for me. "Here, this should help pass the time." I handed her Lucy's copy of *Tiger Eyes*.

She smiled. "You're right. This will help."

I shut the door, leaving Angie and my new life behind to make peace with the only life I'd ever known. I pulled the heavy glass door open and blew out all the apprehension. Russ was waiting for me in the lobby. "Hey, kiddo. Catherine knows you were on your way. She was happy you wanted to talk with her."

"Thanks for letting me. I have a lot of questions for her."

"Just so you know, your visit will be reordered. Anything she tells you can be used against her." Russ ran his hand through his hair. "I really like Catherine. I'm having a hard time with this one. Something doesn't add up."

"I know. None of it adds up. She's not evil. I know what she did was wrong, but she's not a bad person." I watched my feet as I walked to meet my mom, or Catherine. Whoever she was.

"Sometimes good people get caught up in bad things. It doesn't make them bad. They just make bad decisions."

"Kidnapping seems like a pretty poor decision." I gave a half smile. "I hate this."

"I'm sorry, Molly. Hopefully you'll get some answers." He opened the door to a meeting room. "Have a seat, and I'll go get Catherine."

I took the seat closest to the door in case I needed to get out in a hurry. I hated having to think about the woman who had kissed my booboos and sang me lullabies. The singing from my dreams came back to me. *It was her*. She was there when Lucy died. I examined my fingernails as I waited for my mom to arrive. Catherine. She wasn't my mother. She never had been.

A knock on the door made me sit up straight. "Hey, Molly. Your mom is here." I turned to see my mom in handcuffs being led to the open seat, Russ guiding her way.

"Hi, honey. Thank you for coming to see me." The bags under her eyes made her almost unrecognizable.

"I'll be right outside the door; if you need anything, holler." Russ closed the door and disappeared.

"What's going on?" I waited for her to answer.

Her bloodshot eyes were vacant as she stared back at me.

"Please, can you just tell me what's going on?"

"Molly, there's so much I need to tell you, but I can't; not yet."

"Mom." I shook my head. "Or should I call you Catherine?"

"Molly, please."

"You owe me an explanation."

"You're right. I do. And I'll give you one, but now's not the time."

"Why did you want to see me if you're not going to talk to me? What's the point? Did you want to see how you destroyed me?" My anger surprised me, but I couldn't turn it off. "Did you want to throw it in my face that you'd pulled something so huge over on me?"

"You have every right to be upset with me. I love you, Molly. You and Marc."

"Who is Marc? That's another thing I want to know. It's like my whole goddamn life is an illusion. Like what the fuck, Mom? Dad's not who he said he was, Marc's not my brother, and you're not my mother. What's real?"

"I have answers to it all, but now's not the time."

"And you don't seem sick. Was that a lie too?" Rage shot through my squinted eyes.

"Yes, that was a lie. I'm not sick."

"I knew it." I slammed my hand on the table. "All that time you made me stay home to take care of you, and for what? Just to play games with me?"

"I'm sorry. I had my reasons." Mom hung her head. "There's so much I want to tell you, but I can't, not yet. Please, if you can, please be patient with me."

"Why the hell should I be? You knew my whole life was a

lie, and you never told me? You even gave me a bogus birth certificate. How'd you pull that off?"

"Your father had it made. I couldn't tell you the truth. It wasn't safe. That's why I can't tell you now. It's not safe."

"How is it not safe? He's in jail. How are you still hiding behind him? That sounds like an excuse to me."

"Molly, please, trust me."

"Like that'll ever happen. Not again. I can't trust anyone."

"Remember the other day? When you saw me in my room?"

The day played back like a movie. "Yeah."

"The stuff I was looking at?"

I nodded. "And?"

"That will give you some of your answers. But, please don't show anyone else, not yet."

"What happens if I do?"

Mom began to cry. "I don't know. Please just do this one last thing for me."

"Why should I?" I crossed my arms. "What if I don't care about you or your lies anymore?"

"I understand. I don't blame you for being upset. Please know that every time I told you I loved you, I meant it. None of that was a lie. I love you and your brother very much."

I wanted to tell her I loved her too, but I couldn't. I didn't know if I did, and I didn't want to add to the mountain of lies that made up my life.

Russ came in and took Mom away. I waited in the room for him to bring Marc in. I didn't even know what I wanted to say to him. I knew there was no way he was going to tell me the truth, not if Mom couldn't.

The same knock came, alerting me that my next visitor

was here. "Hey, Molly, you know the drill. If you need me, just yell. I'll be right outside the door."

Marc took the same seat Mom had been in. He was as distraught as she was. His eyes were bloodshot. "Molly."

Tears fell as soon as I heard his voice. I wanted to hug him, but I couldn't. He was the reason we were here in the first place. I punched my leg and closed my eyes. I didn't want to feel sorry for him. "Why?"

"Molly, I don't know what's going on. Please believe me. I'm as shocked by this as you. I don't know how this is possible."

"How can you argue the evidence? The test is like a hundred percent accurate. You can't lie your way out of this."

"Do you really think I would have given my sample willingly if I knew this was going to be the outcome? Why would I do that? Think about it."

"I don't know. You got away with it for twenty years. Maybe you thought you were invincible."

"Molly, I'm not stupid." Marc looked up at the ceiling. "I don't understand."

"Yeah, me either. Is that why you left? To throw me away like you did Lucy?"

"You're right. I wasn't even around when you were born." Marc's eyes widened. "See, how could I have been involved? I wasn't even in Vermont."

"No one knows where it happened. They haven't found Lucy yet." I stared into his eyes to see if he was spinning tales of desperation.

"Fuck. You're right."

"I know. And you're a liar. We already know that."

"Molly, I've never lied to you. You have to believe me. I

loved Lucy. I wanted to have a family with her. Why would I kill her?" Marc's mouth dropped open.

"What's wrong?"

"She was pregnant when I left her at the party. That has to be what she wanted to tell me. Fuck, fuck, fuck." He banged his fists down, shaking the table. "This is my fault."

"What do you mean? Are you admitting to killing her?"

"No. But if I would have listened to her, we could have raised you together. We could have had the family she wanted. I should have just let her tell me. Why was I such a dick?"

"That doesn't explain what happened to her. If you didn't kill her, where was she for the nine months she was pregnant? It doesn't add up."

"I have no idea, but I swear to god I did not kill Lucy. How could I kill the mother of my child, of our child?" A tear rolled down Marc's cheek. "It makes sense why you look like her. You're as beautiful as she was."

"That's fucking gross, Marc. Or should I say Dad?" I inched away from him.

"Knock it off. I'm not being gross. You look just like your mother."

"You knock it off. I don't want to play these twisted, sick games. Just tell me the truth. Where is Lucy?"

"Molly, I have no idea. If I knew, don't you think I would tell them?"

"No, why would you? Of course, you wouldn't tell them. But I need to know where she is. If you love me, please tell them. This needs to be over."

"That's not fair, Molly. I don't know where she is." Marc

closed his eyes and leaned his head back. "How come I never saw it before?"

"Saw what?"

"You. How come I didn't ever think you could be Lucy's?"

"I wonder that too."

"I swear I have no idea where she is, or how Mom and Dad ended up with you."

"They're not even your mom and dad."

"What are you talking about?"

Russ opened the door before I could answer Marc. "Okay, okay, I think we've had enough today. Let's go, Marc."

"What is she talking about?" Marc asked Russ as he led him out of the room.

"Oh, nothing. Don't you worry about that."

I was more confused after meeting with Marc than I had expected to be. I should have known he wasn't going to tell me the truth. Not when his freedom was on the line. But what if he was telling the truth? Finding Lucy was the only way to know for sure.

# CHAPTER THIRTY-THREE

Angie brought me back to my house. I didn't tell her about the box Mom had told me about. I didn't know what was in it, and I wasn't sure I wanted to share the contents yet. I needed to get to it before Russ did. The house looked like it had been ransacked. The drawers in the kitchen were pulled out, the cupboards open. Every room I entered looked the same. A hollow pit bore a hole through my stomach. *What if they got to the box first?*

I had no idea what was in the box. Or what the detectives were looking for. I hadn't even thought they would have searched the house. I guessed nothing was off limits when the FBI was involved. I stood in the doorway of my parents' bedroom before I entered. Things would never be the same again. There is no turning back.

I walked over the piles of clothes on the floor to get to Mom's closet. The large box was tipped over on its side, the contents spilling out. Papers and files spread across the floor. I got on my knees and pulled the piles of blankets onto the floor. *Shit.* The box was missing. I fell back onto the floor and sobbed.

In a fit of rage, I pushed the blankets out of the way. Something hard met my hand. The box was wrapped up in the pile. They must have missed it. I took the shoebox to my room to look through it. I couldn't stand being in their room any longer.

There was something eerie about being in the house now. It was like an abandoned warzone. I sat on my bed and took the cover off the box. I removed a stack of photos and mementos from our vacations. I flipped through the pictures and remembered the fun times we had when we went to the ocean. It was the only time I remembered Mom and Dad getting along. The only time it felt like we were a family.

An envelope was the only thing left in the box. I took it out and opened it. The newspaper clippings Mom had been looking at when I walked in on her were inside. I emptied the contents on my bed and started unfolding the pieces of paper. Some of the pages were yellowed with age. Photos of strangers smiled back at me. A young girl, Elizabeth Henderson was in many of the articles. In plays, softball games, graduations, and even a wedding announcement.

There were no answers to any of my questions in this box. Who the hell was Elizabeth and why was the record of her life preserved in my mother's closet? From the dates on the photos, she appeared to be a few years older than Marc. I turned the box upside down and gave it a shake. Nothing else fell out. What was I supposed to take from this?

Elizabeth Henderson became Mrs. Peters in 1998. What were the chances she would still be married to the same man these days? I took out my phone and put her name in the search bar. A Facebook profile was the first result. I clicked on it and saw photos of Elizabeth at a baby shower. It looked like she was going to be a grandmother. The more scrolling I did, the more of her life I saw. Holiday pictures, vacations, and family photos filled the page.

There was no explanation as to who Elizabeth was or why her life was hidden away in my mother's closet. My finger hovered over the message button. I wanted to ask her who she was, but how would I even start that conversation? I went back to scrolling and saw an obituary for her mother in 2018. Clicking on that didn't answer any of the questions I was looking for.

Maybe I was missing something. I went back to Mom's closet and looked around. Was this what she was looking at the other day? Why hadn't she ever mentioned Elizabeth? Frustration replaced the need for answers. Just a wild goose chase. What the hell was she trying to do? She was the one who wanted to see me.

Back in my room, I packed a couple bags with my clothes and the things I wanted to bring to Angie's. I didn't ever want to spend another night in that house again, I didn't even want to go back inside. The heaviness of the lies made it hard to breathe. I had to get out.

I loaded my stuff into my car and started for Angie's. My phone rang before I had a chance to back out of the driveway. I put my foot on the brake and looked to see who it was. "Hey, I'm on my way there now."

"Molly, hurry. I need to tell you something." The pain in Angie's voice made me wish I hadn't left her.

"What's wrong? Is everything alright?" I pulled out of the driveway, squealing my tires on the way out.

"I'll tell you when you get here." The phone went dead before I could convince her to tell me now.

When I arrived at Angie's, Russ' truck was in the driveway. I ran inside and found Russ with his hand on Angie's back. "What's going on?"

"Molly, they found Lucy." Angie dabbed at her eyes with a balled-up tissue.

"Really? Where?"

"She was at the same place where the other body was found but in a different location." Russ pushed Angie's hair out of her face. "We decided to bring the cadaver dog back for one last search of the property. With the results from the DNA tests, we figured we had to keep looking. I didn't want to say anything before in case we didn't find anything or if it wasn't Lucy."

"You're sure it's Lucy?" I asked before I fell into the chair across the room from them.

"Yes, we got a match with dental records. It was quicker this time since we already had them from the last search."

"It's over, Molly. We get to bring Lucy home." Angie let out a sigh of relief.

"You found her at the house in the woods?"

"Yes, on the same property."

"Then Marc didn't do it." I couldn't keep the words in. "He wasn't here when I was born. It couldn't have been him."

"What are you saying?" Russ tilted his head. "You don't think he's involved at all?"

"No, he can't be. Marc said Lucy wanted to talk to him the night she went missing, but he told her he didn't want to ruin the night. When I talked to him today, he said it must have been because she wanted to tell him she was pregnant. He went to boot camp soon after she went missing."

"You don't think he knew he's involved at all?" Angie shook her head. "He has to be, Molly. How could he not have known?"

"He didn't know about the house in the woods. I didn't either. When he was talking to me today, he seemed just as surprised about everything as I did. He loved Lucy. Why would he have hurt her? He said he wanted to have a family with her. He was going to ask her to marry him. If he knew she were pregnant, why would he have killed her? It doesn't add up. It's what they both wanted."

"I don't know, Molly. That seems pretty unlikely." Russ lifted his brow. "You said he was in boot camp? There should be a record of that. If that's the case, you might be right."

"Did you ever figure out who the other person was?" I rolled my neck.

"No, not yet. We have pulled all of the missing cases for the past twenty years, but nothing came close."

"Twenty years? Why only twenty?" Something clicked inside my head when I heard my question. "Can you go back further? Try forty years?"

"Yeah, we can. What are you thinking?" Russ rubbed his chin.

"I'm thinking what Jonathan Rivers did to Lucy wasn't the first time." Russ and Angie turned their heads to look at me at the same time.

"You think?" Angie covered her mouth.

"What if Marc's mom is a missing person too?"

"Holy shit." Russ clapped his hands together. "You might

be right." Russ took his phone. "I have to make a call. I'll be right back."

"Do your parents know about Lucy yet?" I asked Angie.

"No, not yet. Russ came to tell me. We have to break it to them soon, before they hear it on the news."

"So they don't know about me yet either?" I pulled at a loose string on the arm of the chair.

"No, I wanted to introduce you to them. I think they'll know when they see you, though. I didn't want to overwhelm you. You have so much stuff going on already." Angie blew her nose. "I hope you're right. I really hope Marc didn't have anything to do with this."

"I really don't think he would have. You should have seen the look on his face. He was just as confused as I was. I can't even imagine what's going through his head. And to find out that the parents he knew his whole life aren't who he thought they were." I shook my head. "I know how shitty that feels."

Russ came back inside. "I have the guys on it. I have to get back to the station and see if I can get Catherine to talk. She might be our only hope of figuring out what really happened."

"Hey, Russ? Can you do one more thing?" I asked.

"Sure, what do you need?"

"Can you figure out who Elizabeth Henderson is? Her name is Elizabeth Peters now."

"Okay, I'll see what I can do. That seems like an odd request."

I shrugged. "I just have some questions I need answers to."

# CHAPTER THIRTY-FOUR

"You were right." Russ barged into the kitchen without knocking.

"What are you talking about?" Angie set her coffee cup on the table in front of her.

"Molly was right."

My spoon dropped into my cereal bowl. "About what?"

"When we pulled the cold cases from the past fifty years in the state, we found our Jane Doe." Russ pulled out a chair and joined us.

"How did you do it so quickly?" I splashed the milk around, not looking up at him.

"Well, there was one woman from Waterville, Vermont who was reported missing in October 1980. She was five months pregnant." Russ ran his hand through his hair. "We did the math, and Marc's birthday checked out to be right on time."

"So you think she's Marc's mom?" I pushed my bowl away; there was no way I could eat now.

"We're not a hundred percent certain yet, but it adds up."

"What's her name?" My throat started to close up.

"Veronica Brewster. Her car was found abandoned on a backroad, and there was no trace of her. From what we can tell, it looked like she got into an accident and was abducted."

"What do you do now?" I sat on my hands to stop from fidgeting.

"Well, we're waiting to get the dental records or the DNA back. We dropped the ball." Russ shook his head. "We should have run the tests as soon as we found her, but we were certain she was Lucy, and then your DNA results came back. It was overlooked."

"What happens if she is Marc's mom? Then what?" My heart fluttered against my chest.

"We'll tell Marc and then see who Veronica's next of kin is. It's been forty years, so it might be hard to locate them. But one thing at a time." Russ lowered his head and slowly raised it to look at me. "I also looked into Elizabeth Henderson Peters."

"And?" I blew out the breath I was holding.

"Her mom is a missing person. She's been missing since December 1979."

My stomach dropped when the pieces fell together. "What's her mom's name?"

"Carol Henderson. Her name was on the list of cold cases. Carol went missing from Riverside, Vermont. She was walking home from work and was never seen again."

"Where did she work?" I had a feeling I didn't need to ask.

"The hospital. She was a nurse. One of the best ones at the hospital from what Elizabeth had said. Although, she was only a little girl when her mom disappeared." Russ sighed. "I've asked Elizabeth to come into the station."

"To get her DNA sample to compare to Mom's?" I folded my hands in front of me, too numb to feel the world crashing down around me.

"Yeah. How'd you guess?" Russ raised his brow.

"Well, I found a box in Mom's closet with all kinds of newspaper clippings. That's where I found Elizabeth's name. I didn't know who she was. And Mom always talked about her days as a nurse. She never worked outside of the house as long as Marc and I can remember. Did you ask Mom?"

"Yes, but she said she couldn't tell me anything. She just started to cry." Russ looked out the window. "I don't understand why she's not talking."

"She's afraid." I thought back to how timid she had been of Dad, and everything clicked. "If she is Carol Henderson, will she be in trouble? For everything else?"

"That's hard to say. It depends on her involvement. But if she tells us what happened, we can work with her." Russ exhaled, emptying his lungs in my face.

"Can I talk to her again?"

"Okay, but she doesn't seem like she wants to talk to anyone. She didn't really tell you anything before." Russ leaned back in his chair. "It's worth a shot."

"Is there any guarantee I can give her from you guys? Like if she talks?"

"I don't know. It really depends on what she says. I mean, we can't let her get away with murder."

"But can't you give her immunity if she helps you solve these cases?"

"Sounds like someone's been watching too many crime shows." Russ laughed. "I mean, it's a possibility. Why don't you see what you can get out of her, and we can go from there?"

"Okay, let's go." I stood and walked to the door. "Come on."

"Whoa, someone's in a hurry." Russ looked at his watch. "Elizabeth is on her way in this afternoon. We should have time this morning. Give me a half hour head start." He winked at Angie before he excused himself.

"Holy cow, that's a lot to take in, huh?" Angie put our breakfast dishes in the sink.

"Yeah, I'm not sure how much more I can take. Nothing I thought I knew is real. Absolutely nothing." Chills covered my body. "You don't think she was in on all of this?"

"Molly, I don't know what to think. I don't know how she could have been your father's prisoner for all that time without telling anyone. There must have been times that she could have left. Why didn't she?" Angie dried her hands on the dish towel. "I'm so sorry you have to go through all of this."

"Will you come with me? I'm not sure I'll be able to drive back after this. What if she does talk to me? What if she tells me something I don't want to hear?"

"Oh, Molly. I don't know, honey. I'll be right by your side through every step of the way." She put her hand on my back. "I love you."

"I love you too. I'm so grateful we found each other."

"I think Lucy sent you to me. She knew we were going to need each other. I can't wait for you to meet your grand-parents."

"Can we do that after?"

"You'll be up for it?" Angie smoothed my hair. "That's a lot for one day."

"I don't want to keep them waiting any longer. I know Russ wants to tell them about Lucy, and you asked him to hold off until I was ready." I sighed, thinking about the pain they didn't know was ahead of them.

"Actually, they know Lucy was found, but they don't know about you yet. Russ said he had to tell them in case it was leaked to the media. He didn't want them to find out that way."

"How come they haven't been over here? Aren't you close?"

"Molly, they're old. They don't get out much. I go to their house to visit. Mom doesn't like coming here. Ever since Lucy has been missing, she pretty much stays at home. The whole thing nearly destroyed her. I've been making excuses why I can't come over because I didn't want to have to lie, but we've talked on the phone."

"I'm glad they know. I felt bad for taking my time. I really want to meet them." I turned and hugged Angie.

"They are going to be beside themselves. I can't wait to see their faces when they see you." Angie gave me a squeeze before she let go. "Are you ready? I think we gave Russ enough time."

"It's barely been ten minutes. He said to give him a half hour."

"Don't tell me you're going to listen to him." Angie giggled.

"You're in love, aren't you?"

"What? No! You're crazy." Angie blushed.

"I saw the way he looked at you. What are you waiting

for? You should totally date him." I elbowed her side. "You know you want to."

"We'll see." Angie grabbed her keys. "Come on; let's go."

"I like Russ. I think he'd make a good uncle." I was glad for the distraction. I wanted nothing more than for everyone's life to go back to normal. Angie deserved happiness. Lucy was coming home, and there was nothing left for her to do. It was time she enjoyed her life.

"Knock it off." She laughed as she held the door open. "Get in the car."

# CHAPTER THIRTY-FIVE

Russ led me down a different hall. "We're going to have you talk with Catherine in here." He held the door open. "That way I can have a couple of the guys listen in with me. I've told them about your immunity idea, and they think it could work. Just see what you can find out. I'll be right back."

I looked around the small white room and then looked at my reflection in the two-way mirror. It was unnerving to know they could see me, but I couldn't see them. I wanted to talk to Mom alone.

The door opened, and Mom stood, uncuffed, next to Russ. "Hey, Molly, remember if you need anything, holler." Russ disappeared before Mom even had a chance to sit down.

"Hi, Mom." I smiled to try to put her at ease.

"Molly." She sniffled. "I didn't think you'd ever want to see me again."

"Mom, I love you. I know you wouldn't do anything to hurt me, or anyone else. I know you're a good person." I reached my hand across the table. With her hand in mine, the love I felt as a child came back to me. "I found your box."

Mom's eyes filled with tears. "I know. The detective told me. I asked you not to say anything."

"I know, and I didn't really; not at first. I asked about Elizabeth, and he did the rest. Mom, I know the truth."

The color drained from her face. "Molly, please."

"Can't you tell me who she is? Who you are?"

She shook her head. "I can't. He..."

"He what? Did Dad ... I mean Jonathan Rivers threaten her? Is that what you're afraid of?"

Her body trembled. "He..."

"Mom, tell me. You're safe, Elizabeth is safe. He can't hurt anyone anymore." I looked into the mirror. "Can someone please come in here?"

Mom lowered her head and sobbed. "No."

Russ appeared within seconds. "Catherine, or Carol, she's right. Whatever Jonathan told you before is over. He's not going to be able to hurt you or your family. Whatever you tell us is only going to help us and everyone involved." He sat on the edge of the table. "The more you help us, the more we can help you."

"How can you be sure?" Mom lifted her head. "What if he gets out?"

"He's not going anywhere. He's been on the run for over fifty years. He's going to spend the rest of his life behind bars." Russ folded his hands. "Elizabeth is coming in this afternoon."

"She is?" Mom covered her mouth.

"Yes, and you can talk to her if you want. I mean, if you want to tell us what really happened."

"Okay." Mom took a deep breath. "Where should I start?"

Russ held up his finger. "Hang on." He jumped off the table and left the room.

"Molly, I'm sorry."

"Mom, I know you love me. You gave me a good life. I'm not going to be upset with you." I pulled my chair to her side of the table and held her hand.

Russ returned and held up a yellow legal pad. He had three bottles of water pressed against his chest. "I have a feeling we're going to need these." He pulled a chair to the other side of the table. "Okay, ready when you are."

Mom squeezed my hand. "I am Carol Henderson. Wesley, or Jonathan, offered to give me a ride home from work. I never took rides from strangers, but he looked like a nice man, and it was cold. It was the first snowstorm of the year. I've regretted getting into his truck ever since."

"Do you remember when this happened? Where you were?" Russ held his pen to the notepad.

"Yeah, it was December 15, 1979. I had just left Waterville Hospital. Our house was only a mile away. My husband, Richard, offered to come pick me up, but Elizabeth wasn't feeling well, so I didn't want him to have to get her out of bed. I'd walked that same route home hundreds of times before." She dropped her head. "I shouldn't have taken that ride."

"After you got in, what happened?" Russ held the pen to his chin.

"I told him where I lived, but he kept driving. I tried to open the door when I figured out what was happening, but he told me if I ever tried to get away, he'd go to my house and kill my family. I was so afraid he'd hurt my daughter that I stopped trying to fight it. I know how stupid it sounds. I know I should have tried."

"You're not stupid." I rubbed the top of her hand. "That sounds incredibly scary."

Mom nodded. "It was. And then he brought me to the damn house in the woods and tied me to a bed. He said he had to go get some stuff, and he left me there, in the cold and dark. I tried so hard to get out of there while he was gone, but it was no use. I don't even know how long I'd been there before he came back for me. It could have been a night, or ten; I didn't know. There was wood covering the windows, so I couldn't even tell what time of day it was."

Mom let go of my hand to take a drink of water. "When he finally came back, he told me my name was Catherine Jackson now. He said my old life was over, and he threatened to kill my family if I did anything stupid. I couldn't risk it. Eventually, when he figured he could trust me, he gave me a little more freedom. He uncovered the windows and let me stay in the house without being tied up. He started being nicer to me, and after a while I had to go along with it. Carol Henderson had died, and I embraced the life of Catherine Jackson."

"Can you tell us anything about Veronica Brewster?" Russ tilted his head.

"I didn't know her last name." Mom closed her eyes. "But about a year after he took me to the house in the woods, he brought Veronica. He told me he wanted to give me something to do, something to keep me busy." Mom looked down at the table. "Veronica was pregnant when she came to stay with us. I knew she was afraid. I knew he had taken her like he had taken me, but we weren't allowed to talk about it.

Wesley said he had the place bugged, and he'd know what we talked about when he was gone. We started writing back and forth to each other in the magazine, but we couldn't share too much. We were afraid he'd find out and hurt us, or our families.

"When it was time for Veronica to have her baby, Wesley made me deliver him. He knew I was a nurse and told me if I didn't do it, he'd kill us all. After she'd had her baby, Wesley wouldn't let me give him to her. When I was still cleaning up the baby, he shot her in the head right in front of me." Mom hung her head. "I held that baby close and didn't dare let him go. It was the first time I saw what Wesley was truly capable of."

"Was that baby Marc?" Russ stopped writing long enough to look up.

"Yes. Wesley brought a birth certificate back to the house that listed us as parents. Wesley brought us to the house we live in now. I think since I had Marc to take care of, I was less likely to run, either that or I was too afraid to run. I knew he wouldn't hesitate to kill me just like he did Veronica."

"Wow, that sounds terrible." Russ looked down at his note.

"It was like living in hell. I wanted my old life back, but I had this little baby who needed me, who had lost everything too. I felt guilty for wanting to protect him when I wasn't able to be there for my daughter."

"Oh, Mom, I'm so sorry." I took her hand again. I wanted to take the pain away from her.

"So what happened next?" Russ leaned back in his chair.

"Nothing. At least not that I was part of. Not until the

summer of 1999." Mom looked over at me and pushed the hair out of my face.

"Lucy?" I whispered her name, hoping I could turn back the clock.

She nodded. "I'm not sure how long he had her before he brought me back to that house, but she was terrified."

"Did you know she was pregnant?" Russ dropped his pen and folded his hands.

"Yeah, she was about seven months pregnant. Marc had joined the Air Force. He needed to get out of town. He was devastated when Lucy went missing. Once he was gone, Wesley brought me to stay with Lucy."

"That was the first time you found out where Lucy was?" Russ asked.

"Yes. I had been helping Marc and the other kids with the first round of searches. I wanted to find her so badly. I wanted to fix Marc's broken heart. When I saw her tied to that same bed, my heart broke. I already knew what was going to happen, and there was nothing I could do to stop it." Mom held her face and sobbed.

Russ picked up his pen and clicked it before dropping it again. "Can you tell me what happened?"

"I stayed with her in that house. Wesley gave us more freedom, but I was still worried he might be listening to us, so we did the thing where we wrote in the magazines again. I knew Lucy, so it was different this time. She was so scared. I wanted more than anything to figure out a way to get her out of there, but I didn't know what to do. I didn't tell Lucy what was going to happen; I lied to her and told her everything was going to be okay. I told her Marc knew she was there, and he'd be back for her."

"Did he? Come back for her?" Russ squinted his eyes.

"No, he didn't know. He couldn't know. I didn't want him to get hurt. I tried to make Lucy's time there as good as I could. We played card games and read. I let her tell me about her dreams for her baby." Mom turned to look at me. "She named you."

"She did? How did she know I was going to be a girl?"

"She said she could feel it. She just knew." Mom smiled at the memory. "She loved you so much, even before she'd met you. She wanted to name you Molly because it started with M, like Marc and ended with Y, like her name."

"That's really sweet." My heart hurt as I thought about the love that was stolen from me. "Did she meet me?" My body tensed as I waited for her to respond.

"She did. Wesley was at work when Lucy went into labor. She got to hold you until he returned to the house. I wanted so badly to get her out of there, to get us all out of there, but I didn't know what I could do. Wesley was the sheriff. No one was going to believe me, and if they did, I couldn't risk what he might do to my Elizabeth."

"Was Marc involved in Lucy's death?" Russ rested his hands on top of his head and leaned back.

"No, he never knew anything about it. He didn't know that Molly was his daughter. He didn't even seem to notice how much Molly looks like Lucy."

Russ nodded. "What happened next?"

"Wesley brought Molly and me back to our house, and he gave me a birth certificate, just like he did for Marc. I don't know how or where he got them; I didn't ask any questions. It was safer not to know."

"No one in the neighborhood noticed that you had a baby

but weren't pregnant?" Russ scratched his head. "Pine Grove's a small town; how do you pull that off?"

"I don't know. I was gone for a while, looking after Lucy." She shrugged. "The whole town was more worried about where she was than getting in my business."

"And what about Marc? How did you break the news to him?" Russ asked.

"Wesley told him. Marc wasn't himself after Lucy disappeared. He didn't really care about much after that. He had nothing to do with any of this."

"What about the dementia? How come your doctor told us you were sick?" I shifted in my metal chair.

"When you were about to graduate high school, I got scared that if you went away to college, like you wanted to, Wesley would strike again. He didn't tell me he was going to look for another girl, but I didn't want to risk it. I couldn't do it again. I faked the symptoms, so you'd stay home and have to take care of me. If you were home, I knew he wouldn't have to replace you. I'm really sorry, Molly. I didn't want to lie to you. I didn't know what to do."

"It's okay. I don't blame you. That was actually really smart. You probably saved someone's life." I massaged my forehead, letting my cold fingers push out the headache.

"I know I should have said something sooner. I didn't know what to do. I didn't want anything to happen to Elizabeth or my husband." Mom sighed. "Time slipped away so fast. Before I knew it, forty years has passed. I figured it was too late to say anything. And Wesley told me I was responsible for Veronica's and Lucy's deaths, and if anyone ever found out, I was the one who was going to go to jail, not him."

"Did you ever know who Jonathan Rivers was?" Russ rubbed his chin.

"No, I didn't even know that was his name."

"Jonathan Rivers murdered his wife and two children. It was one of the grizzliest crime scenes in the history of Waterville. I won't go into details, but he's a dangerous man. He got away with those murders for over fifty years."

"He killed his family?" Mom gasped. "I thought the only thing keeping us alive was that we were his family."

"It doesn't make much sense, does it?" Russ looked at his watch. "He killed his own family to replace it with strangers. What's the point of that?"

"If Jonathan Rivers killed his family, then who is Wesley Jackson?" Mom took a drink of water, and the plastic bottle crinkled as she emptied it.

"Wesley Jackson is a dead man. He was an eighty-nine-year-old man who died of natural causes. We haven't figured out why or how Jonathan Rivers took over his identity, but it's possible it's because he did it so long ago. The technology we have now was nonexistent back then. It was probably pretty easy for him to figure it out."

"We were all his make-believe family." Mom shook her head. "Why would he do that to all of us when he already had everything he wanted?"

"I don't know. Sometimes it's all about the chase. Getting what you're not supposed to have. The grass is greener kind of thing." Russ held his hands up at his sides. "He's a very disturbed individual. I'm thankful you, Marc, and Molly survived him."

"Me too. I never knew when he might take them away from me. I guess, in a sick way, he loved you kids too."

"I can't even wrap my head around it." I buried my face in my hands.

"I'm so sorry, Molly. I never wanted to hurt you." Mom rubbed my back.

"I know. I hate that you've had to live this life for as long as you did. I'm only nineteen, but you've had to deal with this for over forty years. He stole so much from you, from your family." The pit of my stomach burned.

"He did give me you and Marc. The two of you were the only things that kept me getting out of bed every morning. I wanted to make your mothers proud. I knew in my heart both of those girls were watching over their babies."

"Did Lucy sing to me?"

"She did." Mom smiled. "How did you know?"

"I remember." The dreams came back to me. The ones I'd had since I was little. The ones of my mother singing me the sweet lullaby. She was dead, but she had never left me. Veronica and Lucy might be what kept us alive. I'd never underestimate the power of a mother's love.

# CHAPTER THIRTY-SIX

"Are you sure you're up for this today?" Angie turned the directional signal to take us to her parents' house.

"Yeah, I want to meet my grandparents." A warmth filled me, surrounding my heart.

Angie reached over and took my hand. "They are going to be so excited to meet you." She pulled into the driveway. "Give them a little time to process it all, though, okay? I know they're going to love you, but it might be a lot at first."

"I understand. I can't imagine what they're going to think." I took off my seat belt and took a deep breath. "Okay, let's do this."

Angie moved the hair out of my eyes. "I'm so happy I get to be your aunt. This is a job I never thought I'd be able to have." She placed her hand on her heart.

"I'm happy about that too. I always wanted a cool aunt."

I took Angie's hand and walked beside her toward the house. Her mom was looking out the window. The curtain fell closed, and the door opened. "Angie? What's going on? Who's this?" She covered her mouth.

"Mom, this is Molly. Let's go inside so we can talk." Angie pulled me into the house.

Her mom shut the door and followed us into the living room, where Angie's dad was watching TV. "Henry, turn that thing off." Angie's mom yelled for him to hear her.

Henry turned his head, unaware he had company. "What's this? Angie? Lucy?"

"That's enough, Henry." His wife swatted in his direction. "What's going on, Angie?"

"Mom, Dad, I have someone very special to introduce you to." Angie put her arm around me. "This is Molly, and as you can see, she looks like Lucy."

"What's this about? What are you doing?" Angie's mom sat on the edge of her seat, growing agitated with each passing second. "This isn't funny."

"Mom, the detective told you they found Lucy, but I asked him not to tell you everything. I wanted to tell you myself, with Molly." Angie turned to me before she finished. "Lucy was pregnant when she was taken."

Angie's mom's mouth dropped open. "You're Lucy's?"

"Yes, Mom, Molly is Lucy's daughter. She grew up just a street over. She was raised thinking Marc Jackson was her brother. We found out recently that Marc is her father, and Lucy is her mom."

Angie's mom held her face in her hands and sobbed. "Praise Jesus."

Henry wiped a tear off his cheek. "See, I knew she looked like Lucy." His eyes twinkled in the light.

"Yes, Dad, you are right. Molly looks so much like Lucy."

"Well, come here, young lady, and give your grandpa a hug." Henry reached his arms out.

I bent down and let Henry wrap his arms around me. The love from his touch warmed me to my core. "I've always wanted a grandpa."

"Oh, honey, I'm so happy to meet you." Henry took my hands in his when I stood. "You're so beautiful. Just like your mama."

"Mom, what do you think?" Angie sat on the arm of her mom's chair.

"I don't know what to think." She lifted her head and looked at me. "I can't believe this. It's like Lucy is standing in our living room."

"I know. Molly is a sweet girl, just like Lucy. Guess who her favorite author is." Angie folded her hands in her lap and smiled at me.

"Judy Blume?" She covered her mouth. "Oh my gosh, how is this possible? It's like a gift from God. My baby lives on."

"She is a gift. She's your granddaughter, Mom. You always talked about wanting grandkids. Looks like Lucy answered your prayers."

Angie's mom pushed herself out of her chair and walked over to me. "Come here, sweetheart, give your grandma a hug." She pulled me in to her body and sobbed. "Oh, honey, I'm so happy you're here. I love you already."

"I love you too." And I did. I could tell she was going to be a special person in my life. The emptiness of the life I thought I knew was being filled with love from my grandparents and my aunt. Still having so much to wrap my head around, this was a step in the right direction.

# CHAPTER THIRTY-SEVEN

When the tests came back, everything Mom told Russ was confirmed. Marc and Mom were released. It was the first time the three of us had been together since the tale of deception had been unraveled. Boxes filled the house that was once our home.

"Just throw his stuff in there. He's not going to need it where he's going." Mom pulled the packing tape over the edge.

"What are you going to do with all of this stuff?" Marc loaded his box with clothes from Wesley's closet.

"Donate it to Goodwill." Mom shrugged. "I don't want anything that belongs to that monster anywhere near any of us."

"Maybe we should burn it. No one needs his evil energy that's attached to all this stuff." I tossed my armful in. "What do you say?"

"I don't know. Let's just get it out of here, and then we'll figure it out." Mom laughed. "I do love a good fire."

"When are you going to see Elizabeth again?" I bent down to pick up another load of his stuff.

"We're going to have lunch on Sunday. We have a lot of catching up to do." Mom frowned. "It feels so strange to have her back in my life. Part of me feels bad for wanting a relationship with her."

"Why do you feel bad? You have your daughter back." I sat on the edge of Mom's bed.

"You two have lost so much, and I don't want you to feel like you're losing me too." Mom sat next to me.

"Mom, we all have new people in our life now. It doesn't mean you're not our mom, or that you're going to forget about us." I held her hand. "I have a cool new aunt and grandparents. You don't know how bad I wanted to have grandparents when I was growing up."

"I always felt bad about that. I know how important grandmas and grandpas are." Mom reached for Marc's hand. "And, you have this handsome guy as your father. You'll always have each other."

"That's right. You're stuck with me." Marc laughed. "I'm still having a hard time wrapping my head around the fact that I'm a dad."

"I know; it's crazy, right? You're not my cool big brother, but you're my dad. I secretly wished I had a different dad; I didn't know it was going to be you who answered my wish." I laughed.

"As sad as it is that you didn't get to know Lucy, I think it's so cool that the world still has part of her in it. You're very special, Molly." Marc sat between us. "I always knew I'd never stop loving her, and that's because I needed to take care of our daughter."

"Did Mom tell you how I got my name?" I leaned into Marc. "She named me Molly so I could begin with you and end with her. The M in your name, and the Y in Lucy's. She loved you as much as you loved her."

"It's love, Molly. It's present tense for me. I've never stopped loving her, and I know in my heart she still loves me."

"That's true." Mom reached for Marc's hand. "Lucy loves both of you more than anyone I've ever met. Her love was something out of this world. I knew you were one lucky little baby."

"I'm glad I don't have any part of Wesley in my DNA." My body shuddered. "I don't know if I'd be able to live with myself knowing I was keeping any part of that monster alive."

"It's a very good thing." Mom stood and brushed her hands off. "Let's get the rest of these remnants out of here."

"This is so weird. We were all living in this make-believe fantasy world. Nothing was real. It was all an illusion." I got on my feet to get back to work.

"That's not entirely true." Mom put her hands on her hips. "My love for you two was real, and I know the love between you and Marc was real. Parts of our life were near perfect. Those are the parts that matter. We can't control what Wesley Jackson or Jonathan Rivers did or took from us, but we can embrace what was real."

"I'm so glad you don't really have dementia. I have so much to learn from you still." I put my arms around Mom's waist and hugged her.

"That was pretty genius. Have you ever had an acting career?" Marc laid back on the bed. "Since I found out I'm a father, I'm so tired. Being a responsible adult is exhausting."

Mom threw a pillow at Marc. "Well, I'm a great grand-mother. I'm the one who should be napping."

"That's so crazy to think about. We have all these new families, plus we're a family. It's like we hit the lottery. A very sick and twisted lottery, but we're winners nonetheless." I looked to Mom and Marc when they started laughing. "What?"

"You definitely need to spend more time with Mom so she can teach you how to be poetic." Marc snorted.

"I think it's cute, very creative." Mom put her arm around me. "Nicely done."

"I just mean our family multiplied in size with all of this. When it could feel like so much was stolen from us, we've been given all these new, important people in our lives."

"You're right, honey. Looking on the bright side was the only thing that kept me sane all these years."

"There's always a silver lining when you look hard enough." I had never been one to believe things happened for a reason, or serendipity, but I was a believer now.

# CHAPTER THIRTY-EIGHT

The state released Lucy's remains into the custody of her parents. It was time to say goodbye and give Lucy a proper resting place. After twenty years of being hidden away, the people who loved Lucy the most were going to be able to pay their respects.

Marc, Mom, and I arrived at the church together. The parking lot was full, with an overflow of cars in the street. "Wow, Lucy must have been pretty special." I took in my surroundings, watching people file into the building.

"She was. Everyone who met her loved her." Marc blew out his breath. "This is so surreal. I never thought I'd ever know what happened to her, and now..." He pressed his head into his headrest. "I have you."

Mom gave Marc's knee a pat. "She was a very special young lady. I loved her too. She had a fire about her." Mom turned to look at me. "You have her fire."

"I do?"

Mom laughed. "You do, and her heart."

"She's right. You're so much like Lucy, it's crazy." Marc

gripped the steering wheel and leaned forward. "Oh man, I don't know if I can do this."

"Oh, honey, it's going to be alright. You have so many people who love you here. They know they made a mistake." Mom looked at the crowd of people. "It looks like the whole town is here."

"Yeah, and they all think I killed her. I know they think I had something to do with it." Marc lowered his head. "It is my fault."

"Stop that nonsense. You know you had nothing to do with any of this. Wesley is an evil man, and that has nothing to do with you." Mom's tone was more annoyed than sympathetic.

"If I hadn't brought her home, he never would have known who she was." Marc looked out the window. "I don't blame any of them for hating me."

"Marc, he would have found her with or without you. Do not take blame for what that monster did. You are not him. You are so much better." Mom put her hand on his. "This is not your fault."

"She's right, Marc. He ruined all of our lives, and by the sounds of things, everyone he ever came in contact with. No one was safe with him around. Don't let him steal another day from you. This isn't your fault." I rubbed his shoulder. "Lucy wouldn't want you to feel this way."

"It's so hard. I didn't want it to end like this." Marc's words came through gritted teeth. "This isn't the happily ever after we were supposed to have."

"I know, honey, but you have time to make a new one. Lucy would want that for you. She loved you so much. She would want you to be happy." Mom pulled a tissue out of her purse and handed it to him. "Come on; let's go say our goodbyes."

Mom and I walked Marc into the church. He kept his head down so he didn't have to make eye contact with anyone. People were talking, he was right, but they weren't saying what he thought they would be.

Murmurs of the news circulating town were being gossiped about as we walked past. "Isn't it a shame?" "I knew he couldn't have done it." "That poor girl." Were a few things I heard on the way by.

Angie was at the front of the church with her parents. When she saw us, she waved for us to join them. "Let's go sit with the family."

Marc froze. "I can't."

"Marc, come on. They know you didn't do it. Besides, we are family. We belong up there." I tugged on his hand.

"She's right." Mom gave him a little push forward. "Let's sit with Molly's family."

There was a space for us to sit next to Henry. "Hi, honey, come sit with me." He held up his hand.

"Hey, Grandpa." I leaned in and gave him a kiss.

"Hi Mr. and Mrs. Minor." Marc bowed his head.

"Hi, son." Henry pushed up a pained smile. "I'm glad to see you here today. I know Lucy would have wanted you here."

"Thank you, sir. That means a lot." Marc took the seat next to me.

Mom and Angie took their seats, and the service began. I looked behind me to take in the whole surrounding and saw the church was full. There was not an empty seat. People were even standing outside. All for Lucy, my mother.

It was hard to feel so much pain for a woman I didn't even know I wished I knew. I had no idea what I had missed out on. The anger wouldn't settle in because I knew she was still around, watching over me. She always had been. Any girl would have been lucky to have a mother like Lucy. I just happened to be lucky enough to have Lucy and Mom. I couldn't be mad about that.

Memories flooded me as the service continued. I thought back to the first time I rode my bike and how I almost fell but didn't. To the time I went horseback riding and something spooked the horse, but I didn't get hurt. Or the time I was driving a little too fast on the snow-covered road and should have ended up in the ditch but didn't. There were so many times I knew she was looking out for me. My guardian angel.

In the parking lot of the church, people swarmed around us to pay their respects. The line seemed like it was never going to end. I held Marc and Mom's hand tight as strangers told me how much I looked like my mother. I couldn't smile one more time, or I was going to explode. "I think I'm ready to go," I whispered to Mom.

She tugged on my hand. I saw Beth coming toward us. "Hi, guys. I'm so sorry to hear about everything." She took Marc's hand. "If you ever want to talk or anything, you have my number." Her eyes locked with Marc's.

"Thanks." Marc smiled.

I squeezed his hand, and he gave me a look. The look of a big brother and not a father. "Marc would love that."

He gave my hand a squeeze back. "Yes, I would."

"James has the kids this weekend if you'd like to go get a drink, dinner, or something." Beth pushed her hair behind her ear. "It was nice seeing you again, Molly and Mrs... I ah..."

Mom reached out her hand. "It's Carol. You can call me Carol."

"I'm sorry; I wasn't thinking." Beth frowned.

"It's okay; it's quite the mess. I won't hold it against you." Mom winked.

"What was that about?" Marc snarled at me.

"What? It looked like you needed some help." I shrugged.

"Molly, we're at a funeral, for god's sake."

"Exactly, if anything, you should realize that life isn't guaranteed. You have to live while you can."

Mom laughed. "See, she's a firecracker, just like her mom."

That brought a smile to Marc's face. "I guess you're right. It is time to start living."

"We're going to head out. Mom and Dad are getting tired." Angie leaned in and gave Marc a hug. "It was really nice of you to come today."

"I wouldn't miss it for the world. Lucy was my girl." Marc's eyes watered.

"My parents would like to talk to you. Do you have a minute?" Angie waved for her mom and dad to join us.

Marc ran his hand through his hair and fidgeted. "I'm really sorry about everything."

"You don't have anything to be sorry for." Henry took his wife's hand. "Look, I know this is hard. Angie has told us about everything, and my wife and I have been thinking."

Angie's mom took over. "What he's trying to spit out is we want you and Molly to take our last name."

"You want me to be a Minor?" Marc swallowed hard.

"Yes, if you want to. We were thinking you might not want to keep your last name, with the circumstances as they are. And we'd be happy to have you in the family." My grandma looked over at me. "You too, Molly. We'd love for you to share our last name."

Mom put her hand on my back. "That's so sweet of you, Mrs. Minor."

"I'd like that." I looked up at Marc. "What do you say?"

"Wow, I'd like that. I wasn't sure what to do about my name. I kind of felt like a stranger. I'd be honored to be a Minor."

Henry smiled. "Good. Welcome to the family, son."

Marc put his hand to his heart. "Thank you, sir. That means the world to me."

"I know how much Lucy loved you, and you're our granddaughter's father. There's no getting out of this now." Henry chuckled. "I'm sorry, but I have to get home. It's been a long day."

"It sure has." Marc took my hand, and we walked to our cars together.

"I'll see you later, Molly?" Angie held the door open for her mom.

"Yeah, I'd like that." I got into the backseat of Marc's car and let my body relax into the softness of the seat. Molly Minor, I liked the sound of that.

# CHAPTER THIRTY-NINE

The house was only on the market for less than a month before it sold. I didn't expect life to happen so quickly. I put the last of my belongings into the box before I turned off my bedroom light for the last time. I carried the box to the empty living room and set it on the floor.

"I can't believe this is goodbye. To Molly Jackson, to our life together, to Green Street; to everything." I put my hands on my hips and looked around the bare house.

"I know; it's like the end of the sitcom you love to hate." Marc put his arm around me and laughed. "It's where no one knows your name."

"Are you sure you two will be okay? I don't have to go." Mom bit at her fingernail.

"Mom, we'll be fine. I'll take care of Marc." I hit his chest.

"And I'll take care of Molly. Don't worry about us. You spent the last forty years making sure we were okay. It's time you get to live your life." Marc picked up the box. "Come on; we should get out of here, or we're going to be late."

"I don't know. What if she doesn't need me? What if I'm in

the way?" Mom stood in the middle of the room, a look of panic on her face.

"Mom, Elizabeth doesn't need you to take care of her; she's a grown woman. She needs to get to know you again. She thought you were dead. Having you in her life is a gift she deserves to have, and so do you. You worked so hard to protect her and us. Now it's time to live your life. It's not like we won't need you. You're the only mom we have. You don't get off the hook that easy." I rested my head on her shoulder. "It's going to be fine. You're going to have so much fun together."

"I'm only a phone call away. You know that, right?"

"I know."

"And you know I'm not abandoning you." Mom closed her eyes.

"I know, and you didn't abandon Elizabeth, either. She knows that. You did the best you could. No one thinks you're a bad mother."

"Oh, Molly, I don't know what I'd do without you." Mom kissed my cheek. "We better get out of here, or Marc's going to have a fit."

"You're right. He doesn't want to keep them waiting." I closed the door behind us.

Mom got in her car and followed behind Marc and me. "I can't believe we're going back there." Sweat beaded under my bangs.

"Yeah, me either, but we'll all feel so much better when it's over." Marc turned the music on. "Let's listen to House in the Woods; I think it's only fitting."

"Let me guess, Tom Petty?"

"How'd you know?" Marc's smile grew.

"I mean, because who else?"

"That's my girl." Marc laughed. "It's still weird to think of you as my daughter. You get that, right?"

"I know. It's hard not to see my big brother when I look at you. We'll figure it out. It'll just take time."

"My body is on fire. I can't wait to get this over with." Marc looked in his rearview mirror. "I bet she feels the same way."

I turned and waved at Mom. "I can't even imagine what it was like for her. She must have been so afraid."

"Yeah, I don't even want to think about what happened there. He's such a sick bastard. I'd kill him if I could." Marc's knuckles turned white as his grip tightened on the steering wheel.

"He's not worth going to jail over. He's gone and out of our life now. And the best part is we don't share any of his DNA. He's a nobody. When he dies, he'll be forgotten about. Just a blip on the planet."

"But he caused so much damage to so many people. He stole so much."

"So don't give him anymore of your life. Find happiness, do good, and he'll just be a distant memory. We're nothing like him. We're survivors, and he's a coward. He'll get what's coming to him."

"I sure hope you're right." Marc turned onto the dirt road. "Here goes nothing."

When we got to the pull off at the dead-end, it was already full of cars. We had to park on the side of the road. "Whoa, I didn't know this many people were coming today."

"I guess he really did mess with a lot of people." Marc rubbed his face. "Let's do this."

Mom was already out of her car, walking toward us. "This is crazy. I can't believe the turn out."

We walked the path that led us to the house in the woods. The field in front of the house was filled with people. The fire department was on standby with their hoses ready to go. Russ and Angie met us at the clearing. "Hey, guys, I'm glad you made it. We were starting to think you weren't going to come." Russ shook Marc's hand.

"We had to finish up at the house," Mom chimed in from behind. "It's hard to say goodbye, even to a place with such turmoil. Kind of like this place."

"I bet." Russ adjusted his sunglasses. "Are you up for this today? I can call it off, if you want."

"No, it needs to go." Mom looked over at the house. "Too many painful memories here. It's riddled with evil. Pure evil. It has to go."

"Okay, I'll let the guys know we're ready." Russ walked toward a group of guys with yellow hardhats on.

"It's so hard to think this was the last place Lucy was alive." Angie looked over at the house, and the pain dripped off her face.

"I loved your sister." Mom put her arms out to offer Angie a hug. "I wished I could have done something more for her."

"You did; you raised her beautiful daughter. She'd be proud of the woman Molly became because of you."

Mom clutched her heart. "Molly was Lucy's gift to this world. It's a better place because she's in it."

"Just like Lucy was. Her flame wasn't extinguished, only passed on." Angie took a step back. "Speaking of flame, are you ready? I hear the countdown."

"It's over." Mom's eyes filled with tears. "When Wesley

brought me here, I had no idea what was in store for me. A dark, cold night turned into a life of hell. The only saving grace were you two. You kept me going every day. Without you, I know I wouldn't be here to see this or get a second chance with my daughter. You are my miracles."

"You were ours. Whatever you did to keep him from completely snapping saved our lives." Marc rubbed his eyes. "You worked your magic and sacrificed so much for us. The outcome could have been so different."

"You're free, Mom, just like the others. You made it." I rested my head on hers.

We stood, huddled together and watched the flames grow and dance. The air was lighter. Mom, Marc, Angie and I locked arms as we watched the house in the woods go up in flames. There would never be another chance for this place to hurt anyone else. The pain and suffering went up in smoke with the beams of the building. A heaviness lifted as the house began to fall. Veronica and Lucy were there with us; I could feel it. My mother and grandmother surrounded us with their love and protection. They were free now, just like us.

# CHAPTER FORTY

Marc and I were settled into our new house. We were still in Pine Grove, but in a different neighborhood. I could walk to Angie's house now. "I'm going for a walk," I yelled to let Marc know. He was in the backyard soaking up the sun.

"Have fun. Don't do anything I wouldn't do." Marc sat in the Adirondack chair with his arms over his head.

"That's such a dad thing to say." I rolled my eyes. "Have you been working on your dad jokes?"

"Not yet; that's on today's agenda."

"You're such a dork." When I opened the gate, Russ was parked in the driveway. He was knocking on the front door. "Can I help you?"

Russ turned around. "Jesus, you scared me." Russ put his hands in his pockets. "Is Marc around?"

"Yeah, why? What's going on? He's not out, is he?" My heart began to race, so loud I couldn't hear his answer.

"Hey, what's going on out here?" Marc stood at the gate. "Molly, are you alright?"

"Can we go someplace to talk?" Russ kicked at the lawn. "Somewhere you can sit down."

"Is Mom okay? Did he get to her?" I covered my eyes as images of what he had done to her came at me.

"Molly, your mom's fine. I just got off the phone with her." Russ smiled. "I think you'll like what I have to say. Is there someplace we can talk?"

Marc held the gate open. "There's plenty of room out here."

Russ and I went into the backyard and found a place to sit while we waited for Marc to join us. "So I have some news to report."

"Did Mom have something to do with it? Is there someone else involved?" The different scenarios played out in my head.

"Molly, let Russ talk." Marc sat on the edge of his seat, ready to receive the news.

"There's been an accident. I was told this morning that some of the inmates assaulted Jonathan Rivers."

"Why do we care about that?" I folded my arms, annoyed he had scared me with the possibilities I was cooking up in my mind.

"Well, because there's more to the story. I can tell you, if you'd like." Russ smiled.

"Sorry." My foot began to tap as I waited.

"So as I was saying, a couple of the inmates brutally attacked Jonathan Rivers. They recognized him from his days as the sheriff and had a beef with him. I guess he was the reason these guys were behind bars. A drug bust, or something like that." Russ lifted his shoulders. "Some reason it was overlooked, and Mr. Rivers' requests to be moved weren't approved."

"He was attacked by the guys he helped put away." Marc nodded. "Priceless."

"Well, no, there's more." Russ rubbed his hands together. "It appears the guards that were on this morning didn't hear the commotion. Not until it was too late. It seems as though there was nothing they could do to save him."

"They couldn't save him?" The words hadn't fully computed when Marc started cheering.

"Holy shit, are you shitting me? No way. He's dead?"

"Wait, he's dead?" I looked at Russ and then back at Marc. "Jonathan Rivers is dead?"

"Yup. It happened this morning. He's no longer a problem." Russ clapped his hands.

"My prayers were answered. I wished that sonofabitch dead. Actually, I wished I could've killed him. But this works too." Marc jumped to his feet. "This calls for a celebration."

"I thought you'd be happy." Russ got up. "You okay, Molly?"

"Yeah, it's a lot to process. One day he's my dad, the next day he's a murderer, then a kidnapper, then someone totally different. And now he's dead. It's a lot to take in."

"I'm sorry, kiddo. I didn't think about it upsetting you." Russ put his hands in his pockets. "I thought you'd be happy."

"No, I am. It's so hard to believe. All these years he was a sheriff to save himself, and it's what took him out. That's Karma if I ever saw it."

"Wow, I hadn't looked at it like that, but you're right. He hid behind that badge, and it became what stabbed him in the back. Literally." Russ started for the gate. "You never know what life has in store for you."

"That's for sure." And just like that, the nightmare was over. Mom was safe. Marc was safe. I was safe. We were the only ones to make it out of the house in the woods alive.

# ACKNOWLEDGMENTS

Thank you to my family for allowing me the time and space to create these stories, and for understanding when I have no brain cells left after writing all night! Thank you for Charlie, my rescue dog, who reminds me I have to move away from my desk sometimes (like when he needs to go for a walk!!) and keeping me company into the wee hours of the morning.

Many thanks to the people who helped bring House in the Woods to life.

Shower of Schmidt Designs for the beautiful cover.

Silla Webb for editing and polishing my words.

Debbie Russell and Michele Avery for beta reading.

To the Coffee Queens: Thank you for your support, encouragement and push to keep writing. You have all helped me so much with your friendship and kindness. Who knows, maybe I've got a romance novel in there some place!

Thank you to the readers. Without you, my characters would never have any fun! Your honest feedback is always appreciated and helps improve my craft. Reviews help other readers as much as they help me. Please consider leaving one.

# ABOUT THE AUTHOR

Jessica Aiken-Hall, author of her award-winning memoir, *The Monster That Ate My Mommy* and the *Scope of Practice Trilogy,* lives in New Hampshire with her husband, three children, and three dogs. She is a survivor of child abuse and domestic violence and is a fierce advocate. Her mission is to help others share their story.

She has a master's degree in Mental Health Counseling, with over a decade of experience as a social worker. She is also a Reiki Master and focuses her attention on healing.

When she is not writing, she enjoys listening to Tom Petty, walking along the beach, looking at the moon, and watching murder shows.

To follow what she's doing next check out http://www. jessicaaikenhall.com.